THE DINNER PARTY

NINA MANNING

B
Boldwood

First published in Great Britain in 2025 by Boldwood Books Ltd.

Copyright © Nina Manning, 2025

Cover Design by Head Design Ltd.

Cover Images: iStock

The moral right of Nina Manning to be identified as the author of this work has been asserted in accordance with the Copyright, Designs and Patents Act 1988.

All rights reserved. No part of this book may be reproduced in any form or by any electronic or mechanical means, including information storage and retrieval systems, without written permission from the author, except for the use of brief quotations in a book review.This book is a work of fiction and, except in the case of historical fact, any resemblance to actual persons, living or dead, is purely coincidental.

Every effort has been made to obtain the necessary permissions with reference to copyright material, both illustrative and quoted. We apologise for any omissions in this respect and will be pleased to make the appropriate acknowledgements in any future edition.

A CIP catalogue record for this book is available from the British Library.

Paperback ISBN 978-1-80426-598-7

Large Print ISBN 978-1-80426-599-4

Hardback ISBN 978-1-80426-600-7

Ebook ISBN 978-1-80426-596-3

Kindle ISBN 978-1-80426-597-0

Audio CD ISBN 978-1-80426-605-2

MP3 CD ISBN 978-1-80426-604-5

Digital audio download ISBN 978-1-80426-602-1

This book is printed on certified sustainable paper. Boldwood Books is dedicated to putting sustainability at the heart of our business. For more information please visit https://www.boldwoodbooks.com/about-us/sustainability/

Boldwood Books Ltd, 23 Bowerdean Street, London, SW6 3TN

www.boldwoodbooks.com

For Glenn x

PROLOGUE

I am great at giving gifts. It is my superpower. People compliment me on it all the time, and I am very proud of all the times I have seen utter joy on the faces of the receivers. I take time to think about the small details, really homing in on the recipient, what their likes and dislikes are, if it would be the right gift for them at the right time of year, is it the sort of thing that they need in their life more than anything, going through each option with complete precision until I am confident that I have made the right choice. Then, I go about making that gift or event happen. I spend hours planning right up until execution, making sure every tiny detail is just right. Seeing the look on their face is one of the most satisfying experiences of my life. It is why I do it. I do it to please others, not myself. I mean, why else do people give? But my last gift has caused some problems and made me wonder if I have lost the knack. But I've done it and now I must live with the consequences.

1

'A surprise. You know I hate surprises.' Stig looks at me with that frustrated glare that I have seen so many times. I know it's not real; I know that it's not that he doesn't like getting gifts. It's just that he likes to feel in control. Ever since I have known him, it's been his default setting. He needs to know precisely what is always going on and, generally, if he can, have some involvement. But there is no way I can let this one out of the bag. It's too good an opportunity to tell him. I need to build up the suspense and the drama. It deserves the drama.

'I think you just say you hate surprises when you don't. Listen, have I ever let you down?'

Stig looks thoughtful, obviously casting his mind back to the myriads of gifts and excursions I have planned and executed over the years.

'I am a great present giver, you know that!' I know I don't need to sell myself to my husband. We've been married for five years, and he proposed on the anniversary of our meeting, which is very convenient as we only have one date to remember. I was over the moon when I realised I could give this gift to Stig for our fifth wedding anniversary. I didn't expect cracks to appear in our relationship so quickly, but they arrived regardless. And this gift is hopefully going to give our marriage the lift it so desperately needs.

Stig sits at the kitchen table and rests his chin in one hand. 'So when will I get this surprise?'

'Tonight, obviously.' I sit opposite him like an excited child. 'You did remember?' Even though it feels as though we have been drifting apart these last few months, I want this to be a memorable occasion.

'What? Have I missed something? Today is what?' Stig tries to sound convincing, but he never misses a special occasion. Every birthday, Christmas, Valentine's Day, anniversary, and even Easter is marked extensively despite how things have been between us.

I shake my head. 'Well, I don't care, Stig, I really don't. Because this is such a great gift, I will get so much out of seeing your reaction.'

'So you don't care about an anniversary gift? Five years in, buying for you gets a bit tricky.'

'Nu-uh.' I shake my head.

'Well, I guess I had better have this returned to the jewellery store.' Stig lifts his hands from beneath the table, and I am more shocked about where the long, rectangular, velvet box he is holding has just appeared from. Did he have it taped to the underside of the table? He places it carefully on the table before him and nudges it slowly towards me. I put one hand to my mouth, then I drop it and let my fingers graze the top of the box. I recognise the name of the shop embossed into the velvet. An image of what I think might be inside the box flashes through my mind. We had passed the store a few weeks back and I had pointed out a necklace as I often did. I was intrigued by its ethical value, how it had been lovingly handcrafted, and how it shone from its stand and caught my eye.

I pull the box closer to me as though it might be taken away from me and Stig raises his eyebrows.

'Open it then,' he says earnestly and my heart leaps into my throat because this is the man I fell in love with. This man can joke around but then hold me to ransom with his stare or the sincerity of just three short words.

I open the case, and the necklace is even more beautiful close up, and I gasp.

'I didn't even know I wanted it this much. It's so beautiful.'

'Well, you said you liked it.' Stig stands up and takes a bottle of wine from the fridge. I feel my heart sink; he can't even watch me put it on.

I stand and look in the large mirror in our kitchen diner. 'It's perfect. I love it.'

Eventually, he returns to the table, sits and smiles.

'You're welcome. Now, is my present still better?'

I look at him for a few seconds. 'Oh, absolutely.'

* * *

'Why are you driving so slowly?' Stig says, and I look at him and laugh because he is wearing the eye mask that I asked him to put on so he couldn't see where we were going. It was the only one I could find to grab, and it was covered in pink lace.

'Because it's a surprise, and surprises are surprises until the last second.'

'Well, I hope this place has food because I am starving.' He is starting to sound annoyed.

It had been hard to keep Stig from eating; he is six foot three and eats like a horse most days. I peppered him with snacks all day, but of course, it was evident that the evening would entail food when all I had allowed him after breakfast was crackers and fruit.

I touch the emerald lying just inside the cave of my neck. It feels nice, as if it should be there. And I find it gives me the confidence that I need this evening, a little piece of jewellery that has perhaps brought us that little bit closer.

I glance around for a parking space, and I am amazed that there is one just two streets away from the venue. But it is still going to require a little navigation on my part. I open the car door and help Stig out. I lock the car, hold on to Stig and steer him in the right direction.

'Nearly there,' I say as I almost topple off my heels on the cobbled pathway. It's a quaint part of Oxford, a short drive from where we live on the outskirts. I get us there in one piece, and I look up at the ornate building in front of me, the large, clear windows, the view of the conservatory in the background, and the greenery and plants that adorn the corners and edges, creating an outside-inside feel. The stark, white napkins and crystal tableware glisten from the other side. I feel a flutter in my stomach. I made this happen.

'Okay, I'm going to remove your eye mask now, but please keep your eyes closed until I say open them.'

'Okay.' Stig bends to let me slip the lacy number from his head. A couple walk ahead of us and smile at me. I ignore how exposed I feel at this silly yet intimate moment between Stig and me.

I take his hand and squeeze it hard. 'You may open your eyes.'

I watch Stig open his eyes and squint a little. He stares at the name of the restaurant in front of him.

Sapphire

He blinks and looks like he is trying to work out a difficult sum in his head.

'Stig?' I go to touch his arm again, but I stop myself. It's been a long time. I'm not sure how he will react with too much close contact.

'Is... is this Hector Bolson-Woods's place?' he finally says.

'Yes.' I try to contain my excitement, but it sounds like a squeal. 'And I got us a table for tonight.' I look up in awe at the building. 'I've been on the waiting list for six months. I nearly peed myself when they emailed to say vacancies were coming up and one was on our anniversary. It was meant to be.' I let my excitement bubble over. I am trying to compensate. We both are.

Stig looks stunned.

'This really is a surprise.'

My whole body feels tingly. I knew it. I knew he would be stunned. I knew this would be the best present I had ever given him thus far. And it couldn't have come at a better time. We needed something that would bring us back to one another. We had been far away in our minds and bodies for so long.

'I know how much you admire him. I've seen the algorithms on the laptop; I see you following his Instagram page when he landed at this restaurant in February. It's like you became obsessed. I saw you checking out his book in the store when it came out, and the paper was open on that piece about him the other day. We both loved him on *MasterChef*; we watched it like it was a religion for us, well, me more than you, but still. Now we get to eat his food, for real!'

Stig sucks in a breath and blows it out loud and long. 'It looks expensive.'

I recoil at his words, but I won't let them deter me. I was sure money would be brought up. It had been the theme of our conversations for the last four months.

I move in closer to him. 'If you're worried about money, then don't. Once I knew we had the booking, I put some money away each month. I have enough for us to enjoy an evening here.'

I see the terror in Stig's eyes as he realises this expenditure had not made it onto his monthly Excel spreadsheet and I swallow down my frustration. *Park it, Lily*, I tell myself. *He doesn't mean to be uptight.*

'Sometimes, we just have to kick back and live a little,' I say a little too forcefully and push past him into the restaurant, not caring for a moment if he follows me or not.

Inside, the maître d' is on me immediately as I begin soaking up the atmosphere, inhaling the myriad of scents.

'Reservation for Leonard, please,' I say, and I cannot keep the smugness out of my voice. Stig arrives next to me, and I am relieved he decided to follow.

He rubs under his eye, which he does when he feels self-conscious.

The maître d' taps at an iPad then looks up and smiles. She removes two menus from a pile on the dumb waiter.

'Come with me, please.'

I raise my eyebrows at Stig, and we begin to walk through the restaurant.

Stig stares straight ahead; never one to seek attention, I can sense his discomfort, but I know that will pass when we're tucked up at our table, and when I see where we are headed, I am almost giddy with joy. The maître d' stops at a semi-circular table with high-backed soft furnishing on one side, enough room for both Stig and I to sit close to one another but not on top of each other and not opposite each other. They are called the honeymoon tables, and whilst I had put in a request for one in the *any other information* section on the booking form, I didn't expect that we would get one.

'How nice is this?' I whisper as the menus are placed before us, and the maître d' disappears to let us settle ourselves.

Stig looks shell-shocked.

'I know, I know, it's a lot. This place is on fire. I read many reviews online last week, and everyone raved about the food. There's a wine list here; shall we have a look?' I place it in front of Stig, who stares at it for a second and then looks at me. I know I am babbling, and I'm nervous. I want this night to be perfect.

'It's great, Lil, it really is. Thanks,' he says, but I detect the insincerity in his voice and know he is only trying to appease me. I feel momentarily deflated, but then I know my husband. He'll come round. He picks up the wine list and begins perusing it. He lets out a slow whistle. 'Pretty pricey,' he says.

'I know. But it's a treat.' I touch his arm, then quickly retract it. The warm, inviting surroundings make me feel a sense of intimacy that I haven't felt for some time, but I don't want to make this feel forced or fake. 'Don't feel bad; you work really hard. We both do.'

A freakishly tall waiter appears at our table. He places a plate with something very small and tasty on it.

'Pissaladière,' he says.

I glance at Stig to see if he can remember what that is. I made it once about two years ago. It was nowhere near as good-looking as this.

'Anchovies and red onion tart,' I say, and he nods.

He orders the wine and we both opt for sparkling water.

I sit back and sigh, taking in my surroundings, trying to savour every moment. I take a bite of the tart and let out a small groan. 'Oh my God, that's good.'

Stig takes a bite and I can see he is silently impressed.

The wine and water arrive, and I hold up my glass to Stig.

'To us. Happy anniversary.'

He raises his glass, clinks it gently against mine, but he doesn't make eye contact.

I gulp down my first glass of wine too quickly. The stress of trying to keep this a secret from Stig has been too much at times. I have almost blurted it out on so many occasions, purely by accident. I feel the wine go to my head on an almost-empty stomach, as I had been saving my appetite for this evening, knowing I wanted to savour every flavour.

We study the menu, reading the short descriptions, which consist of single words: fennel, wild garlic, hazelnut, and honey. There are no details about how the dish will look or be prepared. We must trust the chef.

When the waiter returns to take our order, I feel light-headed from the wine. We tell him our selections and then just before he walks away, I ask, 'Is Hector in the kitchen today?'

Stig looks at me. 'Lil.' There is a warning in his voice.

I look at him. 'It's fine, Stig.' I look back to the waiter.

'He is today, yes.' He walks away and my body convulses.

'Jesus, Stig, the actual bloody Hector Bolson-Woods is in there right now about to make our food.'

Stig looks shocked again and I wonder if this is all too much for him. He is reserved, never likes to make a fuss or draw attention to himself. We are opposites in that respect.

'Well, let's just eat up and enjoy it like everyone else,' he says and I hear a tension to his voice, so I top up his wine glass.

'Relax,' I remind him.

'Excuse me, madam.' I look up and see the waiter is back again. 'You have been cordially invited into the chef's kitchen for your meal.' He begins to place our wine and glasses onto a tray. 'Would you like to follow me?'

'What does that mean? What is he saying?' Stig sounds panicked but I'm already standing up, unable to believe what I am hearing but not wasting a second in case he changes his mind or someone else gets there before us.

'It means we've been invited to the kitchen to have our meal cooked for us by, I presume, Hector himself.'

Stig groans, but this time, it's clearly from despair. I know I do this; I know I make him do things slightly outside his comfort zone, but you must grab all opportunities, or there will be no anecdotes. We will just become very boring versions of the people we once were.

I walk ahead, following the waiter, occasionally glancing back at Stig, who is looking less than enthused. I know I'm being selfish now, but I am not about to pass up an opportunity like this; if he finds it desperately cringe, I'll find a way to make it up to him. Right now, all I can see is an Instagram photo and the hundreds of likes and comments.

We pass through a door and arrive in a narrow, stark, white hallway. I see an open door to a room with a large grey sofa, a small table and chairs, and an immaculately tidy large desk with an Apple iMac. That must be Hector's office.

'This way, please.'

We follow the waiter left down the hallway as it opens into a larger space with a seating area; a large dining table that would seat six is set for two; set back behind the table is a small but well-equipped kitchen, again, immaculately clean. Through a large open doorway, I can hear the action of where the central kitchen must be: the clang of pans, the holler of orders from a male voice I can only presume is Hector. The smells are hitting my nose and setting my stomach growling.

'Please, take a seat here. Hector will be with you shortly.'

We slide into our seats, and I look at Stig.

'Fuck!' I say.

'Oh, Lil,' Stig says.

'Come on, Stig. It's a once-in-a-lifetime experience; we are about to have our food, our anniversary dinner, cooked by one of the most famous chefs in the world right now. Why can't you embrace it?' I hiss at him, aware that Hector could walk through those doors at any minute, and I don't want him to see me whisper-arguing with my husband.

I sense his presence before I see him. Looking back, I think not only did I feel the room ignite with an energy I have never felt before, but I noticed Stig squirming in his seat, his eyes drawn to the doorway, his mouth slightly agape.

'I really think we should just go, Lil…' Stig's voice is just a whisper in the background.

Then I hear his voice, a deep, booming sound lilted with the aristocracy that runs through his veins and that he is so famed for.

'Ah, Mr and Mrs Leonard, it's a pleasure to see you both.'

2

Hector is a man who commands a room. He wears a stark, white chef's jacket with black, checked trousers when he enters. I had imagined him to be in something grey or all in black, looking a bit more modern, but he seems to have gone for a traditional chef look. My mouth suddenly feels dry from the wine, and I glug some water before I stand up to shake his hand, hoping that Stig is about to follow suit.

'Mrs Leonard, I presume? It's a pleasure.'

I had words prepared to say to Hector, but they have evaporated, along with all the moisture between my lips. I hear Stig shifting next to me.

Hector has his hand stretched out toward Stig.

'Mr Leonard. It's delightful to have you both.'

Stig stands too but has to lean across the table to reach Hector, who I notice doesn't make an effort to meet him halfway.

'Appreciate you doing this for us. My wife, she loves this sort of thing.' Stig gives Hector's hand a quick limp shake.

Hector has a smirk on his face.

'This sort of thing? Cooking, eating. Is that not your sort of thing, Mr Leonard?'

'Stig.'

'I'm sorry?' Hector cocks his head.

'It's his nickname; it's all I've ever known of my husband, to be honest,' I say with a small laugh, wondering if Stig will feel the need to explain the origins of the name he adopted before I met him.

'Ah ha, of course. Stig. It must be from the TV programme, right?'

There was a pause as though Stig is unsure how to reply. 'Yes. I let my hair grow wild when I was in my twenties.'

'Apparently, some people he met when he was travelling called him it and that was it. It stuck,' I chip in, sensing Stig's discomfort.

'How odd!' Hector announces. 'Trying to shake off a previous persona?'

Stig glares but doesn't respond. I feel a surge of familiarity. The way Stig stays cold about his past. There are so many things I wish I knew about him that he refuses to share. *They aren't important*, he recites each time. Now, here he is, acting the same way with Hector.

'Stig of the Dump,' Hector says and laughs loudly, which breaks the awkward silence, and I laugh along with him. Stig barely cracks a smile. I can see Hector puts him out, and I don't understand why when Hector has gone out of his way to cook privately for us. I want to punch Stig in the arm, tell him to lighten up.

'Yes, that's me.'

'Well, I'd say you've done well for yourself, young Stig. Here you are in your fineries, eating in my restaurant.' He turns to me. 'A beautiful wife. Things couldn't have turned out too shabby for you, Stig.' Hector says his name as though he is trying it out, playing with it at the end of the sentence.

'I have no complaints, Hector.'

The three of us stand momentarily, an inane grin spreading across my face.

Hector claps his hands together and a shock goes through my body.

'Well, now, you didn't come here to stand around. I believe you wish to eat.' He motions for us to sit back down again at the table.

'Maurice!' he calls, and a young, skinny man appears. Hector says something quietly to him, and he disappears as fast as he arrives. Hector walks past the table and behind us into the kitchen.

'This was already here when we bought the place, can you believe it? Saved me thousands.'

Hector opens a fridge and begins to root around.

'I think you were having the pigeon, weren't you, Stig?'

Stig clears his throat. 'I was. Yes.'

'And the fennel salad for you. May I call you by your first name?'

'Lily. I'm Lily,' I say breathlessly. I am still overwhelmed by the whole process.

'Well, Lily, let's get you fed.'

* * *

'That was phenomenal,' I say as a waiter clears our starter plates. Hector brings more wine and pours some into a fresh glass.

'I save this for my finest customers. Try it. It's almost twenty years old. I have two more crates in the cellar.'

Hector hands me a glass, and I swirl it around. I take a sip, and I hear myself moan in delight.

'That is...' I look to Stig. 'Oh my God, Stig, try it; it melts in your mouth, it's so... palatable. Is that the word, Hector?'

'Wine can't melt in your mouth, Lily,' Stig says, and I throw him a stare.

'I've never heard anyone describe it that way before, Lily. It's a beautiful description, and I know exactly what you mean.' Hector looks at me, his eyes are smiling.

I want to give an 'I told you so' look to Stig, but I bathe in Hector's compliment. I am not a wine connoisseur, but I know when something tastes good, even if I don't have the correct vocabulary.

Hector laughs. 'And with that sound you emitted, it has to be something special, right?'

I feel myself blush at my sound of pleasure then I look to Stig to see his reaction. He takes a glass from Hector and sips.

He nods. 'Very nice.'

Hector eyes Stig for a second and laughs again.

'Very humble, your man, isn't he?'

'Ah, he hates a fuss, don't you?' I grab Stig's arm. He looks at me, and I see a flash of anxiety in his eyes, and I realise I am holding on too tight. I know I have had too much to drink, and I need to calm down a bit. But this is too exciting, and Hector is so friendly and attentive. The way my cheeks coloured a moment ago makes me realise that I cannot remember the last time someone had that effect on me. It must have been Stig, in the early days of our relationship. 'Sorry,' I mouth at him and let go.

Hector takes a seat at the round table, opposite us both, and I steal a look at Stig, but I can't read his face.

'So what brought you here tonight, Lily?' Hector leans into me as he speaks. 'Are you a fan of my work?'

I hear Stig suck in a breath next to me.

'Fan makes you sound as though you're a pop star. But yes, seriously, I do appreciate your style, and I have followed you for some time. On the socials,' I add quickly. 'Not round the streets.' I laugh loudly at my joke.

Hector laughs, too, and it doesn't seem forced. He has a pleasant aura, and I feel relaxed around him. And I don't just think it's the wine.

'Well, that's the funny thing, Lily, food has become such a fashionable commodity, and so we, the chefs, have become icons in the eyes of many.'

I nod enthusiastically. 'It is ridiculous, now you've said it, that eating, the fundamental act of survival, has become a hobby, a leisure event, something we spend hundreds, even thousands on at a time. I know this, yet I pretend it's not happening, especially when too many are going hungry,' I say forlornly.

'You are not only beautiful but a wise and perceptive woman, and I admire you for showing such humility. That's why I give a percentage of the bill to help fund projects in Liberia. Wells, schools and projects to help make families self-sufficient. It's very liberating, and my guests feel they are also doing their part. I understand the dichotomy between wanting to eat out and enjoy a meal and wanting to feed the hungry. I'm glad to have met someone who feels that too.'

'Wow, that is something, Hector. I wish others would join you in your plight. You don't talk about that enough on your socials. You should,' I say, and he looks at me thoughtfully.

'I don't. Because I don't wish to sound like I'm pushing my choices down people's throats.'

'I work for a charity, Hector; I push that down people's throats all day.'

'Fabulous, what is the charity?' Hector moves an inch closer, which is not a huge move but enough to say that he is invested in this conversation. In me.

'It's a family charity; we assist families who have lost a parent, who are bereaved, or have multiple children or have a parent suffering with mental health issues. We assist by providing them with a buddy, a volunteer who can signpost, listen, help with the washing up, you know, just spend time with them, a listening ear.'

'I take my chef's hat off to you, Lily; that is highly commendable. Stig, you must be proud of your wife.' Hector turns to face Stig.

'Oh very proud.' Stig manages a smile. He seems a little looser, and I hope he is finally starting to enjoy himself.

'And it's your anniversary tonight, is that right?'

'All day,' Stig says dryly. It was meant as a joke, but it sounds crass under the spotlight of Hector's kitchen, next to the man himself.

'Well, I hope he appreciates you, Lily,' Hector says with a wink. 'And how many years, may I ask?'

'The big five,' Stig says, trying to add a lightness to his voice, but I know it's only going to go downhill from here. Stig has had very little to offer all night.

'And children?' Hector asks, looking at me and then Stig.

A few uncomfortable seconds pass before I eventually speak.

'No children,' I say, looking down at my hands.

'Oh, well, you're still so young. You have all the time.' Hector smiles at me, and I force a smile back at him, feeling the energy pouring from Stig. It's as though I can read his thoughts.

Why don't you want to have children, Lily?

'But you must be, what, forty now, Stig? I can tell by the lines around your eyes.' Hector points to his own eyes. 'I went to

Liberia on my fortieth last year. Spent some time in the orphanage we built over there.'

'Well, now you're just trying to make us look bad,' Stig says, and I look at him to see if he is being serious. But it doesn't matter because Hector is so damn friendly and accommodating and not at all offended.

'I know, it's a privilege. But it's all I ever wanted to do: help others. I fell into cooking; it was never something I intended. It just about pays the bills, and I enjoy it, so that's enough for me.'

I hear Stig shift in his chair; again, it's almost as if I can listen to his thoughts out loud. I wonder, if I weren't here, whether Stig might reveal to Hector how my working in charity drives him to distraction, how I work too many hours for not enough money.

'Don't give up the charity work, Lily. I can see it's who you are and it's in your heart.'

I slurp some more of the delicious wine. I'm feeling lighter than air now.

'I got headhunted by this company; they wanted to pay me double what I was earning—'

'And it was a shame to pass up the opportunity,' Stig butts in.

Hector nods. 'I get it; we become so bogged down with the idea that money can solve all our problems. What I see is a happy, blossoming woman.'

I feel Hector's hand on my arm, and I look down to check I'm not imagining it. Stig has turned his body away from the table and is sipping his wine. He hasn't noticed. I feel the softness of Hector's hand against my skin and, at the same time, the tension from Stig.

Turning down the job was a bone of contention for many months. But I stuck to my guns. Money doesn't matter; my happiness at my job does. He understood it in the end. But I know he still doesn't agree with it. Sometimes, I wonder why he obsesses over money and finances. But that is never something I can talk to him about. He closes up whenever I bring it up. It's as though he is somehow now ashamed of who he is deep down and as though it has left its mark on him in some ways.

'Thanks,' I say, and feel a little goofy.

Hector claps his hands lightly this time.

'On with the mains. No rest for the wicked,' he adds with a wink.

Hector is far too close to us in the kitchen; even with the clanking and banging of plates, starting a conversation about what is happening would be impertinent. But I can slice the atmosphere between Stig and me with the butter knife I am holding. There is so much to say about this extraordinary experience, but we will all have to wait until later. I just hope I haven't made things between us worse than they already are.

3

I wake with my mouth feeling as though it has been stuffed with cotton wool, and my head has been packed with shards of metal. I'm not good after drinking lots.

The latter part of the evening is a blur. The main course was followed by dessert, and then Hector got out the limoncello. There were definitely liquor coffees.

Stig is not in bed next to me when I turn over. I feel the space where he usually lays next to me; it's cold. I check the time on my phone. It's just after ten. I sit up, surprised at how late I slept. Stig will have gone for a run already. Maybe he will stop at our favourite bakery on the way back and pick up the crème-anglaise-filled croissants I love. Then I have a flashback to what I ate last night and realise I have fulfilled my calorie quota for the entire week with the alcohol on top of the four courses.

I spot water on the bedside table and gulp down the entire glass. I pull on a cardigan and wander into our upstairs office, where Stig works from time to time but has also doubled up as a second spare room for when friends come to stay.

I stand in the room and am overcome with emotion for

what this room could and should have been. Luckily, we never got around to decorating it or putting in a cot or a mobile. Every month for the last year, Stig has looked at me with expectation. We talked of having children before we married, and now with Stig getting to forty and wanting to have somewhere to work from when he is at home, I know he is losing hope. The dream is parked, yet the looks of curiosity and eventually... is it disappointment? I wasn't sure; from friends and family. I feel like I am in a museum, a strange artefact that they need to observe. I know only a handful of women who are still childless at thirty-five. I didn't ever imagine I was going to be part of that club. But it still doesn't feel right to bring a child into this marriage when things are the way they are.

My friend Emily told me not to allow a baby to come along to be the glue in our marriage. I think I love Stig, but after five years, I thought he would have revealed more of himself to me. There is still this gaping whole between us that Stig refuses to see.

I leave the spare room, go into the kitchen, and make myself coffee. As I sit at the table, thirstily trying to sip the hot beverage, snippets of last night come back to me and play out in front of me like short films. I begin to squirm at one point as the finger of mortification bears down hard upon me. I had been fangirling hard. Stig probably hates me this morning. No wonder he was up and gone and still hasn't returned. I was certain it was the perfect present, yet as the night progressed, Stig seemed to get more and more uncomfortable. I would apologise to Stig for the big, showy dinner and promise to take him somewhere quieter where the two of us could just 'be'. That was more his style. I wanted the dinner at Sapphire to impress him, to bring the spark back, and to remind him that we are two fun individuals who chose to be together. Right now, I feel I have driven a wedge further between us.

I pick up my phone and open my photo library to cheer myself up. Three images were taken last night. A selfie of Stig and me before we had headed out, one of the starters and one of the three of us. Me, Stig and Hector Bolson-Woods. Me on one side, Stig on the other, and Hector sat between us, rosy cheeks from cooking, a small grease stain on the front of his otherwise immaculate white jacket and a smile that stretches across his entire face and finishes at the tips of his eyes, which are half closed. He looks genuinely happy. We look like three friends. I wonder if it is too early to post to Instagram and if Stig would mind. I strongly dislike people who are barely back from a day or night out before they upload 257 images to Facebook, ready to receive comments and likes to boost their serotonin levels.

But I am partial to the odd Instagram post, showcasing the simple but what I consider sophisticated life. I like to, as Stig puts it, 'show off a bit'. I know why I do it. Whenever we get to do something a bit fancier, I want people to know. It's a terrible affliction, and I hate myself for it. We do okay; we managed to scrape the money together to buy the house we were meant to raise a family in, but we are mortgaged up to our eyeballs. Stig works like a horse to keep the payments up; I do my bit too, but Stig's money tops mine and I am fine with that. But Stig is not. He knows I can do so much more and bring in a higher income, and I agree with him. But I love my job. How many people can say that these days? We appear to everyone as though we are on top of our game, that we are winning at life. One friend even dubbed us a 'power couple', which Stig became disgruntled at. Afterwards, he told me in private he didn't want to be seen that way.

I look again at the photo of the three of us, me, Stig and

Hector, and I can't help but smile. I look drunk, there is no denying that, but I also look happy and dare I say it, pretty. I am always so critical of the images I see of myself; it is rare to see one that seems to capture a speck of my soul, something the static image can't retain.

Without thinking about it for too long, I upload the photo to Instagram and type a few words to accompany it.

> Well, this was an unexpected twist. Thank you, Hector Bolson-Woods, that was a truly spectacular evening.

I tag Hector in the post under his name, where he has some three million followers, and sit back, knowing that the questions will soon begin flying in, along with multiple likes. What was I doing there? How did that come about? What was the food like? Is Hector as brilliant in person as he is on TV?

The front door opens, and Stig walks through into the kitchen in his running shorts and vest. His hands are empty. No treats from the deli then.

'Hey,' I say.

'Hey,' he says back, sweat dripping from him, and I try to ascertain the tone of his voice. Is he mad that we spent the evening with Hector Bolson-Woods? Is he frustrated that I drank so much?

Stig fills a glass with water from the tap and drinks it all whilst facing the window onto the garden.

'Good run?' I ask, trying to sound as though I'm not creeping.

'Not my best.' Stig puts the glass in the dishwasher. Always so neat and tidy.

'How are you feeling? Bit hungover?'

'I didn't drink as much as you, Lily.'

Stig's words sting. I take a deep breath. I do feel rough, so I know it's true. I can't deny how much I drank last night.

'Shall we have brunch?' I feel my stomach turn at the thought. I'm not hungry, but I want to bridge the gap that has opened up even more between Stig and me overnight. 'Maybe just some fruit and toast?' I say, and he nods. I open the fridge. Stig is still next to the sink, looking out of the window. I glance down at his arm and notice a long graze. I suck in a breath.

'Stig, your arm!'

He looks down slowly at it as though he has only just noticed. It doesn't look fresh, but it is new.

'I grazed it against the restaurant wall last night,' he says, and I feel my gut weaken. I had been a mess. I have ruined our anniversary, and now he has marks on his skin to prove my irresponsibility. Stig is not a big drinker, but I should have at least let him be the one to get a bit tipsy whilst I watched out for him, as last night was supposed to be so much more than just a dinner. It had been an opportunity for us to reconnect.

'Oh my God, does it hurt?' I go to touch it, and he flinches.

'It's fine. It's a graze. It's not infected or anything.'

'Okay, as long as you're sure. I'm sorry, I didn't know you had hurt yourself.'

'You didn't know much after the brandy came out. I didn't know you were such a keen brandy drinker.'

I laugh, but I feel my stomach burn with acid and I think I might be sick.

'I'm not, I just... I don't know, I just got carried away by the situation. Hector is very persuasive.'

Stig laughs, but it sounds harsh.

'What?' I say. 'Convincing you to come to the kitchen to dine was an experience. One you'll never forget, right?'

Stig clears his throat. 'Oh, I'll never forget it, that's for sure.'

'I'm sorry it was too much for you. I know you like things low-key, and that was the original plan: go in, eat dinner, and leave. Then Hector invited us in and well, you know, I couldn't say no to that. That will never happen again. It was a once-in-a-lifetime opportunity.'

Stig sighs. 'Yes, it was that.' He looks at me for what feels like the first time today. 'Thanks, Lil. It was a great gift.'

I smile but feel a flutter in my tummy. Is it just my gut still churning from the alcohol?

But before I have time to mull it over any longer, the doorbell trills loudly through the carpet-less hallway, which we still haven't finished. The tiles I have seen and want are way more expensive than I had thought. I'm not very good at reading the small print, and the cost per tile is not within our budget this month. Or for the rest of the year. Not until Stig gets that pay rise he has been edging toward for the last six months. We need it more than ever. The credit cards have been mounting up, and I don't like the thought of being in that much debt. And I am certainly not due any bonuses or rises any time soon.

Stig wanders wordlessly to the front door and swings it open. I begin taking out fruit from the fridge and flick the kettle on for our coffee. I hear a deep, male voice that isn't Stig's, so I peer around the kitchen door to get a look down the hallway. There is a man in a biker helmet handing a small package to Stig. A courier?

Stig slams the heavy door, and the sound echoes through the hallway again. We need to make some decisions soon as the lack of flooring, stripped back bare walls and no furniture means there is nothing to absorb the sound. But I am not ready to say goodbye to my dream tiles just yet.

'Was that a courier?' I ask as he arrives back in the kitchen. I lean over him and look at what is in his hand.

Mr and Mrs Leonard is embossed onto a grey, glossy envelope. Stig remains stationary, staring at the envelope.

'Stig?' I say.

He looks at me.

'Oh, yeah, a courier just delivered this.'

'A hand-delivered envelope,' I muse. 'Well, shall we open it?' I take it from him.

'I'm going to make eggs.' I wonder how he can walk away from such an intriguing envelope when I'm so desperate to know what is inside.

Stig starts cracking eggs into a large bowl.

I lay the envelope on the counter between us.

'Who do you suppose it's from? A wedding invitation, maybe? It can't be a wedding; it's already summer, so it's either very late or ridiculously early. I can't remember the last time I went to a wedding. Oh no, I do: it was the summer we met; I took you to my friend Lara's.'

Stig is whisking the eggs. I can hear the butter sizzling in the pan.

'Why don't you open it and see,' he says calmly, highlighting my anxiety. I feel on edge, and it could only be from the alcohol. I pick up the envelope and turn it over in my hand. It is matt grey, handwritten in swirling italics, and an embossed stamp is on the back. Two or three letters circling within one another; it is hard to determine what they are. I tear at the envelope and tug at the piece of card inside. I slide it out and lay it on the counter. I look at it momentarily, taking in the words and then rereading them to be certain that I am seeing them correctly.

'Stig?' I say questioningly.

'Hmmm?' He has poured the eggs into the pan and is stirring vigorously.

'It is an invitation.'

'Yeah?' He half glances back at me.

I laugh before I speak again. 'Yeah, and it's from Hector.'

Stig stops stirring, I hear the wooden spoon drop onto the floor. He bends quickly to retrieve it and lays it on the kitchen counter.

'He's inviting us for dinner,' I say, barely able to keep the hysteria from my voice. 'At his house!'

4

It has divided us, that I am certain of. Stig says we will talk about it later, and I haven't seen him since. I am getting the impression he is ignoring me and that after our unexpected encounter with Hector, he had hoped that was that.

By Monday morning, the invitation still sits unanswered, undiscussed on the kitchen counter. We are invited to dinner in a fortnight, to Hector's London house. I looked up the address immediately on Google Maps and zoomed in on the property and found it was a six-storey, red-brick town house with a glossy, black door in Mayfair. That kind of building here in Oxford would serve as a flat and home to several people. But the address is not a flat, it is just a number. Hector is wealthy; these buildings are worth millions. I had felt a flutter in my stomach at the prospect of seeing inside the building, walking into the hallway, and through into high-ceiling rooms. I wonder if there is a study, a library or a gym. I bet he has it all.

I want so badly to talk to Stig about it, but it is all too soon for him after Friday night. He needs to decompress for a few days, and then he will realise the magnitude of this. Hector

Bolson-Woods is inviting us to dine with him at his house. I wonder if he will cook, or bring in a chef? One of his own, maybe? I have so many questions and thoughts running through my mind, and I know the only way to satisfy them is to accept the invitation.

The email address is at the bottom of the invitation, and just before it, the words *RSVP*. This is where I need to reply. I will try one last attempt to discuss it with Stig; then I guess I am on my own.

First, I need to get to work. My employers are good; sometimes, I skip the office and work from home. But today, I fancy a bit of human company to speak with my colleagues, to get their approval over the dinner gift that I had organised for Stig. Of course, they knew all about it; I hadn't stopped talking about it for weeks. They thought it was an excellent idea and will be keen to know how the evening panned out.

* * *

I have my own office at work, which is rare and unusual for the charity sector, but the building we rent for Family First has so many rooms, and we have the whole of the lower floor at a rate that has not increased for four years. And each of the three rooms is huge. So, although I have an office, I spend most of my time in the communal office with my colleagues, Hannah and Michelle, where we laugh and chat about life. And, of course, raise money and place volunteers with families.

A coffee shop right next to our office sells the best bagels. Now fully recovered from the weekend's drinking, I am back on track with my eating. I order three for the girls and me and a coffee for myself.

I enjoy having the first half-hour to myself in the office to acclimatise and get through some emails before the other two come in. We get nothing done for the next hour as we socialise and catch up on each other's weekends.

Hannah arrives half an hour later, looking as stressed and flummoxed as she always does, as though every issue from her life has been brought to the office with her. She throws off her bright yellow raincoat, hangs it on the coat rail, picks up the three bags she was carrying, and walks over to me, where I sit at the communal desk.

'Morning,' she sings. She drops one of the bags on the desk. 'I found all those sensory toys I was telling you about; they'll be perfect for the Burns family boys.'

I peer into the bag and see a lot of bright colours and textures, things that look battery operated that will light up or make sounds. I think of the family Hannah is referring to, with two severely autistic boys. We are about to send a volunteer in to give the mother some respite once a week and these toys will be a godsend for her.

'That's great! Mia will be so happy with those. And the boys will love them.'

I push the bagel across the table to her. She snatches at it like a hungry hyena. Hannah has three children at home, all teenagers. When she isn't here, she runs around after her family and never looks after herself or eats properly. Michelle is much better at home cooking, bringing in bits of her batch baking, salads or sandwiches for us all to share.

I let Hannah settle down in her chair across from me. I know she will ask about my weekend; she's that kind of person: thoughtful and caring. But first, she needs to get all her paraphernalia out and check her emails. I make two coffees, one for her and one for Michelle, who will arrive any minute.

And as I put the mugs down at each of their desk spaces, I hear the buzz of the door as Michelle lets herself in.

'Have you seen it out there? It's bloody bedlam,' Michelle comments. She drapes her handbag over the back of her chair and drops another larger tote bag on the floor, spots the coffee and takes a swig. Then she points at me. 'You look like a woman who has been hobnobbing with the rich and famous this weekend.'

Hannah stops typing and looks up at me. 'Oh yes, that Hector thingy's place. What's it called?'

Michelle shakes her head. 'Honestly, Hannah, get with the programme. It's Hector Bolson-Woods.' Michelle looks at me; her long, dark hair glistens from the rain that must have started. She looks fresh and relaxed after her weekend. Her children are in their twenties and don't live at home, so Michelle's weekends consist of baking, gardening and watching Netflix with her boyfriend, George. 'How was it?' Her eyes sparkle with intrigue.

I smirk. 'It was great.'

'Better than great. I saw the picture you posted. You got a selfie with the main man.'

'Better than that,' I say. 'We got to go into the kitchen, and he cooked dinner for us!'

'Woah! So that was where that photo was taken?'

'What photo?' Hannah asks.

'Will you ever get social media, Hannah?' Michelle rolls her eyes dramatically.

'Not any time soon. I prefer the good old days when we brought in our photos that we had developed from the chemist in an hour.'

I smile as I remember the simplicity of those days.

'I have the photo here, Hannah.' I pick up my phone from

the desk next to me and find the photo from Saturday night. I hand her my phone, and she studies it.

'Aww, look at you both, you look so cute. Look at Hector, he looks so handsome.' She hands the phone back to me.

I look at the image again, trying to see it from Hannah's perspective. Did she see a happy couple out for dinner? And Hector, I always thought he was good-looking, but seeing the image through the eyes of Hannah, I realise that he is handsome. He looks like someone with a privileged upbringing and a good education; he has confidence, which is etched within his solid jawline. My mind is thrown back to the moment he placed his hand on my arm at the table.

'That's quite something, Lily. How did Stig find it? Not too overwhelmed?' Michelle laughs; she knows how Stig is and how he likes to spend his time, and I think back to the way Stig has been for the last two days.

'Oh, you know him, doesn't love all the attention like I do. But Hector was charming and accommodating, and my God, the food was divine. I keep thinking about it like it was an illicit night of passion or an affair. I keep getting flashes of the dishes and the flavours in my mind, you know?'

Michelle laughs. 'Well, I don't know what it feels like to have an affair, but I do know what it feels like to have flashbacks of something I had in my mouth the night before.' She says it so matter of fact, her face turned to her computer screen, her expression set. I roar with laughter. Michelle is so dry sometimes; she doesn't even know she is funny. Hannah laughs, too, even though she is not one for a double entendre.

'I think he looks nice.' Michelle slides into her seat. 'Was he nice?'

I try to think back to the evening to recall Hector, and I

realise that I have thought about him and his demeanour quite a lot. He complimented me over and over and stuck up for me over my job and then that touch. Did it mean anything? Or did I allow myself to get wrapped up in the excitement, and the alcohol has muddled my memories?

'I told him what I did here for a living and he was impressed. I can't remember his exact words, but he said he thought it very noble and a worthy thing to do. Words to that effect.'

'How lovely,' Michelle says.

'I mean, Stig never comments like that about my work. You know he thinks I should have taken the better-paid job.'

'Well, I told you that too.' Michelle snorts. 'Remind me, why are you here again?'

I roll my eyes. 'Because I love my job. And you guys.' I nibble on my bagel.

Michelle's fingertips begin to hit the keys on her keyboard. I can also hear Hannah typing.

'Say, Lily, what did you say his surname was again, the chef?' Hannah asks, and I imagine her googling him.

'Hector Bolson-Woods.' Saying his name is like taking a huge bite out of a sandwich, the letters filling my mouth.

'Oh,' she says, 'that's so weird.'

I strain toward Hannah as though I might be able to see what she is looking at on her computer. 'What is?'

'Well, there was a deposit made over the weekend. And it is in the name of Bolson-Woods.'

My heart thuds hard in my chest. I think back to the conversation I had just relayed. Hector had been impressed by my altruism. He himself had built an orphanage, for goodness' sake. 'He's given to the charity?' I ask.

'Err, yeah.' Hannah's voice has become quieter; her brow furrows and she stares hard at her computer screen.

I swallow hard and ask, 'How much?'

She stares at the computer for a few seconds more then looks at me. 'Twenty thousand pounds.'

5

I stand and walk to the other side of the desk and stand over her shoulder, my hands on the back of her chair, staring at the screen. Michelle is leaning on my shoulder, her hand pressing into the muscle just below my neck; I ignore the pang of pain and focus entirely on the figures bouncing around in front of my eyes. Hannah does our accounts and deals with everything from the money we spend, petrol money for our volunteers, any marketing and advertising costs, our wages and of course the donations. Of which there are usually just enough to keep us afloat. We are a self-run charity with no help from the government or any other bodies. We've been going for five years, and in that time, we've received a few generous donations, as well as regular subscribers and, of course, the fundraisers we do throughout the year, which brings in enough to cover the basics. But we have never received a lump sum this high before, and immediately, I feel sick. How much had I gone on about my job and how much I loved it? Had I bombarded Hector so much that he thought he had to gift that much money? Was I responsible in some way for making him feel he needed to do it? I cast my memory back to Friday evening again and nothing jumps to the forefront of my mind. This is a purely altruistic act. Hector is a charitable man; I remember him talking about the work he had done abroad, somewhere in Africa, was it?

Michelle steps back and removes her hand from my shoulder.

'My God,' she whispers.

I look around at her, my eyes wide, my mouth slightly open.

'You must have made quite an impression on him.'

I can't think how I had made any impression on him. I had made an impulse decision to ask if Hector Bolson-Woods was cooking in the kitchen that night and it turned out he was. I guessed that not many people asked after him or maybe he was feeling particularly generous that day. Or maybe he never said yes, but it was a one-off that day; he was feeling frivolous. I didn't know. I did understand that Hector was wealthy; I had read articles about his multiple businesses, and I presumed he must also have investments and that he was from the aristocracy. I had read in *The Times* an entire article about how he had come to food from a young age by shadowing the family's private chefs. But twenty thousand feels like such a huge amount of money. I wish that amount would just land in my personal account so we could finish the hallway, maybe start tackling the kitchen and buy a few bits for our bedroom. I could make that amount stretch and do so much with it. And Hector – or whoever worked for him and managed his money – had just pressed a button and transferred the money to us. Just like that. He would never think of that amount of money again. It was obviously pocket change to him.

But what am I doing thinking about all the things I could do with the money, when I should be thinking of all the things we could do with it here. The toys we could buy, the marketing we could do to reach more people like Hector. I have been dreaming up a marketing campaign for some time which involves celebrities the way big charities like UNICEF bring in the likes of actors such as Ewan McGregor – I wonder if it would be a step too far to ask Hector to be a face in a campaign?

I am getting carried away with myself. I have some money to play around with now. A nice chunk we could spread about the departments and do so much good. Twenty thousand would see us through for a long time and we could do things we had only dreamed of doing.

What a good man Hector is. He understands the importance of what I am doing, and while I know it took seconds to transfer the money, his heart was in the right place; he wants to help.

'I can't believe it, Lily! How much did you tip?' Hannah laughs a little nervously, I notice, and rightly so. This is the most significant deposit we have ever seen.

'It's mad,' Michelle says.

'We should schedule a meeting; we have some money to play with this month. I'm tied up until two, but after that, we'll talk,' Michelle says, suddenly putting on her manager's hat, looking thoughtful, and heading back to her seat.

There is silence amongst us as we all return to our morning tasks. The occasional sigh emitting from one of us, each understanding its meaning. I have an overwhelming desire to call Stig, but Monday mornings are his busiest times. For a moment, I wonder if I should tell the girls about the invitation, but suddenly, it all feels a little weird and intimate like a relationship with a new boyfriend that has accelerated at a rate beyond its own capability. For some reason, I think Hannah and Michelle would feel it was too much. Going out for a meal, meeting the chef personally, getting an invite to his London town house, and now this gift. And although I can sense those feelings lingering, mostly I just feel as though it is all purely innocent. We met Hector; he liked us as a couple, he is a generous man who likes to give to charity and probably has a lot of money he likes to put to good causes for tax reasons. That was what all these celebs did, wasn't it?

* * *

I stop at the supermarket on the way home and pick up ingredients for a paella. Stig and I ate an amazing paella on our honeymoon in Marbella, and it has become our special thing. Stig will know I've cooked it because I want to discuss the Hector invitation. I know that hobnobbing with celebs is not something he enjoys. I know he would rather have a takeaway in front of the TV, but how can we possibly decline an invitation like this? After the generous donation today, I am wondering if Hector is interested in a collaboration after all, and this invite is a means to discuss business. These sorts of random meets happen all the time whereby people are thrust together for reasons only the universe knows.

When Stig arrives home, the smell of fish, prawns and garlic, and chorizo fills the air. I hear him drop his briefcase on the floor in the hallway. It makes a dull thud, and I imagine a crisper, cleaner sound when the tiles are laid and the hallway decorated.

Stig comes through into the kitchen.

'Hey.' He stands over me, peering into the pan. 'Paella?'

'I just really fancied it,' I say, partly lying, but also, it is our favourite dish, and I can and would eat it every week. But we try and limit it to keep the specialness of it alive. I was lucky enough to be able to blag the waiter at the restaurant to get the chef to give us part of the recipe. He wouldn't give us the full recipe, and we believe he withheld one or two key ingredients, but whenever we eat it, it tastes the same as it did that night in Marbella, so who knows?

Stig doesn't say anything else. He doesn't try to infer that there is a hidden reason behind the paella coming out tonight. I try to think back to the last time we ate it; it has been so long since we have had anything to celebrate. Then I feel sad. But now we do have something to celebrate. And whilst the restaurant date overwhelmed Stig, I wonder if an intimate dinner would be less stressful for him.

'Also,' I begin again, 'I thought it would be nice to have it as I had a good day at work today.'

'Oh yeah?' Stig sounds mildly interested as he takes his phone out and begins bashing out a text.

'Yes, we had a healthy donation.'

'Oh yeah?' Stig says again. And I frown at the repetitiveness of his responses. I take a seat opposite him at the kitchen table. I think about what Hector's dining table at his house would look like, and I picture something five times as long.

'Twenty thousand pounds,' I say and feel a flutter of pleasure as Stig stops typing and looks at me.

'Twenty thousand?' he repeats.

I nod.

'And was it anonymous?'

'No. They gave their details.'

Stig shakes his head and opens his eyes wide as though to ask who without saying the word.

'It was from Hector.'

'Bolson-Woods?' Stig confirms.

'I don't think we know any other Hectors, do we?'

'Sadly not,' Stig says so sincerely that I pull a face. I wait for him to tell me he is kidding.

'You know we can't turn down his invitation now, can we?' I say tentatively.

'Well, of course, that's exactly why he did it.'

'What?' I snap. 'You think he just donated twenty grand to Family First so that we would go to dinner with him?'

Stig is silent as he stares at me as though he is looking right through me.

'I think we should accept the invitation,' I say, and he looks away.

I hear him exhale.

'I think this could be a business proposition. I think this could benefit Family First. He's donated some money and I think he would be interested in being an ambassador. I could convince him to be an ambassador.'

Stig gives me a weak smile.

'Come on, I'm good at my job. I'm good at marketing. That's why that other company wanted to poach me. I have skills. I know you think the charity pays me peanuts, and it does, but it's a worthy cause; I get an enormous sense of satisfaction, especially when people like Hector invest.'

'I really don't know what you think is going to happen. He's a man with a bit of money, and he's obviously...' Stig pauses, seemingly thinking about his words. 'Done a good thing, and I think we should leave it at that.'

'So you don't think we should accept the invitation? We could have a nice night out in London. Book a hotel and take the train.' I look longingly at my husband. 'I think we need this, Stig. Things haven't exactly been great between us recently.'

'You don't need to remind me,' Stig says. 'You do know why that is, Lil? I don't have to reiterate it, do I?'

I feel the rage building from the pit of my stomach as it

always does when Stig brings this up and tries to pin the blame on me for all our issues.

'I tell you what, why don't you *reiterate* it again? I don't think I've heard it enough.'

Stig snorts. 'Do you know what, it's not worth it.'

I laugh. 'I'm not worth it? We're not worth it?'

'A baby!' he hollers.

I shudder at his words.

'The baby isn't worth it,' he says more quietly this time.

I feel all my energy deplete. I can't keep rehashing the same argument over and over. And I can't explain to Stig why a baby won't come. I can't tell him how I still feel we aren't where we are supposed to be as a married couple. Couples aren't supposed to feel that something is missing. And I do feel there is a piece missing between us. I don't know what it is and so I can't communicate it to him.

'It's a free meal, for goodness' sake, and I imagine it will be exceptional,' I say, feeling defeated. I know Stig is no longer into this, but I don't want to go alone.

'I have no doubt the food would be exceptional,' he says flatly.

'So, what's stopping us?' I say, hopefully.

Stig sucks in a breath, shakes his head again. 'It just feels weird.'

'I think things like this happen to people, and it's happened to us. I think you just need to accept it,' I say, matter of fact.

Stig laughs demonically. 'There are certain things I am forced to accept, like how I will probably never be a father. But I am uncomfortable accepting dinner dates as fate with a super-star chef.'

'We've only been trying for...' I do some quick mental arithmetic. 'Well, less than a year,' I say, remembering the conversation between us when Stig told me he was ready to be a father.

Stig shakes his head. 'These things shouldn't take a year; it's basic human biology.' He sounds exasperated.

I know how much Stig is ready to be a father. I feel the weight of the responsibility hard. I am the bearer, the one who should be walking around blooming, baking a baby, meeting new expectant mothers, filling the nursery with baby clothes and mobiles and baby monitors, feeling maternal, feeling purposeful, as though I now have something truly remarkable to offer. Listening to Stig's family give me advice about what to expect from a baby he created.

And it is this part that I struggle with. The missing piece of our marriage. How can I bring a baby into a marriage when I know so little about Stig and his family? I talk about my parents all the time, but from Stig, there is nothing. I can't just accept that he came from nothing. He had parents, that I know. But that is where the conversation always starts and ends.

'I don't see you exploring other options; I don't even see you upset each month when the pregnancy doesn't come.'

I pull a face. 'Er, sorry. What do you want me to do? Make an Instagram post about it?'

'Well, you do about everything else.' He snorts.

'Well, I wouldn't do that about something so personal and private to us.' I touch my lower stomach, feeling the empty, cavernous space, thinking how rightly it should be filled with a growing foetus. I have failed my husband. I haven't given him the one thing he needs more than anything. Instead, I am trying to fill the void by going out to fancy restaurants. Then posting about it on social media. I think about the other events I have lined up this year, things to do with Stig, museums, shows, picnics under the stars at music events at our local park, and

Tough Mudder runs. I even booked tickets to Bear Grylls live at the Theatre Royal; who knows what that will involve, but it is a way to get us out and distract us from the one thing I know I'm not giving Stig. And the things he isn't giving me: an insight into his past and who he really is. But I fear he will never tell me what his life was like before I met him; I will never know.

'It will come when the time is right,' I snap. I want this conversation to end.

'I'm forty, Lil. I never wanted to be an old dad. I want kids.'

My heart speeds to a furious beat. The weight is all on me. Again.

'I told you, I'll book myself in for the tests, wank in a pot, do whatever I need to do, but you need to do the same.'

But will you ever tell me who you really are? I silently ask because I am tired of asking it out loud.

'It's slightly more invasive for a woman, more poking and prodding.' The thought of someone putting anything inside of me makes me shudder.

'I get that,' Stig says, but I know he doesn't. No man can understand what a woman goes through, what she feels and experiences compared to men. But neither do I. I have only heard the stories from generations before me and the relatives and friends who already had babies.

I think for a moment before I speak again.

'Can we please just go and live our lives before a baby comes along and we can no longer do these things?'

Stig lets out a small sigh and nods. 'Sure. Accept the invitation. Let's have a nice night out in London. But book accommodation; I don't want any last-minute offers to stay the night at his house.'

I almost smile. 'You think that's a possibility?'

'Did you think any of this was a possibility?'

'No.' I snort. 'It is all very surreal, but a good surreal.'

Stig pushes past me. 'Just book the accommodation.'

I feel his brashness, but then I think that we are going to London to visit Hector Bolson-Woods in his home. I feel a thrill of electricity shoot through me.

* * *

Stig stays up in his office overnight and, for once, I do not try to coax him to bed or complain about how he has brought too much of the office back home with him and that he needs to switch off at some point.

Instead, I take my time getting ready for bed, and when I am bathed and dressed in my favourite leopard-skin-pattern, silk cami shorts and vest, I reach into my bedside drawer, take out a small make-up bag, one I used to travel with in the past, and unzip it. I take out a rectangular foil packet with the days of the week etched onto small, raised lumps. I pop the one that says Monday and take out the tiny, white, sugar-coated tablet. I look at it for a moment, recalling my conversation with Stig downstairs before dinner. It is amazing, really, that such a small, tiny pill can be responsible for preventing me from getting pregnant. I see Stig's face, hear my words of promise to him, pop the pill in my mouth and swallow it.

6

I pace from one end of the bedroom to another, stopping occasionally to look out of the window to see if Stig's car has arrived. I know it hasn't; it has a very particular sound, and I have become used to hearing it at a specific time most nights. He was due home an hour ago. Our train to London is in an hour. I look at my suitcase packed on the bed, my handbag next to it with my Kindle in it, and a couple of cans of Aperol Spritz for Stig and me to guzzle in the carriage. Mainly for me, as my nerves have not stopped fizzing since I replied to the email to Hector's office to say we were accepting the invitation.

It is so daunting, what we are doing, and now Stig is late, I have begun to weigh it all up in my mind. Is it worth going all the way to London? Is the invite really from Hector? What if they don't like us, and we stand out like sore thumbs? Who else will be there? Will walking through the door and into the grand dining area be embarrassing? Because in a house that size, I can only imagine a grand dining area. All these thoughts swirl in my head like a mini tornado as I pace the room alone. Much in the way a detainee might when they have been left purposely alone for longer than necessary in a locked room awaiting the interviewers so they will confess their crimes. Faced with only my thoughts and no one to share them with, I, too, begin to doubt what it is we are doing and feel ready to throw in the towel. Sod it; let's write again to say we are both ill and call in a takeaway instead. After all, it is what Stig and I are good at: staying away from the world; it is what we have become good at this last year. Stig is always buried in work, which is why he is late now. He knows what time our train is; I reminded him countless times and messaged him this morning to remind him once more. There is no way he can have forgotten. I know he is doing this because he is more absorbed in work than in our life and time together. And deep down, I know this is to do with me. And my empty womb. The more times my period arrives each month, the more Stig retracts and cocoons himself amongst his paperwork, becoming that husband who puts work before anything and everyone. But who can blame him? He wants something that I am not giving him.

It makes my blood boil that he would choose to do this today, of all days. He would choose to leave work later than we had organised and not be home on time. Now, he will be rushing, and it won't be the fun trip I had anticipated because he will be stressed, and I will be angry.

I hear a car door slam; in my rage and pacing, I hadn't even heard him pull into the drive, but I recognised the way the door closed on the Mercedes. I race down the stairs when he walks through the door, my rage bubbling. Expletives might be hurled, but I am ready.

Stig opens the door, and it takes a moment for me to see that he isn't in his work clothes but is wearing a light-blue shirt, unbuttoned at the top, light-khaki trousers and his Rockport shoes.

'Hey,' he says, dropping his sports bag and his briefcase on the floor with a thud. 'I just had the best game of squash of my life.'

My body shudders with anger. 'Squash?'

Stig nods and flicks through the post on the one tiny table in the hallway.

'I thought you cancelled your membership.'

'I will. I'm just finishing out the month.'

'You said we were skint, Stig. We agreed, no luxuries. I cancelled my gym membership.'

'Good. We can't afford your membership on your wage.'

I clench my teeth. I don't bite back but I do think of the credit card and loan repayments that are stacking up and the minimum payments keeping us in the red every month.

'Oh, for fuck's sake, Lil, I can feel you condemning me. It's all I have right now; I need it for my mental health more than anything.'

'Is that something that runs in the family?' I dare to ask, knowing I won't get my desired response. Knowing that Stig will not reveal anything more than he has to about his family.

'It runs in every family, Lil.'

Clever answer, I concede. 'I thought you would be home an hour ago. Our train leaves in an hour.' I move the conversation on; time is ticking, and I don't want to be late.

Stig gestures to himself. 'And I am ready to rock and roll.'

He chose to go to the gym, shower, and change there, and I don't want to jinx things. He looks very smart, and as I look at his familiar features, I remember that he is handsome. But my anger still simmers.

'Why didn't you text me and tell me? I was worried, actually.' This is partly true as the worry would have been after my anger and frustration. Worry that he had been hit by a truck, his car had swerved off the bypass; he'd had a heart attack driving home. He is young, but I often hear about men who drop down dead with aneurysms and all sorts at Stig's age. It is all things I would never be able to control, yet they invade my thoughts occasionally.

'Because I knew I was going to be on time,' he says plainly, and I feel stumped. Is he trying to punish me, get one over on me? I try to assess his behaviour. Is that a hint of smugness? I can't decipher. I think back to last night, to popping that pill, the one preventing my body from releasing an egg each month, meaning Stig's sperm is effectively redundant inside me every time. I feel a swirl of sickness, and I push my hand against the wall to relieve some of the intensity. I haven't eaten all day again, except for a few fruit pieces. I want to save myself for the feasts that we will be experiencing at Hector's house. Has Stig in fact found out about the pill? Is he trying to call my bluff, act all cocky and clever and then he will bring it up on the train to ruin the evening? *Christ, Lily, get a grip*, I tell myself internally. I did know how to overthink everything.

'I'm starving.' Stig walks past the bottom of the stairs toward the kitchen.

I hurry after him. 'You can't eat anything. We're about to go to dinner. We have no idea how many courses it might be.' I know I sound panicky.

Stig turns from where he stands at the fridge doorway. He has a smug look on his face, and I feel a surge of anger, the anger that has been building since I began pacing, waiting for him to arrive home.

'Relax, Lil. What time does the dinner invitation say?'

'Seven.' The time has been etched on my brain since the invitation arrived.

'Right, well, our train is at five. We'll get to the house just before seven, and I doubt we'll eat before eight.'

'You sound as though you know what you are talking about.'

Stig closes the fridge and helps himself to a banana. He peels it, bites almost half of the fruit, and swallows it without barely chewing.

'I know how these things work. No one will eat before eight. Maybe a canapé or two.'

I also know how these things work, of course, but I do not want Stig spoiling his appetite. This feels like an act of defiance already.

I watch him swallow the rest of the banana, feel my gut churn and turn on my heel.

'I'm going to get my stuff.'

Upstairs, I sit on the edge of the bed thinking about what we are about to embark on: a journey into London, the accommodation. All are paid for on a credit card with money we can't afford to repay. Will Hector be able to sense that we are in debt? Will we exude poverty? People with money can spot those differences between the classes and we are going for dinner at a world-famous chef's house. For some reason, now that Stig is downstairs acting all nonchalant, I am beginning to have doubts. Sometimes, it works that way with us; whenever he is unsure, I am always straight in there, guns blazing, as though his uncertainty fuels my certainty. I think it's a reaction to the way he is so closed off; it's as if I see his weakness and find a way to overpower it. And now he is, ready and organised, looking carefree and casual. I begin to worry. Have we made the right decision? Will we make fools of ourselves? Does Hector think we are something we aren't? What if no one there likes us? What if the conversations are stilted, and we have nothing to discuss past the entrées?

I take down the dress I have selected, which has been hanging on the back of the bedroom door for a few days now. I am ready to go once I slip it on. Suddenly, it seems drab and unsuitable. What if everyone there is dressed super trendy? I am not sure who these hypothetical people are going to be. I can't imagine Hector only invited us to his house to dine. Surely it has to be an event with other people as well?

I take the dress off the hanger and lay it on the bed. It is pink and black with large, geometric, abstract shapes. It looked good a few hours ago; now I am not so sure.

I am teaming it with a vintage jacket and pink heels. It's too late to change the outfit now.

I strip and dress. I touch up my make-up, which I did before I began to get tense from Stig's lateness, and throw the last few essentials into my handbag. A little confidence booster. Stig seems to be confident all of a sudden but the anxiety is rising. Maybe they didn't mean to invite us, and it was all a mistake.

I take one last long look at myself in the mirror. 'You are brave, strong, capable,' I say to the reflection and head downstairs.

* * *

The train is muggy and busy, but Stig and I manage to find two seats together opposite a large woman who keeps letting her feet touch mine and doesn't even seem to care. I keep snatching one foot away, only for hers to find its way back to mine again like a magnet. I eye Stig a few times, to get his attention over the matter, but he is already absorbed in a podcast with his earbuds tucked in. He hates having conversations on trains. He says it feels too intimate, as though people are watching us having sex or something. I think the way he thinks is a little weird sometimes.

I said he was being overdramatic, but I do feel he has a point. I don't like how cramped trains are and how people can hear every word you utter. The number of conversations I had been privy to on a train is unreal. People are either just oversharers, or they don't understand the proximity between other passengers and how their voices travel. I have so many things I want to say to Stig, but I know it will have to wait until we are off the train. I take out a can of Aperol Spritz and wave it at Stig; he shakes his head. I open it for myself, and a little of the fizz sprays out in front of me. The woman with her wandering legs frowns and tuts. I nearly laugh out loud at the audacity of her.

By the time the train shudders to a halt at our station, I have drunk both the spritzers. I feel wobbly as we walk along the platform and head up the stairs. I automatically go to place my hand in Stig's as the crowds bustle around us and the alcohol has given me a boost of confidence. He loosely takes it and then drops it once we are on the street. I'm not sure if Stig noticed I had both cans. I was sure he would berate me, tell me what I already knew: that drinking on an empty stomach is a bad idea. I think back to Stig's banana, and how his stomach is nicely lined, and now I wish I had done the same.

It is another Tube ride or a short walk, and we opt to walk the twenty-five minutes or so right to Hector Bolson-Woods's house.

'Are you nervous?' I ask Stig once we are away from the crowds of the train station.

'A little,' he says and I am glad he has acknowledged his feelings, and isn't trying to play the big man in front of me.

'Me too. But I think it will be fun. Let's just make it fun, yeah?

We only live once. This is an experience, right? Let's be ourselves.'

'I wasn't intending on being anyone else,' Stig says, that serious tone slipping back into his voice.

'And if either one of us feels uncomfortable at any time, we just—'

'Let's have a safe word,' Stig interrupts, and I spit out a laugh.

'A safe word? Okay. What sort of safe word? It can't be any random, weird word that will sound as though, well, it's a safe word.'

'Maybe a safe sentence, then?'

'Yeah,' I agree.

'Do you remember that time we went to Margate?' Stig says.

'Eh, Margate?'

'It's a safe sentence. I just made it up then,' Stig says.

'Oh right. Yes.' I giggle. 'Margate.'

'Do you remember that time we went to Margate?'

'Yeah, it's the kind of thing you can say, and it won't sound too weird if it came out of the blue.'

'Yes, that's good. I like it. Margate.'

'Have you ever been?' I ask Stig, imagining him there on a family holiday and willing him to tell me about it.

'Never. You?'

'No. We should go. Have a weekend away. It's got a beach right?'

'I believe so.'

'Right. Margate.'

I try to ignore the pinching in my toes. The shoes haven't been broken in properly. I only wore them once to an office party, and I was walking on carpet. This is the first time they have been walked in outdoors. Why I have chosen this evening to wear them, I'm not sure. I think about the inside of Hector's house and how, after a few hours, I could kick them off under the table and no one would notice.

We round the corner to the long road that will take us to Hector's house.

'About a minute's walk or so down here,' Stig says.

In the end, it takes us almost five minutes as we pause to marvel outside every house that we pass. Stig seems to come alive and comments on the brickwork and talks about the history of the buildings.

Eventually, we arrive. The house looms down at us. It appears to be mocking us: *who do they think they are?* It feels ridiculous now we are here and even though Stig practically rejected my hand earlier, I grab on tight to it now; part of me is ready to turn and drag him back the way we have come.

'All good? Any final requests?' he says with a hint of joviality.

'All good.' I gulp, my mouth suddenly dry.

We walk up the steps together, Stig still muttering away about brickwork.

'Here we go,' I say.

Stig presses the doorbell, and we hear the sound trill through what I imagine to be an expansive, carpet-less corridor. My feet ache at the sound as I long for a plush, thick rug underfoot.

I hear footsteps and a male voice calling loudly to someone before the door is pulled open. There stands a man, not Hector, but someone who looks very similar to him. He pulls a face, showing he doesn't recognise us. My stomach plummets. Is Hector even home? This is a mistake.

'Hello?' he says enquiringly. He turns his head slightly to one side, a smirk appearing as though he is mocking us. I feel the plummet turn to a flutter of rage. This man has annoyed me, and all he's done is open the door and say hello.

He holds the door open with one hand and a bottle of beer in his other. His shirt is open at the collar, and he is swaying.

'Mr and Mrs Leonard,' I say. 'We're here for Hector, we were invited—'

'Oh Christ, well then come on in!' he says enthusiastically. He pulls the door back. I look at Stig; he nods and walks in ahead of me. I watch as the man looks at Stig first, taking him in for a good few seconds before I walk across the threshold after him. He closes the door behind me, louder than I expected, and I jump.

'I should say,' he shouts to us, louder than necessary, 'I'm Hector's younger cousin, Tristan. It's just down the hall there; keep going until you hit the kitchen.'

I follow Stig, who is good at following his nose anyway, and that is literally what we're doing as unique smells of food cooking fill the air.

Inside the kitchen, Stig and I stop and wait for Tristan to come in past us. There are two women and a man standing at a massive kitchen island. The whole kitchen is marble and chrome. A complex-looking cooker and hob system is behind the island, with two ovens built into the walls and an array of machines on the surfaces. The island is filled with colourful ingredients: chillies, mangoes and a few things I don't recognise. Plus, a fresh piece of monkfish on a piece of baking parchment. The two women and the man look up at us and stop their conversation. Tristan announces our names.

'This is Mr and Mrs Leonard.'

One of the women steps forward. Stig stares, and she, in turn, stares hard at Stig, and for a moment, I am in the shoes of others. I have stopped really seeing him, but I know he is attractive. And this woman is looking at him as though she finds him attractive. 'Hi, I'm Ruby.' She holds her hand out; her fingers are long and bony, and the rest of her body is skinny, too. She wears a black dress with spaghetti straps, and her bony shoulders show through the see-through wrap she is wearing. Her skin is tanned, her long, black hair loose and wild like the look in her eye I can see now. Stig holds her hand and appears speechless. They are just staring and holding one another's hands.

I thrust my hand out. 'I'm Lily and this is Stig.'

Ruby shakes my hand loosely and then turns back to Stig.

'What an unusual name. Is it short for something?'

'It's a nickname. After the TV show *Stig of the Dump*,' Stig says robotically.

'So what's your real name then, Stig?' Ruby says, and she has that same mocking tone to her voice that Tristan had at the doorstep. I already feel that we are the outsiders, the jokers of the pack.

'Nicholas,' he says, 'but no one has called me that for years.'

'Nicholas,' Ruby says, mulling the name over as though she has never heard it before and as though it were more unusual than Stig.

Ruby is looking intensely at Stig, and I grasp his hand.

'Can I get you guys a drink?' Tristan calls over from a huge, American-style fridge, full on one side with food, the other with beer, wine and champagne. My mouth almost drops open, and I see it all when I think of our measly one-door fridge at home, with a few vegetables and one bottle of Chardonnay.

'Beer, please,' Stig says, and he is looking at me. 'Lil?'

I return to looking at Ruby, who has now dropped her intensity and is moving back to the other side of the kitchen.

'Um, wine. Please. Anything.'

'I'm having champagne, Lily. Why don't you have champagne?' Ruby calls as she walks away.

'Um, yeah, sure,' I say. I think of the two drinks I had on the train. My empty stomach gurgles. I can see bowls of spicy rice crackers and pistachios on the island. I begin to make a move toward them.

I want to ask where Hector is but I am sure he will arrive any minute.

'Hi,' the other woman calls over. 'I'm Henrietta.' She looks less intense, yet more conservative, in a simple, blue shift dress. 'This is Daniel.' She nudges the man who is part slouched over the island. He stands up and I can see how tall he is. I presume they are a couple, but Henrietta doesn't elaborate.

'It's nice to meet you both,' I say. 'Have you come far?' It sounds like a stupid question when it leaves my lips, but I want to keep the conversation going. I don't want to be the new kid who's just arrived and doesn't know anyone. Even though that is exactly who I am.

'Richmond,' Henrietta says. 'You're both Oxford, aren't you,' she adds without question as though she already knows the answer.

'Yes, that's right. Littlemore.'

'How quaint.' Henrietta squints, as though she is forcing a smile through her eyes.

'Yes, I suppose it is.' I haven't thought of it like that before, having grown up in the countryside, but just then, I see our life through the eyes of a stranger, and it does seem idyllic on the outside. An image of the little packet of pills flashes in front of me, the long silences and sleeping in separate rooms. The baby that is never coming that Stig presumes would have already.

Tristan hands me a flute of champagne.

'Thank you.' I look at the bubbles floating to the top and I feel my stomach gurgle again. I take a tentative sip. I see Tristan eyeing me; he lets his glance slip away slowly, purposefully.

'When will our host be joining us?' Stig asks with conviction, and I am thankful for his intervention at this stage. I haven't found the confidence to ask it out loud, although it was all I could hear in my mind.

'I apologise for my lateness.'

We both spin around, and we're face to face with Hector. He is wearing a crisp, white dinner jacket over a black shirt and black trousers. His face has a natural glow, his thick hair swept to one side. Hector steps forward and grips my hand. I think I am imagining it, but as he holds my hand, one of his fingers rubs back and forth on my palm.

'Lily, it is so good to see you. Thank you for accepting my invitation.' He holds my gaze, an intensity in his eyes as though he is trying to convey more without words. There was no way anyone would have seen what his finger had been doing.

'Thank you for inviting us, Hector; your house is beautiful.' I glance at Stig and Hector releases my hand.

'You wait till you see the rest of it!' He laughs and winks at Stig.

My eyes widen.

'Oh, yes.' He nods. 'No areas off limits; take yourself on a tour whenever you're ready.' He holds out his hand for Stig. There is an awkward moment between the two of them that I had seen so many times between men, a fluffing of the feathers, sussing one another out. I hadn't noticed it at the restaurant, the first time I met Hector, I had been so caught up in the excitement of being brought 'backstage' to meet the star of the show. Now, in a calmer environment, without the loud clattering of pans or seventy other guests surrounding us, I can see how the two men interact with caution. I don't know Hector well at all, but I can see he is exercising restraint. I wonder if he is worried about the large donation and how Stig might be feeling about that. Or perhaps it is just that male ego thing. Hector is a successful, wealthy, celebrity TV chef with multiple restaurants around the world. Stig is chief commercial officer for a merchandise company.

Does Stig feel threatened by Hector's wealth and status?

'Good to see you, Hector. We appreciate the invite.'

'It's my pleasure, my pleasure.' The men drop their handshakes. 'I see you have drinks, good. Now, we're having my menu this evening; I'm not cooking it, so you'll have me all to yourselves.' Hector's eyes land on me again. I feel a flutter in my stomach, which rises to my chest, then I feel a heat spread across my face. It isn't the first time he has looked at me like that. An image of Hector's hand on my arm at the restaurant and, just now, the movement of his finger across my palm, knowing no one else could see.

I look to my left at Stig. 'Sounds great!' I say, and I slip my hand into his for comfort or for show, I'm not entirely sure. I wanted to be here more than anything, but now I am, I have never felt so out of place. Perhaps it's just nerves and paranoia. Henrietta and Ruby both seem like a different breed of women to me. Ruby oozes wealth, as well as a kind of sex appeal that men adore, that innocent yet over-flirtatious approach, coupled with the laid-back personality bordering on nonchalant. Henrietta seems a lot more worldly and mature. I imagine her as someone who has lived and worked in a lot of countries, the sort of woman who has family money to support her. I feel slightly intimidated as the one thing that binds them is money. I would probably discover myriad ways that we could connect as women, but the one thing that would separate us is money. They have it. I don't.

'Marvellous. We're eating in the green room,' Hector announces as though we are all familiar with the room.

'Oh, lovely, Hector. I love the green room; I had my thirtieth in there,' Ruby drawls. She could be in her late thirties, possibly older. I look at the glass of champagne in her hand, and I can't help but presume it is a regular fixture. Her skin certainly seems as though it has taken a hammering from alcohol over the years, as I spot dry and red patches under the make-up.

'I remember. And you would have slept there as well if we hadn't come back for you, you silly tart,' Tristan pipes up, and Ruby snorts out a laugh which actually sends a shudder through me.

'We'll just wait for Gordon to arrive and then we're good to go. He's always late,' Hector scoffs and I am already forming an image of Gordon in my mind when the doorbell trills and Ruby skips out of the kitchen, her heels clomping along the wooden floorboards. The next moment, there is a squeal so loud that Stig and I both jump and turn around. No one else seems to flinch, and then we hear the snorting laughter of Ruby, who seconds later comes falling back into the room, her hand clasping that of a very tall and striking man, as though she were dragging him into the room.

'Everyone, darling Gordon is here,' Ruby announces whilst Gordon looks a little sheepish.

There is a little chorus of 'hellos' from the others. I smile meekly and Stig holds his hand up in a stationary wave.

Gordon is handed a beer by Tristan, and Hector vigorously shakes his hand, throwing around phrases like 'old chap' and 'jolly nice threads' as he does.

Then Gordon's eyes meet mine and he moves over to us. He holds his hand out and I reciprocate.

'Gordon,' he says. 'I see you've been dragged into this charade as well.' A genuine smile spreads across his face, and for the first time since I arrived here, I feel at ease with someone. I still can't get my head around the Hector thing, and it feels alien

The Dinner Party

to me that we are spending time socially with him. But Gordon, despite the upper-class name and slight plum tone to his voice, seems quite normal, a bit more like Stig and me.

'Hi, I'm Lily; this is Stig,' I say.

Gordon turns to Stig. 'Interesting name. I like it.' Gordon doesn't push for an explanation which relieves me, and I imagine Stig too. His nickname has stuck so much that it is impossible for us ever to introduce him as anything else, and it is a pleasant change when someone accepts it rather than digging to know the origins or wanting to know his real name.

'I think Regina is ready for us. Shall we head into the green room?' Hector says, and I feel a rush of relief that we will soon be seated, and I can relax, maybe kick off my shoes and focus on a delicious meal. Maybe it will be fine, and I have been worrying for no reason. We can fit in with these people.

Then Ruby is next to us. She squeezes Stig's arm and has hold of Gordon with her other hand.

'Come on, Nicholas, dinner time!' she squeals and trots out of the room, clinging to Gordon.

I look at Stig and roll my eyes; he reciprocates with a tiny shake of his head, silently asking me not to make such gestures. Why would an eye roll bother him so suddenly? I wonder.

I am curious about this collection of people. I can sense something strong-binds them all together, which isn't obviously on display for all to see.

7

The green room is exactly as I expected. It is heavily wallpapered in dark shades of green with flecks of lighter shades throughout. The darkness is lifted by the chrome fixtures in the lighting, candelabras, and a huge, chrome-framed mirror, which gives the illusion of an even bigger room. The oval dining table, which is the only black thing in here, is set for eight but could easily seat double that amount.

'Sit anywhere!' Ruby squeals, still as excited as she was when Gordon arrived. I am intrigued to know more about this relationship that appears to be one-sided and not reciprocated. She is sidling up to Gordon, who looks so far to be tolerating her.

'Should we sit together?' I ask Stig, but I don't need to decide as Hector marches in and begins directing people to seats. I end up opposite Stig, between Tristan and Henrietta, and Stig is in between Hector and Daniel, I am already wondering how that conversation might pan out. Stig looks over at me, and for a second, I think he might give me a reassuring wink. But he looks quickly down and fiddles with his napkin.

A waiter begins to circle the table with bottles of wine. Music begins in the background which Ruby looks to be managing via her phone.

'Wine, madam?' I jump when I hear a voice speaking directly into my ear.

I turn my head, and my hand goes to my chest.

'Sorry, you startled me,' I say and see I am almost nose to nose with a finely dressed man in a white shirt and black waistcoat. He is holding a bottle of white wine.

'This is to accompany the amuse-bouche,' he says.

'Oh, okay. Thanks.' My heart punches my chest. But he is oblivious to the shock he caused. I wonder what it is like to work in the home of someone as famous as Hector. He must get to see and hear all sorts. And a little unknown guest like me, jumping at the mere sight of him, hasn't fazed him at all.

He pours the wine and I take two big gulps and smile to no one in particular.

'Head for the door,' I hear, and I swing around this time, wondering if my ears have deceived me even though the same man who just poured my wine has his chin almost touching my shoulder, his lips inches from my ear. Am I supposed to be standing up again, moving to another room?

'Pardon?' I ask.

He looks at me, but he doesn't answer.

'Sorry, I didn't quite hear what you said.'

'I said, would you like me to pour?'

I look at his hands. He is holding a jug of ice water, the condensation dripping onto the napkin he holds beneath it.

'Oh, I... I thought you said head for the door,' I say with a laugh, and again he looks at me but doesn't answer. He must think I am a total idiot and I decide to refrain from interacting with the staff too much from now on.

He pours the water into a tall water glass, the kind I would have used to drink a large glass of wine out of at home. I mull over his words, weighing up the two sentences. It was noisy with chatter and shrieks of laughter from Ruby from the end of the table and clinking glasses. It is obvious I have misheard because it would have been a ridiculous statement to make, unless I hadn't misheard him and it was a snobbish response to my being here. This brings me back to my original feelings of not fitting in here and all of this being a ridiculous mistake.

I take a sip and then look at the waiter as he moves to Henrietta next. I watch as he pours water, noting how he doesn't ask her anything before. I can put it down to familiarity, the fact that Henrietta dines here often, and I am a newbie, but the logical part of my brain is being nudged by the notion that perhaps, just perhaps, the waiter had whispered something else to me first. My face must have been displaying a muddle of emotions because when I look up, I catch Stig's eye.

'You okay?' he mouths.

I let my face stretch into a smile.

'Yes,' I mouth back.

He keeps his eye on me for a few moments more before he is pulled back into a conversation with Daniel. My gaze falls to the left, and I find myself locked into an unexpected look with Hector. He holds my gaze for a few seconds and then smiles broadly. I was about to take this as my cue to thank him for the generous donation when a plate is placed in front of me.

The amuse-bouche is a simple smoked salmon and whipped crème fraiche and cream cheese topped with capers and caviar. It is classic, a perfect introduction to Hector's menu, which represents who he is and the way he cooks. He doesn't aim for gastronomic menus featuring odd and out-there combos, which, whilst I understand the science behind, can often seem off-putting. Hector's cooking is simple and flawless yet exquisite. I gulp it down and dab my mouth.

I drink down the wine that accompanies it, briefly noting how the saltiness of the caviar and capers, the sweetness of the salmon and the creaminess of the crème fraiche compliments it perfectly. *Damn, that is good*, I think to myself. My stomach and palate are ready for more.

Eventually, Stig and Daniel's conversation comes to a natural break as the starter arrives, some sort of chicken terrine beautifully presented. I take a bite of the feathery-light texture before I seize the moment.

'I just want to say, I very much appreciate the donation we received at Family First; it was a very unexpected but much-appreciated surprise.'

Hector looks down at his plate and then back up at me, swallowing what was in his mouth before he speaks.

'My dear Lily, when you told me about your work with those families, it stole my heart. I was captivated by the story behind the charity. I couldn't help but show my support. It is one of the most worthwhile organisations I have come across in a long time.' He places his knife and fork down, takes a sip of the wine: a different one which has been poured by the sommelier. 'I think what you are doing is wonderful. I want to show my support. I hope I have been able to do that with my small gesture.'

I gulp. 'Small, it was... Well, let's say...' I lower my voice; I don't want to make a thing out of Hector's money in front of his friends and family and with Stig back in a conversation with Daniel, I am safe to mention it. 'It was the largest amount we have ever received, Hector. It will do so much for the charity.'

Hector looks down at his plate, this time out of modesty. 'I am sure it will, and I am happy it could help. And you're staying over somewhere this evening, I hope?'

'The Winchester.' I think of the modest hotel we chose to keep the costs down.

'Ahh, I know it well. You'll have a lovely stay.'

I want to say more to instigate the next level whereby Hector becomes an ambassador for Family First. But he is speaking with the waiter who is now at his side.

'It was a very kind gesture,' comes Henrietta's voice next to me.

I look at her. 'It was. I'm still in shock. Well, about all of this: meeting Hector, receiving the donation, and now being here. It's all a bit of a whirlwind.'

'Hector's way. He likes things to be memorable. He likes to make a lasting impression on people.' She leans in a little closer. 'When Hector does something, he doesn't do it by halves. He is a master at inclusivity.'

'Wow, I didn't know this about him. I just thought he was a good chef. Now I know he is a perfect guy as well!' I scoff.

Henrietta doesn't laugh; she simply looks at me as though she is observing me. I break her concentration with a smile, and she allows her expression to break into a semi-smile.

'Hmmm.' She looks me up and down. 'I think you two will get on very well.' Then she turns to the waiter, who is removing the starter plates, and begins thanking him profusely.

'You're going to love the next course.' She leans into me again. And I nod and smile, but I can't shake the notion that Henrietta hasn't warmed to me. There is an air of something between us, and maybe she feels she is better than me. The way she looked me up and down just then. I wonder if she is an old flame of Hector's and if it's a jealousy thing. I am simply taking advantage of a very excellent, one-off opportunity. I am sure after tonight, I will never hear from Hector again. After this evening, I imagine Stig and I will fade into the background.

The main course comes and goes. The monkfish I had seen when we arrived is devoured, and then the dessert, a play on the s'mores dish with home-made marshmallows, individual pots of booze-infused chocolate and sesame biscuits. Wine is topped up; the bottles are left on the table. The noise level has gone up a notch, as has the music, I note by the way Ruby is swaying along to the beat, which has a Cuban feel, and I can't stop my body, fuelled by wine, moving along as well. Ruby catches my eye.

'Lily, come.' She stands up and walks to my chair with her hand out. 'Dance with me; these men are being so boring.'

'I... um...' I look up at Ruby. Her wrap has been abandoned, revealing her bony shoulders. I can see her true weight, and I glance across the table at her plate, which is the only one still full of monkfish.

I stand and take her hand, and Ruby grins. She carefully navigates us to where the dining room opens up a little, giving us enough space to move.

To begin with, Ruby holds on to my hands and sways, a sweet, naïve expression playing out across her face. For the first time, I see a small girl within her, and I feel a wrenching in my gut. I wonder if it is some maternal pull because I want to put my arms around her and hold her close like a mother would to her daughter. I see a flash of the aluminium case and the months and months of putting the pills into my system so I won't become a mother, yet always ignoring the pain which sears beneath the surface. I must admit to myself that I may never become a mother; the longer we are in debt, the longer Stig stays clenched up about his family and past, the more likely it is I will continue to pop one of those tablets every day.

I feel the eyes of the others on us, and I glance at Stig. He is smiling, but I see that he looks uncomfortable behind his expression. The other men look on with intrigue but not as if it is a new sight. Ruby lets go of my hands, lifts her long hair and flicks it over her shoulders. She throws her head back in a sultry way as she becomes more absorbed in the music. I feel obliged to do something similar, so I put my arms in the air and swing them gently from side to side, moving my head in the opposite direction to my arms. I can sense Stig's gaze, but I don't look over at him, in case his expression is sombre. I feel relaxed and more in the moment than I have all night.

'Whoo-hoo!' Ruby squeals as she dances around me, nudging her bony bum against my hips as she passes. 'I'm so glad you're here,' she coos. 'You're perfect.'

'Oh, thanks,' I say.

'I've been waiting for someone like you to join our little clan. The others have been so stuffy. You seem fun.' She wiggles her hips. 'That's why Hector likes you,' she says quietly this time. 'You're a breath of fresh air. He needs that; it's been a while.' She stops dancing and leans her weight against me, her breath sour from the wine. I can feel the heat from her body against my skin.

'Did you say the others have been?' I ask Ruby, wondering if I misheard because of the music.

'Hmm?' she says questioningly but grabs my arms and spins herself around me.

I was drunk and I didn't ask Ruby again, but the words play on my mind for a few more minutes.

And why did she say that is why Hector likes me? I have noted every look and touch from Hector, but it is madness to think he likes me in any way other than a new acquaintance.

I see Henrietta approaching from behind Ruby.

'Hey, Rubes, how's it going?' Henrietta has the look of a startled rabbit.

Ruby swings round to look at Henrietta and then back at me. She rolls her eyes. 'Oh, here we go.' She turns her back to Henrietta, who puts her arm around Ruby's shoulder.

'What's the plan, babes? We made the soufflé suite up.'

I smile at the notion of the soufflé suite, it sounds soft and luxurious, and I wish to go and lie down in it myself.

Ruby nods.

'Too much to drink,' Henrietta mouths to me and I nod, feeling a little disappointed that it seems the night is almost at an end.

'The boys are all off to the drawing room for cigars,' Henrietta says without a hint of irony.

'Are we in a Jane Austen novel? Will we retire to the library for sherry and cards?'

I realise immediately by the look on Henrietta's face that she thinks I am mocking them. Henrietta looks seriously at me. 'Well, yes, that seems like a nice idea. Ruby? Can you manage a sherry before you retire?'

'Yes,' Ruby slurs and then grins at me, yet her eyes do not show the same meaning, and I presume the alcohol has got the better of her.

'I'm just going to use the facilities,' I say and Henrietta looks at me with a puzzled expression. 'The bathroom,' I say, realising *facilities* was far too formal and I sound as though I am trying too hard.

'Sure, sure.' She waves her hand, and Ruby falls against her shoulder like a defeated child.

I find the toilet just down a hallway adorned with artwork and odd-shaped statues and figurines set on ancient-looking furniture, presumably from Hector's travels. The bathroom is small and darkly lit, with deep-purple wallpaper. It wouldn't have been my choice for such a small room.

I wash my hands, and when I open the door, I collide with Hector, who is walking along the hall.

'Lily, my God, I am so sorry.'

'Don't be sorry,' I gush. 'I think I walked into you…'

'Tomato tomayto,' he says in a mock American accent. 'Have I covered you in whisky?' he asks, holding his tumbler aloft to inspect the contents.

I look down at my dress. 'No, I'm good.'

'Ah, that is a shame; we could have had a *Notting Hill* moment.'

I feel my heart race as I think of the iconic scene where Hugh Grant takes a soaked-through Julia Roberts back to his house to help her clean up.

'Shame,' I hear myself say, shocked that I said it.

'My bedroom is just there,' Hector says, pointing along the hall.

My heart races in a panic as I am stuck for the words to reply, and then I realise he is just playing with the line from the film.

'Give it to me in yards,' I say in an American accent, trying to emulate Julia Roberts's style.

'That's very good, Lily.' He laughs. 'Have you watched the film a lot?'

'It's one of my favourites.'

'Mine too,' he says. 'I'm a bit of a sap when it comes to romantic comedies.' Then he looks at me. 'I'm a bit of a sap when it comes to romance, actually.'

Oh God, my mouth is dry as we both stand in the dimly lit corridor. I'm not sure what I am supposed to say that is appropriate.

'I didn't know that about you, Hector,' I say eventually.

'There is a lot you don't know about me.' He leans back against the wall. 'I hope you will come to know more.'

'You do?' I ask.

'I do. I think you are lovely, and I have thought of you often as it happens.'

'I...' I am stuck for what to say and then I hear Tristan's voice, and he appears at the end of the hallway.

'Come on, old chap, we need you for the poker.' He looks at me. 'Lily,' he says, nodding and then looking at Hector.

'Right, coming.' Hector stands up straight and walks toward his cousin. He doesn't look at me again and I wonder if he is embarrassed by what he has just said, but I can't ignore the rousing sensation in my chest.

* * *

The library is, in fact, a library and not what I had expected to see in Hector's house. He doesn't seem that academic, although I know he attended one of the most prestigious schools in the country. He seems so creative these days, yet this room displays an array of books from floor to ceiling. In the corner is an old bureau and a worn leather chair. Somewhere, Hector does his admin. Was that where he had been sitting when he had transferred twenty thousand to the Family First charity?

Henrietta goes to a drinks trolley in the corner and pours three sherries. She brings them over to us on a tray. Ruby has already claimed the chaise lounge and looks like she might fall asleep.

I take a moment to browse the shelves, noting plenty of photos of Hector on a large, round table. Behind the table is a large framed one, the classic school year photo with several hundred boys in school uniforms standing upright. Underneath the image, inside the frame, it reads:

Blythewood School for Boys, 15 July 2000

I scan the rows of slightly blurred faces until I find who I think is Hector. He would have been around sixteen. I smile at the thought of a young Hector Bolson-Woods, wondering if he ever knew what his life would be like and that he would be a celebrity chef, and everyone would know his face and name worldwide. And now, I suddenly seem to fit into this period of his life, dining in his house and popping into his thoughts from time to time.

Henrietta places the tray of drinks on a small, glass-topped table and we each take a seat on either side of it on a soft chair.

She glances over at Ruby, who appears to be asleep now.

'Did you have a good evening?' she asks quietly.

'I did,' I say. 'It was quite unexpected, but now I'm here, I don't know; it feels like it was always meant to be. Do you know what I mean?'

'He's a lot more delicate than people think,' Henrietta says, and I frown, wondering what she means and hoping she might expand on that comment.

She opens her mouth to say something else, but then she smiles at me. She stands and goes to the record player in the corner of the room, and within seconds, the crooning sounds of Frank Sinatra are floating around the room. I lay my head back against the chair and close my eyes for a moment, hoping and praying that this isn't just a one-off fluke and that we will find ourselves amongst Hector and his friends again soon.

And as the evening finally draws to a close, I feel a tugging in the pit of my stomach; I am already despondent as our departure grows nearer. After all the worry and stress of getting here and wondering if we would fit in, I feel very much a part of this. I may not be a Henrietta or a Ruby, but I know I can't walk away and say goodbye. I am hungry for more. I have a sensational appetite not just for the exceptional food, which far exceeded any menu I have eaten anywhere in the world, but for the buzz of the evening, for the feeling of inclusion, to know that despite the noticeable class difference, I am welcome here, I have conversations to offer, as Ruby said. I am someone amongst this motley crew. And as Henrietta had hinted, there is a side to Hector that he doesn't let just anyone see. Maybe in time, I might get to see that more vulnerable side to him. And then there were the words that Hector spoke to me in private in the hallway: I am someone he thinks about often. I feel the familiar flutter in my stomach again. The sensation I once felt when I first met Stig. I fit in well. And so I am going to take Ruby's words and hold on to them.

As we stand at the door, Stig clutching my hand – I'm not sure who was holding who up – I glance a final look into the hallway and see the waiter pass on his way to the kitchen. He glances up and looks at me, and in that look, I see something quite distinctly. It is a look of sorrow, as though he feels sorry for us.

The drunk woman in me wants to shout at him. *What is your problem?* But I snort out a laugh, kiss a final goodbye to our host and lead Stig and me to the waiting car.

8

We both crash when we get back to the hotel room. We don't discuss the evening, and I don't ask Stig what he spoke about with Hector and Daniel. Instead. we both sleep well in the comfortable suite, both of us glad of a good night's rest.

The following day, neither of us can manage much for breakfast; we both opt for coffee and a slice of toast.

Stig's phone rings just as we are leaving the room.

'Stick it on the joint account,' he says quietly, covering the mouthpiece, then mouthing 'Work' so I knew he will be a good twenty minutes.

I go to reception and slide the door card across the counter.

The receptionist stops typing and smiles at me. 'Was everything okay for you?'

'Yes, too good. I could have slept for a week.'

'They are good beds.' She smiles again and looks at me. I take my purse out of my handbag and place our joint bank card on the counter, thinking of the dwindling figure.

'Could I get the printed invoice as well?' I ask, knowing how Stig likes to keep a record of all our expenditure.

The receptionist glances at her screen. 'The balance is paid, Mrs Leonard.'

'Paid?' I quiz. I look at my phone and at the recent texts from Stig to see if he had somehow paid and forgotten. There is nothing. Then I flash back to last night and to a conversation with Hector.

And you're staying over somewhere this evening, I hope?
The Winchester.
Ahh, I know it well. You'll have a lovely stay.

'Are you sure?' I say again.

The receptionist taps at her keyboard and squints her eyes a little. 'Yes, the bill was settled last night around midnight. Surname Bolson-Woods.'

The receptionist looks at me and I quickly look down, shoving my card back into my purse and the purse into my handbag. She must recognise the surname; there can't be too many of them in London.

'Is that okay?' she asks.

'Yes, yes, that makes perfect sense to me now. My... our friend kindly paid for our accommodation as we went for dinner with him last night.'

'That was a very kind gesture.' She smiles.

I nod, thinking of the twenty thousand in the Family First account and now a two hundred hotel bill settled.

'Well, it was very nice. I'll see you again,' I say, almost certainly looking as flustered as I sound as I scurry away.

Stig is outside pacing the driveway as he finishes up his call.

'Everything okay?' he asks.

I smile, tight-lipped. 'Yes.'

'I called us an Uber to get to the station. Figured you wouldn't fancy walking in those shoes.'

He points at the heels I am now wearing with the jeans I had packed in my overnight bag; there wasn't enough room for a pair of trainers with all the make-up, toiletries and nightwear.

'Great.'

I take a bottle of water from my bag and sip until the Uber arrives; all the while, the words hang on the edge of my lips: *Hector paid for the room*. But I dare not say them.

We climb into the Uber and ride the journey to the train station where we travel in silence. All the while, the words do not come out.

* * *

It takes a while for me to come down after the dinner party at Hector's. The taste of all the food and wine lingers in my mouth for days afterwards. I think a lot about the conversations, which had been surprisingly varied and not all about money. Politics featured heavily, as did other topics such as poetry and literature, naturalism and philosophy. I didn't get to speak with Hector as much as I had hoped, but there had been that moment between us, and that was what I held closest to me.

I adored how he had seemed almost bashful when I mentioned the donation, as though he didn't want to speak of it over dinner and show what he had done. I appreciated him even more and felt satisfied that it was a transaction between us that need not have been mentioned again. Perhaps he didn't want it to seem as though he had bought our company, although when I thought of it that way, it seemed ridiculous because why would Hector Bolson-Woods need to buy the company of someone like me and Stig? Yet he had paid for our room.

Stig and I were both quiet for a few days, exhausted from all the excitement. The trip to London had worn me out, and I was sure it had done the same to Stig, who had kept himself to himself for the rest of the weekend, and then it was Monday again and time for work.

Because I had neglected to tell the girls at work that I had been invited to Hector's for dinner with Stig, I was worried about their reaction. Still, I had called my best friend Emily and filled her in on everything from the first meal at the restaurant to the donation, and she had been texting me since Saturday morning.

Finally, she calls me on Monday morning. She is on the school run as I walk the short distance to my office after parking.

'Tell me and quickly; the beasts are particularly feral this morning. Milo, get back here!' Emily half shouts into the phone, and I hear a rush of traffic and children screaming in the background. I pull the phone a little away from my ear.

'It was brilliant. I was worried, as you know, but things were good, and everyone was nice, and he paid for our hotel room.'

'What? Lily, what the actual fuck?' she whispers. 'This guy is off the scale. So are you like proper mates now? This is nuts.'

'I don't know. It doesn't feel like we are friends; I mean, we haven't exchanged phone numbers, although he must have all my details on the restaurant system from my booking. But yeah, he just keeps doing these nice things.'

'And what does Stig think of all of this? Has he come out in hives yet with all this socialising?'

'He's not been too bad, actually. I know he isn't as thrilled as I am, but he seems to be getting on okay with the guys and…' I trail off and stop walking. I am metres from the Family First office building. A woman is staring across the road, and as I stop, she ducks into the Waitrose supermarket. She looks exactly like Ruby.

'Getting on with the guys, hey. It sounds so macho. What are the guys like? No, wait, you'll have to tell me on your lunch break. MILO!' Emily screams into the phone again. And then she is gone.

I stand for a minute longer, waiting for the woman to reappear, and then I consider going in and following her to check to see if it is Ruby. But why would Ruby, who lives in London, from Hector's dinner party, be in Oxford, standing outside my place of work on a Monday morning? I conclude I am seeing things, my mind still awash with the excitement of the dinner party; it has, after all, been playing over in my mind for most of the weekend. I am still living in the moment, and now I need to get back down to earth and get on with my job. It was a chance encounter where something good came out of it. Hector had been altruistic, donating to Family First and then paying for our hotel room. I was the one who had approached him, I had got us into his restaurant that night, and I was the one who had instigated the entire thing.

But now I am preparing myself for the fact that it is over. Despite Ruby's comments about how much fun she thought I was, she had been waiting for someone like me to join their clan. Despite the touches and comments from Hector about how he felt about me, I just had to put it down to a lucky, one-off experience. Two experiences. I can't help but think that Ruby is 'that' friend—the one who feels everything a little harder and needs love and affection a little more. Who doesn't quite fit the mould of the others, yet they let her hang around so they can feel entertained, loved and complimented. She gives off positivity because they are perhaps incapable.

As usual, I am first into the office and spend half an hour firing off emails and replying to those received over the weekend. Once I am done, I make a coffee, and then Michelle and Hannah arrive, and we have our usual catch-up. I want to tell them about the dinner party at Hector's so badly. Still, as much as I am friends with them both, I feel that they would see fault in it, that perhaps the money arrived due to the nature of the sudden relationship I had formed with Hector. I had spent time in Hector's company twice, and with the conversation in the hallway playing heavy on my mind, I knew they would see it as inappropriate. And in a way, I can see how it is.

By lunchtime, I decide to take a walk as there is a hint of spring in the air. Sitting in the park for half an hour is an excellent tonic; my energy levels have depleted somewhat after the weekend. It has been among the highest forms of socialising I have done for a long time. I find a bench, kick off my flats and wish I wasn't wearing tights today. Then I flick my legs up, position my handbag so it sits behind my head, lay down and close my eyes.

Someone calling my name wakes me from a delightful snooze. I open my eyes and see a figure in front of me. I shade my eyes from the sun and immediately recognise who is standing there.

'Ruby,' I say and sit up. 'How are you? What are you doing here?' I instantly regret those last words as they almost certainly sound rude and abrupt, but I am shocked to see her.

'Lily, hello. It's so nice to see you.'

I slip my legs off the bench to give Ruby space to sit. I pat the space next to me and she lays a white and black chequered blazer on the bench before resting her small, pert bottom down.

I shake my head. 'How are you? I'm sorry, I didn't mean to ask why you were here; I'm just shocked to see you.'

'That's okay,' she says. Her voice sounds different to how it was the other evening. It still bears the plummy tone of a woman who is sheathed in wealth but today, it offers something softer. I suppose it is because she doesn't need to shout to be heard over the others; that, and the lack of alcohol in her system.

Her face seems mellower, yet the lines of her life that cross it are still prominent. I put her at a few years older than me, more Stig's age. But it feels impolite to ask.

'I had a little business to attend to, so I thought I would come and see you. I didn't have your number, and well, I remember you saying you worked for a charity called Family First, and so I googled it and found you.'

'So that was you across the street this morning.'

'Oh... yes, I... I'd just got the train, actually, and was feeling a little faint. I popped into Waitrose for a pastry and an iced coffee. I saw you briefly, so sorry. I didn't mean to look stalker-ish.' She chuckles and I laugh.

'No, not at all, I wasn't sure if it was you. I thought I'd imagined it. The dinner party is still so vivid in my mind. The food, the wine, it was all so lovely.'

'Yes, it always is in the beginning,' she muses, looking away across the park.

'I'm sorry?' I quiz her. I want to hear what she said and understand what she meant this time. It isn't the first time she or Henrietta have made a comment about Hector, but this time, I am sober.

Ruby looks at me. Her eyes are tired, and her make-up is a little greasy in the afternoon heat. A few strands of grey shimmer as the light hits her hair. She shakes her head. 'I meant that's how it is: when something is new and novel, you think about it a lot. Like a new lover.' She flashes a smile at me, and I see a flicker of what I had seen at the dinner party on Friday night: a cheeky yet naïve woman who seems younger than she looks, who just want to party and be liked.

'Right. Sure,' I say. 'So, what business are you here for?' I dare to ask as she has yet to offer the information.

'Oh, a bit of this a bit of that.' She grins. 'Sounds a bit dodgy, doesn't it?'

I smile, bewildered. *This is all a little strange*, I want to say. I just met Ruby in London at the weekend, and here she is, in Oxford, outside my place of work. It could hardly have been a coincidence, could it?

'Well, is it illegal?' I say jovially. I don't know these people well enough; how am I to know how they make their money?

Ruby pulls a funny expression and looks away, then waves her hand about as if to shake off my comment. 'God, no.' She turns to me again. 'I'm very straight down the line. I'm a good girl, really.' And I swear I see tears in her eyes before she looks away again. 'I'm thinking of investing in a property here: a house I'd seen and when you said you lived here, it prompted me to consider it again. I guess I'm tired of the hustle and bustle of London, all the socialising and the partying. It's been a long couple of decades. Time to hang the sequins up and start winding down.' She lets out a small noise that sounds like a whimper, but I guess was supposed to be a laugh.

'So where's the property?'

'Well, it's two. One is in Wytham. The other...' She waves her hand about again. 'I can't remember the name. I'd need to look at the paperwork.'

'Wow, exciting!' I say. 'Will you be living alone, or—'

'Alone, at least for now. Until everything falls into place. It shouldn't take too long, I hope.'

'So, Gordon, are you and he not an item?'

Ruby lets out a sigh. 'No, sadly not. I'm just not his type or something. I do try, I do.'

'That's a shame, Gordon seemed like a nice fit.'

Ruby giggles. 'He was.' She raises her eyebrows cheekily. 'But alas, he has a girlfriend. I was only useful for one thing. To fill the gap on a lonely night a few weeks ago. When he came to the dinner party, I had hoped he would see me and realise I was the one for him.'

'And he didn't?' I confirm what she was only about to tell me.

'He did not.'

'And did you stay there? The night? At Hector's?'

Ruby glances away quickly. 'Yes, as per.' She sounds resentful. I think back to Henrietta saying to Ruby that the soufflé room had been made up.

How idyllic to have somewhere to retire to whenever you were too drunk to make it home – and at a friend's such as Hector's house as well. We didn't get to tour the house as he had suggested. The night led very quickly into drinking, eating, and then dancing, and besides it felt impertinent.

I glance down at my watch, I only have a few more minutes left until I need to wander back to the office. Not that Michelle and Hannah would mind if I was late anyway, and certainly not when I had been the instigator for the 20k donation from Hector.

Ruby sees me look at my watch. 'I'm keeping you. Say, would you mind if we swap numbers? I want some advice if I do decide to buy here.'

'Of course not,' I say. I am happy to swap numbers, and not just for the reason she suggested; it would be nice to keep in contact. There is something quite endearing about Ruby. And besides, there is a part of me that wishes to keep my foot in the door with Hector. If the dinner at his house was the first and only time I would be invited to spend time with him personally, it would be nice to know I had a contact if I ever felt I wanted to reach him. Even now, I hear the echo of my lie to myself. I also want an in with Hector for my reasons. He awakened something in me that night at the restaurant with his subtle touch, the way he believed in me and the cause I worked for, and then there was the last conversation where he revealed he had feelings for me. Things have been so dire between Stig and me for months now, and this early on in our marriage, I'm not sure if this is something we can salvage. Hector is proving to be a welcome distraction right now.

Or had the chance meeting with Hector been just that, and trying to imagine myself as part of his life was trying to force something I had instigated? Yet with Ruby here before me, this was the catalyst to make the relationship a little more authentic.

We exchange numbers, and Ruby stands to leave. She looks down at me, and then, as though it is a last-minute thought, she bends down and kisses me on the cheek.

'You seem like a really nice person, Lily,' she says, and she waves. I watch her wander away, clutching her jacket and pulling her handbag further up her shoulder.

I ponder over her parting words for a minute because they seem pretty random and perhaps carry more meaning than I can fathom. I don't seek out people to like me, and I have never considered how likeable I am or am not. I let the thought disappear because I like Ruby too.

When I return to work, I find it hard to concentrate. I am riddled with thoughts of Ruby, of her sudden appearance, of the memories of the dinner party, of the things everyone said. I try to recall how Hector had been: friendly, amiable, a good host.

By the end of the day, I feel I have achieved very little, something I do not reveal to my colleagues, who are always on form and never look like they aren't completing their to-do lists.

By the time I am walking back to where I parked my car, I am overcome with an emotion I am finding hard to put my finger on. Eventually, I realise it is melancholy. I am feeling utterly despondent after the weekend, like a massive comedown;

one minute, my emotions were high and stretched, worrying about the evening, then meeting new people and being with Hector again, plus worrying about Stig, hoping he was okay and not too stressed. And then I was back home and at work, and it was all a lot, I supposed.

I almost crawl through the door when I get home, tired and overcome with a muddle of emotions. Then I see the envelope on the floor and recognise the signature embossed style as the same one that had come via the courier last time. My heart thuds against my chest as I bend to retrieve it, desperate to open it, already feeling a rush of ecstasy that we have been selected again. Hector has been thinking of me again, and so soon after we left. There is no postmark on the letter so it must have been hand posted. I have a sudden thought that maybe it might not be another invite but simply a thank-you card; after all, that was what the rich did: hosted parties, thanked each other afterwards. It feels quite an aristocratic thing to do, and I know that Hector is from that background.

I think about waiting for Stig, to open it together, but I already know his reaction; he will think this all preposterous. This way, I can mention it casually to him later, as though receiving an invite from Hector Bolson-Woods is an everyday occurrence for us. So I rip the envelope open and I can see immediately this is another invitation.

But this time, the address isn't in London. I don't immediately recognise the postcode, and when I look it up, I'm thrilled to see it is in the Cotswolds. I google the entire address to see if I can find the house, but all it shows me is a long, empty country road. The house is hidden somewhere behind the trees along the sides.

'My, my,' I whisper to myself and brace myself to share the news with Stig.

* * *

I don't plan a special dinner this time; I stir-fry chicken and vegetables, add pineapple (Stig's favourite) and drop some egg noodles in water. He comes through the door just as I am just about to plate up, always prompt with his timing.

'Dinner smells good,' he murmurs and, for a moment, I think we can put everything behind us by the time we have finished our meal. But I know there are so many issues bubbling away under the surface that it can't happen.

'Just a stir-fry.'

'A welcome relief from all the rich food we've eaten of late,' he says frankly and I feel we are business associates, not man and wife.

'Well, be prepared to eat more,' I quip as Stig's expression turns solemn. I flash him the invitation from the kitchen counter. 'Surprise! Another invite!'

Stig stares at it for a few seconds.

'Well, I can't say I'm surprised.' He brushes past me to the stove and begins plating up. I sit at the table just as he does, and he slides a plate in front of me.

'What do you mean by that?' I ask, because I hadn't expected that response. Now he sounds as though he is almost resentful of the invites.

'Well, it was obvious that they all liked you and that I was just able to fit in. It seems to me that Hector Bolson-Woods is bored with his aristocratic friends and wants to make some good old working-class friends.'

I stare at Stig.

'What do you mean, working class? You know my parents are, but what about you, Stig? You tell me nothing about your family and where you came from. I know the town you grew up in and you have no siblings, and you have nothing to do with your parents any more. Why is that, Stig? Why? Tell me about your working-class background. I mean, you clearly see yourself as that, as you have just admitted.'

I have two parents who are still together, and they brought me up well, but my sister and I always wanted for something. I am sometimes shocked to find I am back in the same situation, with never quite enough money for what we need. We still want lots, the decorating and building work for the house being the main thing.

'Whatever, Lil, we're not like them, are we? We don't deal in stocks and shares and have several properties, we're not celebs, and we don't have a sixteen-seater dining table, for fuck's sake.'

Stig's swearing makes me flinch.

'So now you are using the class difference to say why we can't be friends with Hector and his lot? Before, I put it down to your shyness and how you despise attention in any form, but now, this? Am I deemed to live my life only hanging with those who exist in the same socioeconomic bracket as us? Whose payslips are reflective of ours and whose hallways also resemble a building site because their monthly wages don't stretch to that as well as car repairs and an annual holiday aboard?'

Stig breathes out a laugh. 'I don't know, what's wrong with that? Sounds pretty simple to me, none of this pretending—'

'I try to get information out of you about your past, about your family, and nothing, Stig. So who's pretending? I'm certainly not; I made it clear exactly who I am and what I do. I'm not ashamed of working for a charity and earning half of what you do. Because I know I can earn more, but I choose not to. I choose to help those in need and that doesn't often come with a hefty salary.'

Stig rolls his eyes and shakes his head. 'Go on then, accept the invitation, as I know you're dying to.'

'What's wrong with you?' I pick up my fork, run it through some noodles and drop it back on the plate, my hunger suddenly dissipated.

'Nothing is wrong with me, but can't you see that maybe there is something wrong with this situation? We met the guy two weeks ago by chance and we've had dinner at his London pad and we're now being invited to his Cotswolds mansion.'

I squint at Stig. 'How do you know he has a Cotswolds mansion?' I knew that because I had googled the address. But Stig had barely looked at the invitation.

Stig sighs. 'I recognise the postcode.'

I think about Stig's reluctance based on not knowing Hector for long enough, but I cannot help but think it is not that at all. I recollect the two times we met Hector and then his friends and cousin. There was something about the way Hector and Stig were around one another, never quite falling into sync and always with that air of defensiveness. I hadn't thought too much of it at the time because I was wrapped up in my own moment, but yet again, I get a feeling that Stig is holding something back from me.

I shake my head, slightly bewildered. 'Right, well, do you think the credit card would stretch to Soho Farmhouse?'

'Absolutely not. Find a cheap Airbnb as you seem so intent on spending time with these people. Do you even know how much it costs to stay at Soho Farmhouse?'

'I know you have savings just sitting there; can't we just dip into those?' I make reference to the bank statement I saw on Stig's desk a few months ago that showed several thousand pounds.

'Because that bit of money I have put aside is supposed to

cover us for a year's maternity leave. You know, when your job stops paying you after a few weeks and you're living off a hundred and fifty quid a week from the government? It's to stop us going into even more debt and so you can enjoy the first year of motherhood without worrying about money.' Stig sounds exasperated, his voice cracking on the final few words.

'Well, how do you suppose I'll be able to wheel a pram down that hallway? The wheels will be getting stuck in the gaps in the concrete, not to mention the flipping cold coming through. You told me we'd be sorted, that we'd have nice house ready to welcome a baby,' I shout back at him, even though having a baby is not on my agenda. But he can't have it both ways. He can't keep me closed off and then expect me to bring his baby into the world when I still know so little about him. It sounds ridiculous to say that when we are married. I sometimes think we did marry too soon, just twelve months after meeting, and we've only been married for five years. Is it enough to really know someone?

'If you wanted to go for the cheaper tiles, we would be getting there, but no, you have to have the ones that cost almost three times the amount,' Stig says a little spitefully.

'Because they will last longer and yes, they look a lot nicer and this is my home, and I want to feel comfortable and look at nice tiles.' I retaliate.

I push my plate away this time and I notice that Stig hasn't touched a thing either. We both sit very still and do not say any more; our words echo and burn through the silence around us.

I stand up and go to walk away.

'Accept the invitation, Lil.' Stig sounds defeated. I turn and he stares into his plate. For a split second, I feel sorry for him, and then for us, at what we are becoming. For whatever reason, the meal at Sapphire didn't bring us closer together, and

Hector's invitations keep coming. Is it me Hector wants to see? What I do know is that the invitations are doing nothing to salvage the mess of our marriage. With every meal we take, I feel another wedge between us. But Stig is intent on keeping a part of his life to himself and here is Hector wanting to spend more time with me. Right now, I ignore the divide opening up and feel the pull toward Hector.

'Okay,' I say. 'I will.' And I go upstairs to take a bath.

9

I have just over one hundred credit on my store card, so I buy a new dress for the dinner at Hector's Cotswolds house. I also buy a new pair of shoes: sandals which are comfortable but still stylish. I try to imagine who could be at this dinner, maybe there will be more famous people, perhaps celebrity neighbours. As we are travelling to such a wealthy area, I want to make sure I make an impression but also that I feel comfortable, and the dress doesn't look as though it was from the sale from an online, high-street store.

It is Thursday, and there are only two days to go. I had almost forgotten about bumping into Ruby when my phone pings on Thursday afternoon while I am eating lunch at my desk.

> Hi Lily. How are you? I heard you and Stig received an invite to the Cotswolds for this Saturday, and I wanted to say how thrilled I am, and I am really looking forward to seeing you both.

I message her back immediately.

> Hi Ruby, I'm doing very well, thanks. Yes, we are invited. It will be good to see you too. I am looking forward to it x

I feel a thrill that we are being talked and thought about and I wonder how much longer our luck will last. Stig and I have very little to offer, which keeps bringing me back to the real reason we are mingling with someone as rich and famous as Hector Bolson-Woods. Hector is making a play purely for me, or it is, as Stig says, Hector likes having the working class around him. But I can't imagine it's in a menacing way; perhaps it just keeps him grounded. Either way, both options are driving me forward to discover precisely what will happen.

I finish my lunch and just as I am clearing up and getting ready to get back to working, my phone pings again.

> Hi Lily, it's Ruby, I don't suppose you're free this afternoon? I'm looking at a house and could do with a second opinion.

> Here in Oxford?

I ping back.

> Yes. What time can you meet me?

I can't is the answer I want to write. I have just finished my lunch and have a ton of work to complete.

> I'm still at work until 4

I write back.

Great, meet me at five. I'll drop you a pin.

I text back a smiley face.

It feels a little strange that Ruby is suddenly here in Oxford and looking for a place to live but I remind myself that she was doing that before I met her, and I had collided with her world too, not just the other way around.

At 4 p.m. I pack up my desk, leaving it as neat as I like it for when I return the next day. I say goodbye to the girls and head into the street with Ruby's location on my phone.

I press start on the pin she dropped me and set off once the directions start.

I begin the drive without thinking, following the voice on the satnav to turn left, second exit at the roundabout. Then it occurs to me, these roads are already familiar to me, and I am turning without much thought because this is how I would drive home. I am now out of the centre and countryside surrounds me.

When the satnav shows I'm one minute away, I realise I am just around the corner from my house. I slow and approach a set of three detached cottages which sit back from the road. I have passed them a few times and thought they looked quaint. There is a *For Sale* sign on the first lawn, and Ruby stands next to that, tapping away on her phone. When she hears my car door slam, she looks up and waves enthusiastically. I can't summon the same enthusiasm because here I am about to walk into a house that Ruby is about to buy, which is a mere few minutes' walk from our own home, and I randomly met her just a few weeks ago. I don't want to feel suspicious, but I am desperate to know her reasons for choosing here.

'Lily, you came. Thanks so much,' she drawls. She drops her phone into her bag and grins her endearing smile. 'Shall we go inside? The estate agent left me with the key – so trusting around here. Wouldn't happen in London,' she scoffs as she turns to the door and opens it.

'Yes, sure.' I allow myself to be led by Ruby into the house.

The smell of fresh paint hits me. Although the cottage is at least a hundred years old, it has been renovated and bears a fresh, slick look. The hallway has an expensive-looking, wood-panelled floor. It looks like oak, a brushed yet rustic finish, and I feel my gut tense at the sight of it; envy grips me like a vice.

Ruby shows me around the rest of the house: four double bedrooms, two with en suites, all with the same flooring throughout, where I have already imagined different colours and styles of rugs adorning them. The sitting room has a wood burner, and the kitchen is huge, country style, with a ten-seater kitchen table in the centre.

'The last owners couldn't be bothered to get it out in the end; they were buying something a bit more modern, so they left it – isn't it wonderful?' She spins around, and I watch as she almost staggers to a halt. She giggles. 'Oops, not quite the ballerina I once was.'

'It's lovely, Ruby,' I say, looking at her more than the house. It is moments like these in the few times that I have been in her company that I get a slight insight into the fragility of this woman. It is as though she is putting on a play, but the performance has been running her entire life and she is so tired and ready for a rest. Maybe this is what this house is; as Ruby said, London wasn't quite doing it for her, and she needs a bit of peace and quiet.

'I only wish I had a kettle so we could have had a cup of tea.' She looks around despondently.

'You do know I live just around the corner,' I say, feeling now is the time to let Ruby know she is buying in my area.

'Is it? Now I did wonder when you told me where you lived. I barely know the area, you see, and this house popped up on my radar, and as you can see, I simply had to come and see it.'

She walks to the kitchen window, a large one that looks out on the perfect, rectangular garden that runs about twenty-five metres until it reaches a fence and beyond, the fields. 'I think I might buy it, you know. I got a feeling the moment I walked in here. Did you, Lily?' she asks, and I agree, even though the only feeling I have is that it is weird that this woman I have met once is now buying a house close to me.

'So you think I should do it. I should buy the house?'

I gulp and force a smile, not knowing what to say, feeling as though I ought to tell her to buy somewhere a little further away, yet at the same time, who am I to say who can buy what and where? Ruby looks so innocent and excited, and this is probably exactly what she needs. And I am an altruistic being. I help people; it is in my nature. Maybe it is meant to be, and she needs me somehow. I am sure I can be there from time to time, a helping hand, a listening ear. So I nod and smile.

'I think you should buy it,' I say, and a look of relief spreads across her face.

'Thank you, Lily. You have no idea what this means to me.'

And she is right. I do not know anything at all about Ruby, but somehow, she is now going to be very much a part of my life.

10

The drive to the Cotswolds is beautiful. We set off at lunchtime with an overnight bag packed.

'He's hardly going to let us drive home. He'll have rooms, and we are obviously invited to stay the night,' I say to Stig. 'If he offers us a stay, we should stay.' I think about the tiny Airbnb we've rented for the night: an annexe in the host's garden.

'But it wasn't on the invite; it didn't specifically say that we would be staying overnight.' Stig sounds cross.

'I know but come on. I know we don't live that far away, but it's still an hour's drive each way. He knows that. I guarantee he has reserved a room for us in his pad.'

Stig doesn't look convinced. I would go so far as to say he looks annoyed. I feel as though we are not on the same page at all. He's doing this because he thinks I'm going to be ready to think about children now. But what can I do? I can't pass up this opportunity, I feel a longing to be in Hector's company again, for him to compliment me and tell me that he has been thinking about me. And there must be a business offer.

'We'll have a great time. Won't we?' I add as an image of

Hector and I in a clinch flashes through my mind and I shake it away.

Stig doesn't reply; he is focusing on driving. He hasn't confirmed that we will have a great time, but he hasn't denied it either. I am frustrated after we argued over having a baby. I understand Stig's frustration as he is forty, and I think I need to make a decision. But what will that decision be? It used to be simply that I wanted my husband to be more open, more honest about who he is. I want to know about every past family member that he can remember, but I need to know about his parents mostly. Why will he not speak of them? What if there is a terrible hereditary disease in the family, or his father is a serial killer? These are important to me to know before I commit to children. Stig does not understand, and the more he doesn't understand, the more I fall a little bit out of love with him.

Hector seems the opposite of Stig. He is open about his life and where he went to school. He hasn't mentioned it, but I know he is estranged from his father, a multi-millionaire businessman, and he is very close to his mother. I have gained all this information from newspapers and social media. Hector is supportive of the work I do, and I know he is in a much more fortunate position than Stig, but Stig has never congratulated me on what I do the way Hector has. And the twenty thousand donation illustrates Hector's selflessness and recognition of my work.

As we drive, I decide I will enjoy myself this evening no matter what amount of noise my mind is making. There is suddenly a battle between Hector and Stig going on in my head and I had not expected it. I had initially just wanted to fit in and now I want so much more. I want it all. The meals, the conversations, the friendships. The touch on my hand. The words about how much I am thought of.

The Dinner Party

A second visit must mean we are liked, and they might want us as their friends even if we are just outside their clan, not special or privileged enough to be let into every event. Still, we are allowed a glimpse and would be invited around for occasional soirées and dinners. And I think I could be happy with that. But three encounters with Hector within a month. That is a lot.

I ponder on the drive if I should mention Ruby to Stig. He has been quiet for the drive, and it would give us something to chew over together.

'I saw Ruby the other day,' I say.

There is a definite pause before he replies. 'Oh yeah,' he says coldly.

'Yeah, she was in town, right next to my office.'

Stig swings me a look, then turns back to the road. 'That's odd,' he says with a little laugh.

'Yeah, I thought so too. It turns out she has been wanting to buy out this way for some time; London life just got the better of her, and she wants a pad in the countryside.'

'And where is she looking, do you know?' Stig sounds perplexed.

'Well, this is the weird thing: she picked somewhere just around the corner from us. Little Grove. There are three detached cottages—'

'I know where Little Grove is,' Stig snaps. 'Did you tell her it was inappropriate?'

'Why would I tell her it was inappropriate?' I ask, confused by his immediate response.

Stig glares at the road for a few seconds. 'We barely know her is what I mean. She can't just decide she is buying a house around the corner from us.'

'But I don't think she did just decide. It seems she has been looking for some time, and this house came up just recently, and she has been pondering on it for a while and so she asked me if I thought she should buy it and—'

'You went with her?' Stig interrupts again.

'She asked for a second opinion,' I say, noting my calm tone against Stig's vexed one.

Just then, Stig's phone pings. He almost jumps at the sound.

He doesn't pick it up, and I can see it is in the gap between us: a safety precaution only, never so he can use it when he is driving, yet always somewhere within reach for an emergency. I like that a lot about Stig, I recall with fondness as I glance at him, thankful that is the sort of person he would be around children if we ever had them.

'So?' I say enquiringly. Stig is angry about Ruby and sees her house move as an impertinence.

'So?' Stig asks.

'You think it's weird that Ruby is moving near us?'

Stig is quiet for a few seconds. 'No, not weird. It's just a coincidence is what it is. Forget it. People can live wherever they like.' He doesn't sound like he is putting the conversation to bed; he still sounds angry.

I try and think of other things to talk about with Stig to make the rest of the journey pleasant, but I can't think of anything to say that will appease him. I feel my presence annoys him these days, and he is only here out of politeness.

I don't want to make small talk with my husband; it sends pain to my gut, which in turn goes to my head, and I don't want to have a headache tonight. Stig's values and ideals are different to mine, and I can't change him or the way he perceives things. I have always been more of a fly-by-the-seat-of-my-pants kind of girl. Stig is sensible and that is the only word I have for him. I close my eyes and welcome a short nap, the hum of the car lulling me to sleep.

The car slams to a halt, the seat belt snaps against my chest, and my eyes shoot open. My heart beats furiously inside my ribcage. In front of us, on a country road still, I glimpse a deer bounding across a fence, having just come from the road.

'Did you hit it?' I whisper, trying to scan the road for blood and then glancing back at the deer as it disappears into the foliage.

'No... I don't think so.' His voice is airy and light. He is clutching his mobile phone in his hand.

'Who were you going to call? The RSPCA?' I try to sound jokey, but my heart is still hammering, and I feel anything but jovial.

Stig looks down at his phone. 'No... I... erm...' He drops the phone into the inlet next to him and slowly starts manoeuvring the car forward. Luckily, the road is quiet and there is no one behind us.

'One of the hazards of living so far out in the sticks,' I say after a while and Stig nods. He must still be in shock.

I look at his hands, now firmly gripping the steering wheel so that his knuckles have turned white, and think about how he had been holding his mobile phone when I had jolted awake. I had presumed he had picked it up when he had hit the deer and was preparing to call someone, perhaps predicting a fatality or a fault with the car following a collision. But we hadn't hit the deer. And Stig hadn't picked his phone up after he had slammed on his brakes because it had happened so fast, he wouldn't have had time to have grabbed it.

Stig had been using his phone whilst he had been driving, and that was the reason we had almost crashed. His eyes hadn't been on the road; they had been on his phone. The shock had temporarily distracted me from what I now know I saw. Stig's phone had been open on WhatsApp. He had been engaged in a message, so we had almost collided with a deer. As shocked as I was by what had happened and what could have been, it could have been so much worse. Stig is not a risk-taker; he would not have been texting unless he had felt it was an absolute must. What had been so important that he needed to text while driving and put both of our lives at risk? But I am still shaken by the near crash that I can't even find the words to ask Stig what had happened. And he certainly didn't want to admit anything to me. Probing him will only lead to an argument, and I do not want that before we arrive at Hector's.

We arrive at the Airbnb, and Stig carries our overnight bags through the back gate. It is only 4 p.m. and we had intended to drive around for a while, find a cosy pub and have a few pre-dinner drinks and nibbles before we headed over to Hector's country manor. But as small as it is, I am glad we are now somewhere we can relax. There is a lock box on the wall as we enter, and I tap in the code Stig reads out, and we retrieve the key.

The room is more spacious than I had thought from what I had seen but we are still in someone's back garden and I definitely see a figure observing us from the top window of the main house opposite as I pull the curtains closed.

I lie down on the bed, and Stig goes straight to the bathroom.

'I need a shower,' he says, and I imagine sweat-drenched armpits from the stress of almost hitting a deer. I toss about, trying to get comfortable to finish the nap I was so rudely woken from earlier.

I hear the shower turn on, and I realise I am on Stig's side of the bed when I see he has placed his overnight bag next to this side of the bed. Then I see his phone peeping out the inside pocket. He must have dropped it in there when he collected his toiletry bag. I have never had an urge to look at Stig's phone before. Overall, I know he leads a simple life, and if I go snooping, I am unlikely to find anything earth-shattering. But that near-crash earlier and the fact that I knew Stig had been texting before he slammed on his brakes has made me curious. And again, I ponder the obvious. What had been so important that he felt the need to text and drive, something he has never done the entire time I have known him?

I reach my arm out, grab the bag and tilt it so I can slip my hand in. I grab the phone quickly enough. He has a passcode, but I've never paid much attention. Again, the simplicity of Stig makes me put his date of birth first as the six digits. It isn't that. Damn it. I try my date of birth next. It isn't that either. The shower still pumps out hard and fast, and I know I have a few minutes until he is finished.

I give myself one more try today and if the urge still persists tomorrow, I will try again.

I type in 030319, the date we met, and the screen bursts to life. I open WhatsApp straight away, and the recipient at the top is someone named Delilah. My heart skips a beat, and my stomach lurches.

There are two simple messages.
One from Delilah:

> I miss you.

One from Stig:

> I can't do this now.

11

It is easier to carry on with the afternoon and evening than I had imagined. When I first read this Delilah woman's message, I felt sick. I had envisioned asking Stig who she was when he came out of the shower and demanding an explanation. But I don't know where to start. How would I explain why I was snooping through his phone in the first place? But none of that matters now, as I know why my husband has recently been so tetchy and distant. Despite him claiming he wants to have children with me, I suspect that is now a cover-up. He probably knows that will never happen due to how little he has revealed about this past. And it seems there is still more I don't know about my husband, like why a woman named Delilah is missing him and why he cannot talk with her right now. Could he not have said, *I am with my wife*, or does she not know he has a wife? My mind is a tornado, and I will flip out if I do not stop the storm of questions now. And Stig will not ruin my evening with Hector.

Confronting Stig now would only cause even more animosity between us, and I don't wish that mood upon us this evening. I want things to go smoothly, for Hector to carry on liking us, or rather *me*. I no longer care if he likes Stig, as Stig is not someone who even wants to be here. I now imagine he wishes he were with Delilah. I know that if another invite comes our way, I will accept it. Alone.

I dress slowly and apply my make-up carefully to accentuate my eyes and not overdo the blush and powder. I want to look natural and bronze. I complete my routine and feel satisfied when I see myself in the mirror. This is the moment, if we were a normal, loving couple, that Stig would come and put his arms around me.

But he barely looks at me, and I can see a look of tension spreading across his face. Both our minds are on the message, the unspoken words filling the air between us. I am determined not to allow it to taint this evening's activities, so all I can do is push all my knowledge of it away and deal with it tomorrow.

Stig is wearing a pair of khaki trousers, a dark-pink patterned shirt and a mauve jacket. He always dresses smartly and with style, a slight quirkiness that I don't always see in every man. I enjoy the way he takes a little risk with colours and fabrics. It is a side of him that is removed from the rest of his personality because he is usually so safe and organised and not in the least bit risky. But I don't allow the things that first drew me to him to compensate for the message I discovered. A message that almost caused us to crash. I try not to think about how much worse that could have been.

I take out the wine I brought and pour it into the tumblers they left for us. I don't say anything to Stig, but he picks it up and downs it in one. I had brought nibbles, but now, the thought of eating anything makes my stomach churn.

We order a taxi to take us to Hector's and when the driver pulls up outside the driveway, there is an intercom to let us in.

I ask him to drive forward enough so I can talk through the window, which he does, and I press the button.

It rings for longer than I hope, and I glance at Stig a few times, a part of me wondering if this is a joke and we have been pranked. Even after everything I have experienced with Hector so far, a part of me still thinks it will come to an abrupt and embarrassing end, like now, if someone answers the intercom and says, *Er no, I don't think so.* And hangs up.

But eventually, a male voice answers.

'Oh hi, it's the Leonards. We are here for dinner?' I say questioningly, part of me wishing Stig would squeeze my hand for comfort, the other wishing he wasn't even here.

Whoever is at the end of the intercom doesn't answer but the gate suddenly jolts and then begins to open with a steady whirring sound.

'We're in,' I whisper, more to myself than to Stig and the taxi heads slowly down a long driveway until we see a large house that looks like a bungalow with great, big, glass windows. The car takes us to the other side of the house, which isn't as new, and several barns frame a pebble courtyard. Several expensive-looking cars are parked around the courtyard and two giant fern trees mark the beginning of a path that leads to a large, wooden door that looks like a giant might live behind it.

The driver doesn't speak, but he has driven down this way before as he knew which part to arrive at. As soon as we step out of the car, the big door opens slowly and I am surprised to see Hector behind it.

He is beaming, wearing a white shirt, a few buttons open at the top, exposing a slightly red chest that looks like he has been caught out in the sun. I imagine him sunbathing. It has been a glorious day, and I am sure I glimpsed a pool on the other side of the house as we arrived. I can imagine Hector sitting around the pool, drinking and generally living the wonderful life of Riley.

'Guys!' he croons. 'So good to see you, come in, come in.'

I feel my stomach flutter at the way he greets us, as though we are old friends and not two people he randomly met just a few weeks ago at his restaurant.

I walk in front of Stig, who is finishing off paying the driver and probably giving him a far too big a tip as he is renowned for doing.

Hector pulls me into an embrace.

'Lily, you look divine,' he says huskily, as though he only wants me to hear those words. Then he releases me. Stig is only just walking up the path behind me. 'Go through, go through. Excuse the mess; it's been a day and we're a housekeeper down.'

I walk into a grand, open-plan entrance area. A round table is in front of me adorned with scented candles, a huge bouquet, and what I called accessory books; they are there to decorate an area and not to be read. However, one does catch my eye as the words *food* and *photography* jump out at me. I am already itching to flick through the pages. Hector won't object once we were all suitably inebriated and fed, surely?

I can hear a lot of chatter from my right, and as I turn, I see a few faces. I recognise Henrietta, Daniel, Tristan and Ruby, who are all in the kitchen area. Henrietta catches my eye and waves me over. I turn to check on Stig, but he is locked in an embrace with Hector. Stig looks strained as Hector says his greetings. I doubt if his words are as personal as they were when he whispered in my ear just now.

I arrive in the kitchen area and Henrietta holds out a drink for me.

'Oh, what's this?' I look at the orange concoction.

'Aperol Spritz. The boys have been on beer all afternoon, so I am trying to wean them off it and onto something more sophisticated.' She laughs, and I inhale her infectious vibes and warm demeanour. I had picked up on some prickly vibes the last time in London, so this feels like a welcome relief. As Ruby gives off the notion of someone who needs a little protection, which is endearing and welcoming, Henrietta is the sort of woman who commands control of a room. Even though this is not her place, and neither is the London pad, she has the air of someone who has everything under control. I had picked that up at the town house and dinner, and now here she is again, giving off the idea that she is running the show today. Even though, as I glance around, I can see people who look like staff milling around.

Ruby had been in conversation with Tristan and now they were both next to me, kissing me hello. I want to reach for Stig's hand as I feel the need for that little bit of security again. Then I see the words from the text on his phone, and I can still smell Hector's aftershave on my skin and hear his warm words in my ear.

'We're drinking Aperol Spritz, Stig; does that suit, old chap?' Tristan shakes his hand before handing him a drink.

'Nicholas.' Ruby arrives breathlessly next to us and leans in and kisses Stig. I find it strange how she can comfortably converse with him using the name he has not been called for so many years. He has always been known as Stig, and although he no longer represents the caveman-look of a children's TV show, it has never occurred to me to call him anything other than by his nickname. I guess the rich find a nice, sturdy name like Nicholas much more appropriate.

I watch as Ruby moves away from Stig and turns to me again.

'I signed the papers,' she says as though this a topic she has reserved just for us. 'The cottage is mine!' She flings her hands in the air. A little of her Aperol Spritz spills from her glass.

'I hope Hector doesn't mind sharing this evening, as I would like to celebrate,' Ruby choruses and Tristan and Henrietta look at her but say nothing. I wonder if they have already had their fill of Ruby's excitement over her new home.

'I'm so happy for you,' I say to Ruby, although I have a mixture of emotions about the proximity and the reaction from Stig. 'You must be thrilled to finally have your dream house.'

'I am so happy,' she says. 'Honestly, it's all just slotting into place. You guys here, and Hector and now my house, it's like I have been waiting years for it all to work out, and now it is.' She looks at me and cocks her head. 'Thank you, Lily, for everything.'

I frown. 'I don't see what I have done,' I say.

'Ruby, can you help me pick out the napkins?' Henrietta calls. She saw Ruby and I were conversing; she had been looking our way. She eyes me as Ruby walks over to her, and I wonder if she feels she is saving me from Ruby being too overbearing. I know Ruby's insecurities and vulnerabilities already, but I have never felt the need to push her away. I almost feel a need to protect her.

Ruby looks back at Henrietta and then back at me and rolls her eyes.

'Honestly, you think they would be able to figure out a damn napkin. It seems my skills are indispensable,' she says theatrically and walks away, that slight swagger to her walk that makes me wonder how much she has had to drink already. And then my thoughts are back on Henrietta and why she pulled Ruby away from me, when it was clear we were speaking. It feels like she did it purposely, as though she doesn't want Ruby talking to me. It is reminiscent of the night at the town house when Ruby and I were dancing; suddenly, Henrietta was there, scooping her off to bed, although she didn't go to bed straight away. I have already noted that Henrietta seems to be the one who is in control in some way; maybe she feels she needs to babysit Ruby too. I have seen an inner child within Ruby that needs attention, and maybe that is what Henrietta also sees as her role. Perhaps she feels as though I am treading on her toes now that Ruby is going to live so close to me. I feel as though I want to broach the subject with her and let her know that I'm not a threat. I swig back my drink, knowing I will need a few more of them before I have the courage to speak with the matriarch that is Henrietta.

'Help yourself to an amuse-bouche.' Hector is next to me, speaking to me as though I am the only one in the room again, without the same intensity at the door.

'Hector, your place is lovely,' I say as I home in on a blini.

'Why thank you, as I said, we are in a bit of a mess, but the staff we do have are working around the clock to get the place back in shape.'

I look around again.

'I mean, it looks perfectly fine to me,' I say, glancing at the dining table, which is being set to perfection by two housekeepers. It is overlooked by Henrietta and Ruby, who hold two separate napkins in their hands, musing over which to choose. The rest of the open-plan space is immaculate.

'Well, my dear, things might sometimes seem neat, but scratch the surface a little and you will find the dirt. The ugliness, the parts one is hiding,' Hector says profoundly, a sombre tone to his voice.

'Oh,' I say, taken back by the sudden change to his tone. I have never heard him speak this way before. But something about what Hector has just said makes me think about what Henrietta said.

He's a lot more delicate than people think.

Then I think of Stig and the message from Delilah. I had

always thought that Stig was a straight-up guy who did things by the book and didn't want to upset the apple cart. But he is hiding something from me. Something happened with this Delilah girl, or it could have happened, or maybe it might still happen. Why do I feel as though Hector's analogy is a little too close to my own issue right now? And that our two worlds, which have already collided spectacularly, are now falling into sync?

Stig shifts uncomfortably next to me, and Hector looks at us one at a time.

'Let's retire to the, erm... well it is a patio, but I think the word *patio* sounds a little common, like something from a council estate. I know, I know, snobbish of me, but what can I say.'

I feel the comment like a soft punch to my gut, but I let it slide because although I wasn't raised on a council estate, it wasn't far off. It is the first time I have heard Hector refer to his class. I hope I am now making strides to remove any boundaries between the rich and poor here and that Hector sees us as equals.

We follow Hector outside, where a sturdy-looking man is moving a heavy-looking parasol on wheels.

'Yes, just there, Jack,' Hector says, then turns to us. 'Jack is security, ex-Marines, but occasionally, I ask him to move and lift things because I am less fit than I look,' he quips and eyes me again. I can't seem to get enough of his comments and looks. It feels like a drug that Hector is dispensing in small doses, and I am always ready to receive more.

'It was so bright and warm earlier, but we don't need it now. Thanks, Jack,' he says, and Jack nods. We sit, and as we do, I look at Jack as he locks the wheels into place. As he rises up again, his eyes meet mine and for a nanosecond, it is as though he is looking right into my soul. I shiver despite the heat of the early evening. *Maybe this is what it feels like to be protected*, I think as I watch Jack walk away. His broad back and shoulders are striking. Stig is tall but he has never been muscly in that way. I have never looked at a man of Jack's stature in that way before, but then I have never felt the protective presence of someone highly trained so keenly.

* * *

Dinner is, of course, delicious but not overly fancy. It consists of five courses of delectable delights, which I savour so I can talk about them with Emily, Hannah, and Michelle.

We are into the third course, a seared ribeye with a spicy tiger dipping sauce, which tastes exactly as I expected it to be: sweet and sour with chilli.

I stand up after I have finished the meat course and Hector glances up at me.

'Okay?' he asks. I glance at my husband, who puts a piece of meat in his mouth and chews with intention as he holds Hector's eye for a moment. I try to ignore what I have seen because I don't want to think anything of it. But I feel a stirring in my gut, and the words Hector said earlier about hidden things beneath the surface seem more than just an observation on the cleaning. I am still feeling frustrated over the message from Delilah.

'Just popping to the…' I trail off. 'The ladies,' I finish with a bit more decorum.

'Use any of the guest rooms at the end of the hall there, Lily; much nicer, and you'll find some fancy smellies in there too. Help yourself.' Hector grins at me; his eyes are shiny and he looks healthy and happy.

I sense a negative energy coming from my husband, and

when I turn to him, his face matches my feeling. Stig picks up his wine and takes big gulps his eyes hard and focused on Hector.

I walk through the kitchen until I see the corridor Hector had referred to. The first room I come to is beautifully decorated with what looks like satin, white sheets, huge pillows, fresh flowers, and scented candles. I lift the lid on one to smell it.

'Mmmm,' I say as the scent lifts me. Like limes and coconuts, I feel transported to a tropical beach.

I look around the room and feel the freshness and cleanliness of it. There is a lot of light coming through, and I imagine myself waking up here in the morning and I wonder if it is already made up for Stig and me.

I leave that room, continue down the corridor, and find another guest room, similar in style but set out slightly differently. Light streams in at the end, and I realise it is a patio door. I walk over and pull back the see-through curtain, and there is the view I had been looking at when we had been sitting outside earlier. The sun is beginning to set, and I stand and watch it for a minute, a pink and orange blanket pulled across the sky.

I turn back into the bathroom. and sit on the toilet. I look around at the pristine tiles and ceramics. The flooring catches my eye, and I think how nice it would look in the hallway at home. I wash my hands and dry them afterwards. There is another scented candle, and I smell it, feeling the same sensation it gave me. I wonder if Hector chose this because I am impressed with it all: the colour combinations, all the little knick-knacks. Even if he hadn't brought everything together himself, he would have had to agree on it. Hector has good taste. This house is very me. I can imagine myself living here.

As I walk back down the hallway to rejoin my diners, I pass a photo on the right-hand side of the wall I had not noticed before. It's the same school photo I had seen in the town house. It looks a little out of place amongst the modern artwork and minimalism. I pause to find Hector again and smile when I see him.

'There you are,' I whisper and lightly touch the glass.

12

I return to the table and slide back into my seat. Hector catches my eye.

'Guest suite to your liking? Ruby and Henrietta advised on the products; I don't know what you girls like.'

'It was lovely, Hector,' I say, and we share a look and smile. Then I glance over to Stig to make sure he hasn't seen. He is in conversation with Daniel and hasn't even looked my way.

I try to slide back into the flow of the evening, but when dessert arrives, I barely touch it, and Hector picks me up on it.

'Not for you, Lily?' he asks, gesturing to his take on a walnut whip, and I shake my head.

'No, it looks lovely; I'm just so full. Can I get a doggy bag?'

'Of course, but you're not leaving already, are you?'

'Of course not,' I say.

'Good, well, I think we all need a strong brandy after this,' Hector says, 'and to retire to the blue room for some chill time.' Hector stands and we all follow suit.

'Just one, and we get the cab back to the Airbnb,' Stig says as he walks past me.

The blue room is just that: blue wallpaper and a lush, rich, thick carpet – the only room with any softness underfoot. There is a bar, and Hector is already behind it pouring brandy. Henrietta points out a chair for me. 'Here, Lily, take this one; it's the comfiest.'

I do as she suggests and sink into the soft fabric. Stig is still standing and has his hands in his pockets. He looks awkward there and I want to tell him to sit down.

Hector brings the brandies over on a round, mirrored tray and hands them to us. I notice then that neither Ruby nor Tristan have joined us.

'What about the others?' I ask. 'Should we wait for them?'

'Oh, I don't think so; Ruby is probably passed out somewhere,' Hector says, and I hear Stig let out a loud sigh. I feel he has reached his limit.

'Cheers,' Hector says when he only has his brandy left in his hand.

He glances at Henrietta, and she clears her throat and seems to nod at him.

'Stig, please, sit,' Hector instructs, and Stig quickly slides into a chair next to mine, reaches over and grabs my hand. I didn't like how he did it, and a part of me wants to scream and pull away.

'You seem like nice people and the sort of people who might need a helping hand?' Hector says, and I feel my heart sink. Oh, this is what this is. We are the charity case. All this time, we thought, or at least I thought, that we were becoming friends and Hector thought we were here because we needed money. I cast my mind back to our initial meetings to see where I might have hinted at this; had I said something to suggest we were looking for assistance? I couldn't recollect one conversation or comment. But maybe this was something that

Hector saw all along. How silly I feel. Of course, couples must turn up at his restaurant all the time and try and align themselves with him. He has been generous enough with the donation to the charity, but I feel this next phase would be embarrassing. I shift in my seat, ready to move quickly as soon as Hector says anything else; I am already feeling uncomfortable.

'What I would like to propose is a business deal.'

'Oh,' I say, surprised. I look at Stig confidently. I had thought about the donation that Hector had made a lot. And he was a businessman at the end of the day. He had seen potential in me and us, which was a sobering thought. My eyes saying, *This could be good for us*. He stares blankly back at me.

'Well, we're all ears,' I say, jovially.

'That's good. You seem very amiable, and I liked you from the moment I saw you. You understand that my life revolves around the public domain; I am what people like to call a "celebrity".' Hector puts two fingers in the air and makes speech marks.

I smile. 'It is the world we live in now.'

'Indeed and it can, as I am sure you can imagine, mean I have very little time to do the things I really want to do.'

I nod. I think I understand what he is trying to say.

'Especially when it comes to things I am passionate about. I am very private; I only choose to spend time with people I feel I can truly trust, and I feel, Lily, that I can trust you.'

This is all aimed at me; he looks at me the entire time and does not glance at Stig once.

'I have had some unfortunate incidents in the past where people have taken advantage of me. Put me in very painful situations, and well, ever since then, I have found it difficult to trust people...'

'Oh, Hector, I am sorry to hear that,' I say over what I think is a snort from Stig, and I hope no one heard it.

'I will come straight out with it, Lily, as I can see you are an intelligent woman. I propose that you help me set up a charity and then run it for me. The charity will focus entirely on family and community, creating safe spaces for young adults to spend time in, helping parents with basic skills, and giving them invaluable help so they can parent their children better. Henrietta has drawn up a draft business plan.'

I look at Henrietta, glad of the break from looking at Hector because I am in shock. Henrietta hands me two pieces of A4 paper. I glance at them before I turn to Stig, but he has a look on his face that says he's had enough.

I glance through the plan and I see a figure jump out at me that has my name next to it. It's a salary, and it's three times what I am earning now.

'You have to be bloody joking?' Stig suddenly says. 'You think my wife is going to start working for you because you have money to throw about?' Stig shouts, and I wonder how he even knows what the figure is as he hasn't looked at the business plan.

'Stig!' I say, horrified at his outburst. It's as though he has been racking up all his emotions these last few weeks and is now letting them out.

'I think it's time we left,' he says to the room. I am thankful we booked our room at Airbnb because things have just gotten more awkward.

'I know this seems a lot to take in, but this is a business proposition and I know I haven't known you that long, Lily, but already, I feel we have a connection, a shared interest and passion in helping people. And I know the money will help...' Hector stands and walks over to me. I feel myself shrink a little at his closeness. He drops a business card into my lap. 'This is my number. Think about it; call me any time.'

'We don't need your money,' Stig says sternly, 'and we won't be calling you. Lil.' He holds out his hand, and although I stand to follow him, I ignore the gesture. I don't feel this is an act of solidarity. Stig is angry and it makes no sense.

We leave the blue room together. I am still clutching the business proposal and Hector's card. I feel the smoothness of it in my palm.

'Bloody fucking cheek, the absolute cheek all this time, this was what he was planning, the canny, scheming little bastard.' The obscenities fly out of Stig's mouth as though he uses them every day, except I know this is a different side to him that I am seeing. One that I have never seen in the years we have been together. I'm not sure if it frightens or thrills me.

'Why are you this angry?' I struggle to keep up with Stig's long strides as we head to the huge door we came through when we arrived. Stig pulls it open. 'What will we do?' I add.

'We will tell him to fuck right off, and if he calls or sends another invite, we tell him to fuck right off again.'

I listen to Stig and then say quietly, 'I meant about getting home.'

'Oh, right.' Stig pulls out his phone and calls the number of the same taxi firm that brought us here.

'They'll be here in five minutes,' he says, and we walk across the driveway.

I hear my name being called in a high-pitched wail. I turn and see Ruby coming out of the door and making her way toward us.

'For fuck's sake.' Stig turns and marches toward her. He reaches her, but they are too far away for me to hear what they are saying.

'Everything okay?'

I spin around, and Jack stands next to me. I hadn't even heard his feet crunch on the gravel. My head spins, and I suddenly want to cry in his big, protective arms.

'I...'

'Do you have a taxi coming?'

'Yes,' I say.

'Good.'

I feel the protection of Hector's staff, from the way we had been looked after at dinner to the housekeeping to Jack, his bodyguard. He has a whole team orchestrating his life, and the idea of being in that world feels good. If I worked for Hector, I would be looked after, protected. The salary alone was enough to convince me this was where I need to be now.

I glance back at Stig to check on him and Ruby. Ruby is gesticulating, her hands thrown in the air. She has no reason to be angry with Stig. I am about to walk over to them when he turns and heads back to me. I look around and see that Jack is gone, as though I had imagined his presence next to me just a moment ago.

As Stig reaches me, we begin walking toward the driveway. We pass a small hut, and I see Jack sitting at a desk, a host of monitors around him. That must be the security HQ of the house, where Jack keeps an eye on the comings and goings. Again, I feel a rush of adrenaline at the sheer protection around Hector. How simple his life is. He can suddenly decide to set up a charity and make it happen just like that.

By the time we reach the end of the driveway, the taxi has arrived. We climb in and Stig tells the driver the address. Neither of us speaks the short drive back, and when we climb out at the Airbnb, there is a party happening at the house next door; outside, a huge gazebo has been erected in the time we have been away, and a lot of loud music and laughter is all around us.

We walk to our annexe and close the door.

'Why, Stig, why?' I ask as Stig moves things about the room noisily. 'You need to tell me what the hell is going on.'

'I'll make us a tea,' he says and fills the kettle.

'Are we going to talk about it?' I ask as the kettle whistles to life.

'No,' Stig says firmly. 'I never want to speak about this ever again. I never want to see that man or his creepy clan again.'

'But you need to tell me why. Why have you taken such a dislike to him? Why did you come to the dinners if you hate him so much?'

Stig doesn't reply and I know I am fighting a losing battle. When Stig decides he is going to be mute and not explain himself, I just need to give up. Although I am angry and desperate to know the reason for his behaviour, I am thinking more about what just happened there in the blue room and the text messages I found on Stig's phone. Despite my husband's protests, I know I will not decline Hector's offer.

13

The letter arrives at my office this time. It is a clever tactic because Stig would have no access to it, and it is up to me if I wish to share it with him.

'Ooh, one for you.' Michelle drops it on my desk. 'Looks fancy,' she observes. And I see the same familiar silver-grey envelope and embossed lettering.

I push it to one side and wait until both Hannah and Michelle are out to lunch before I open it.

Dear Lily,

I hope this letter finds you well. May I begin by offering my sincere apologies for what happened on Saturday evening? I did not mean to offend or shock you.

The offer is a simple contract between two people, and may I emphasise its privacy? It is the very epitome of what I stand for and what this whole contract represents.

From the moment I met you, I saw a passion and desire that mirrored my own, and I hope I can help you channel those emotions.

> *I noticed you did not refuse the offer, and this is why I am writing in the hope that you have not yet made up your mind and that you will consider spending time with me at my chateau in France to discuss the proposal at length, away from the distractions of modern life.*
>
> *Please get in touch with Henrietta as soon as possible. I hope to enjoy your company very soon.*
>
> *Sincerely,*
> *Hector Bolson-Woods.*

My brain is considering all the wonderful things I could buy with the extra money each month. The entire house could be fitted out exactly as I have always envisioned it, and I would still have money to spare for a luxury trip or a new car, all of which are not essential but would be beneficial. Stig has barely spoken to me since the meal in the Cotswolds and, of course, I have not mentioned the texts I saw on his phone.

I hadn't contested the idea when Hector spoke on Saturday night. It was Stig who was quick with his response. And this is what bothers me more than anything because it is another missing part to the everlasting Stig puzzle. Why does he not like Hector? Why is he so angry? Why does he not see me working for Hector and making much more monthly money as a good thing? It is a win-win situation. I get to do what I love and enjoy and I make more money from it. Perhaps with time, he might see the benefits the way I can, but right now, I can't see past the deceit with him and a woman called Delilah.

* * *

That night, when I get home, I hear music coming from Stig's office. It's classical, which he plays when he is stressed and on a tight deadline.

'I'm home,' I call, but Stig does not answer, and besides, the music is too loud for him to hear me.

I place my hand on the study door handle and begin to open it slowly so as not to startle him; he hates it if I barge in too quickly.

Stig is at his desk. But his hands move quickly and papers slide into his briefcase next to his feet. He looks up, his face a muddle of stress and of someone who has been caught doing something they shouldn't be doing.

'Okay?' I ask with sarcasm. Whatever had been on his desk, he does not want me to see. And now it is tucked safely in his briefcase. The briefcase will soon be locked, and I will never know.

'Yes,' he says breathlessly. 'I'm going to go for a run.' He bends down, twists the lock on his briefcase and stands up.

'Are you making dinner?' he asks. 'Or shall I?'

'No, I can make it.' The atmosphere has been tense since we left Hector's on Saturday night. Every subject that needs broaching has been ignored.

'Right.' He walks past me and upstairs to get changed.

I am in the kitchen chopping vegetables for a stir-fry when he comes down in his running gear.

'See you in bit then.' He walks out, slamming the heavy door behind him.

'Just close the damn thing,' I say, wondering how he would ever cope if we did have a baby in the house.

I wait five minutes to ensure he hasn't forgotten anything or changed his mind before I go into his study. I scan the desk to see if anything looks strange or out of place. Then I bend down to the briefcase. I twist the numbers to different dates to see if it will open but it won't. Then, my eyes are drawn to something under the desk to the left. A sheet of paper. Something must have slipped from the pile when Stig was pushing things into his briefcase in haste.

I lean in and grab it. Then I sit on the floor and turn the paper over.

For a moment, I am not sure what I am looking at. It is a copy of a photo. The image is of lots of boys all in school uniforms; a sick feeling in the pit of my stomach rises to my mouth. Why does Stig have an image of young boys? Then my eyes are drawn to one boy, a face I recognise as I have seen it so often recently. A young Hector stares back at me from the past. Then I realise I *have* seen this image somewhere before. It was in Hector's town house, but this image is different somehow. The picture at Hector's house was more prominent, and had more students in it, hundreds in fact, but I recognise the sloppy smile of Hector's as the same one in the photo at the town house and the Cotswolds. This photo has been enlarged. And all I can wonder is, why has Stig taken a copy of Hector's school photo?

Had Stig taken a photo of this image, and printed it out for an unfathomable reason? It makes no sense to me why this would be in Stig's possession. A man who shows no interest in Hector Bolson-Woods, who appears even to despise the man and certainly does now because of what he's proposed. Then my thoughts turn to why this section has been selected and I scan the rows of faces to see who else I might recognise. Perhaps Hector had been to school with others who had gone on to become celebrities. Maybe this was why Stig had it enlarged and why he had it in his possession. I know I am clutching at straws here because it is all a muddle and makes no sense. But as I scan, it isn't long before my eyes begin to rest on each young face for a second before moving on to the next; there are only about twenty, so it isn't a chore. And then my eyes stop on one face, and they don't move again.

My heart speeds up and my mouth dries up simultaneously. My initial thought is it's a joke, that the face I am looking at has been superimposed onto the photo, to make it appear as though he had been at that school at the same time as Hector, but the more I look, the more I know it hasn't been doctored. It is very obviously part of the image. It is very obviously part of history. A part of history I was not privy to, but I should have been. And as I stare, a whole new rage begins to build inside of me and I feel ready to scream. I look away and then back again in case I imagined it, in case my mind has tricked me, in case I am drunk again even though I had only sipped some wine in the kitchen. But it doesn't matter how many times I look away or try to make my eyes adjust better, it doesn't change the fact that the face I am looking at is my husband's. I drop the photo, and even with the distance between me and the image, Stig's face still stares back at me.

14

'There we go, enjoy your jelly and ice cream.' Martha Leonard placed a large bowl with red, wobbling jelly and two scoops of pink ice cream on the table. Nicholas knew it was strawberry because that was his favourite flavour and his mother had bought it for him because... well... Nicholas thought for a moment about why his mother had bought it for him and he realised that there was no reason; it was purely because she liked to. Nicholas gobbled up the jelly, enjoying the way the wobbly texture ran down his throat, and then he slurped the ice cream. He marvelled at the contrast of textures, even though this delightfully sweet and cold combo was something he had experienced a hundred times.

When Nicholas had finished eating, he pushed his bowl away and looked at his mother. She was standing at the kitchen window looking out, but not in the way that Nicholas did when he caught sight of a squirrel or a particularly interesting-looking bird. No, his mother was looking as though there was nothing there at all, as though the window and the fantastic view of the countryside had been erased. Nicholas recollected that she had been doing this for some time now. He couldn't say how long, but he knew it tied up with the date when his father had left. He also realised that there had been an increase of sweet treats that came his way since his father's sudden disappearance. And he could classify it as a sudden disappearance because one minute, his father was there smoking his cigarette at the kitchen table and turning the pages of his newspaper with such vigorous force, and the next he was getting into his car and hadn't been seen since. Nicholas reckoned it had been about three weeks, as the new episodes of *Ballykissangel* had begun. They hadn't been showing when his father had been sitting at the kitchen table reading his newspaper and filling the kitchen with smoke. Nicholas could remember when something happened based on what was on the television at the time, because his mother let him watch a lot of television. Even more now that his father had left. He was allowed to stay up very late. His mother didn't seem to notice the time either or she was just grateful for the company on an evening. Nicholas would stay up until his eyes couldn't stay open any more and then he would climb up the stairs and into bed. When he woke each morning for school, he felt groggy and irritable. Snacking at night-time had become a regular occurrence too. He would help himself to bags of crisps and jam tarts while watching all the shows with his mother. He looked a lot older than his twelve years; he was tall and had been for some time, and now he had just begun secondary school, he was one of the tallest boys in his class. His mother praised him for his height; he would be such a big, tall, handsome boy. But Nicholas had started noticing the extra skin and flab that hung over his trousers when he took off his shirt. It also wobbled a little when he ran. But he supposed this was all part of getting older and like his mum said, he would soon turn into a big, tall man, lean and strong like an athlete. He just needed to keep eating everything he was given so all that food would turn to muscles.

* * *

Nicholas rode the bus back from school as he did every day and pushed his key into the door, but his time, he didn't have to unlock it as the door pushed open easily. He walked through into the lounge, where he heard low voices, and was surprised to see his father standing in the middle of the room. He turned when he saw his son standing in the doorway.

'Ah, Nicholas,' his father said formally, as though he were a teacher addressing a student.

Nicholas quickly assessed the situation. His father stood in the room; he was sure he had been pacing when he first arrived. His mother stood facing the mantelpiece; she hadn't looked up when he had arrived, even when his father announced his presence.

'Come, sit down.' Nicholas's father gestured to the couch where Nicholas himself would sit every evening with his mother to watch their TV shows. It felt odd that his father was now asking him to do something he did of his own accord and without his father's input. But Nicholas did as he was asked and took a seat on the spot on the sofa where he usually did, noting how it yielded to his weight and shape as he had occupied it for such extended periods.

Nicholas partly expected his father to quiz him about school, ask him how his day was, the way he had done from time to time in the past, but something about the way his father stood up very straight and tall and the way his mother did not move from her rooted spot by the mantelpiece told him that he was not about to begin small talk.

'Now, as you know, your mother and I no longer reside in the same property,' began his father, and Nicholas nodded. Although, thought Nicholas, whilst he had been witnessing his father's absence, he had not been formally informed or told officially that this was the case. 'It appears that your mother is…' His father paused momentarily to consider the following words that were about to come out of his mouth, but he didn't complete the sentence.

Nicholas heard a slight sound come from across the room and presumed it had come from his mother; it sounded like a balloon deflating.

'So we have decided that for all of our sakes, it would be best if you were to spend some time at a boarding school.'

Nicholas pulled a face that he hoped expressed his misunderstanding of the situation. If his mother was struggling with the separation, then surely the best place for Nicholas to be was here, at home, where he could be company for her – sit with her in the evenings as he had been doing for the last few weeks. He was sure that was what was needed. He knew his mother; they seemed to be getting on fine, much better, in fact, than when his father had been around.

Nicholas was scowling now; he could feel his whole face contorting. He knew his father had noticed this, and he could see that it was making him uncomfortable. For a few short moments, he was glad – glad that his father was finding this difficult, that he might for a second consider him in all of this and what it was he wanted.

'Mum?' Nicholas eventually found his voice, and his mother looked around from where she stood. She glanced at Nicholas. Nicholas gasped and threw his hand over his mouth because he could hardly believe what he saw. His mother's face was all bruised from her eye down to her arm. The most alarming mark of all was the two bruises on either side of her neck.

'It's for the best, love,' she said in a small voice and looked away again.

Nicholas went to speak; he wanted to mention the bruises and to run to her. Then he looked at his father and realised that there was only one place those bruises could have come from. Only one person in a woman's life could harm her in that way. Nicholas had seen enough thrillers and crime dramas in his life, staying up and watching TV with his mother, that he knew. He knew what his father was capable of, and what he had done. But he was scared now, and saying something to his father would worsen the situation. He might hurt his mother again. He might take it out on him. He had never seen his father act violently toward his mother before, and he had never seen what went on behind closed doors, but he knew that they were all the things that adults didn't want children to hear or see.

Everything changed in that minute. He felt a rage burning inside him that he didn't know he was capable of. It scared him so much; it was such an enormous feeling.

'So, that's settled. You are lucky to have been given this opportunity, son; they are at capacity, so don't mess it up.'

'Then don't send me! If they are at capacity, don't send me.' Nicholas heard the unfamiliar word 'capacity' on his lips. He didn't think he had ever used the word, and it felt alien to him.

He saw his mother flinch. His father stood still; a firm look on his face. He needed to be here with his mother to look after her, surely?

'The decision has been made. You will begin at Blythewood after the half-term.'

Nicholas did some quick sums in his head. It was less than three weeks away. He felt a strange sensation in his gut, a worry that was beyond any concern he had felt before. But somehow, he managed to push it down into the depths of his body. Then he stood up and walked over to the other side of the room. He placed a hand on his mother's shoulder. She flinched before looking at him briefly, and then, unable to hold his gaze, she looked away again. Nicholas wasn't sure if his physical connection with his mother was a subtle way to get her to intervene, to try and get her father to change his mind, or if it was simply a gesture to let her know that he was okay and didn't blame her. And that he would protect her no matter what. He felt it was a bit of both, but one thing was for sure: Nicholas knew that he was no longer the baby of the house and that he needed to grow up quickly and prepare himself for what was about to be a very different life.

15

Stig returns from his run, showers and as we both sit down to dinner, I force a smile even though my insides are churning, and my mind is racing with thoughts. The words that are plaguing me the most are that Stig knows Hector. Hector knows Stig. Should I be angry at Hector for not making it evident that he and Stig had gone to school together? From that reels, many more thoughts, such as, why? Why did Stig not say anything? Why has he continued to keep it from me? Unless I have got this all wrong? Am I being pranked? Or maybe I imagined Stig's face there when it was someone else entirely. But something tugs at my thoughts: the picture I had seen when I was at the town house is the same as this one here, but this one has just the portion that contains both Stig and Hector together. I had looked intently at Hector's photo because the faces were smaller. I had found Hector among the hundreds of faces because I had been looking for him. I hadn't expected to see my husband, therefore I didn't pick his face out of the tiny, grainy mass. But in this picture, from our study, Hector and Stig were above and below one another and then six or so people apart. But Stig does not want me to see it because he is trying to hide it from me, and when I had stepped into his study earlier, he made it obvious he wanted that paperwork away from my prying eyes. He does not want me to know that he and Hector are old-school buddies. He does not want me to know that he went to one of the most prestigious schools in the country, a school that costs thousands every year to go to. And this image of Hector and Stig was taken when they were young men, at least sixteen or seventeen, meaning that it is likely that Stig spent many years at school with Hector prior to that. And from that, I have ascertained that Stig not only knows Hector but could know him very well.

Stig has implied he is estranged from his parents and that is all I know. There is no way of finding out the truth from either of them unless I can track both of Stig's parents down. But I shouldn't have to do either of those things. I should be able to speak to my husband and receive the truth. Still, after the near deer crash on the way to Hector's Cotswolds home, and discovering the text from a Delilah, who is probably someone he knows from his expensive schooling days, I am beginning to wonder if I know Stig at all. All these secrets suddenly come to light, exposing the lies he has already told me about the way he was raised, the schools he attended, and where he grew up. Was my husband rich or poor? Had he been raised in a privileged home? Had he spent time with Hector and his family growing up? He did not reveal any of this to me when we met. The man I married is an enigma.

I look at my husband chewing intently on his food, sipping his beer, and wonder what he is thinking about. What is he worried about? And I want to know what the history is with Hector. Why have we been drawn into the lives of the rich and famous? Does it mean he knows Tristan, Henrietta and Ruby? I think back to the comfortable manner in which Ruby called him

Nicholas. Was it all a coincidence when their worlds collided again at the restaurant? I hadn't told Stig where we were going that night. He did not know that he was about to bump into Hector Bolson-Woods, his old school buddy, on our anniversary. Did he? My mind is a reel of unanswered questions on a constant loop and one way I am going to get some truth is to spend more time with Hector. I was never averse to Hector's business proposal, it was a pleasant shock, but after everything I have discovered about Stig, it seems our marriage is built on nothing but lies. I am being offered a role as a charity manager, a salary which could do a lot for us. If there is an *us* after this. I know it wouldn't be the act of working with Hector that would ruin our marriage because Stig has already done that with his lies. I no longer know who he is. He has experienced private education; he could be sitting on a lot of money for all I know and keeping it to himself while I walk on a rickety hallway that he refuses to shell out for.

Right now, I am angry at my husband for what he has done and for what he has kept from me. I want to be as far away from him as possible while I try to work out what the hell is going on. I know that I will go to France with Hector. But I will tell Stig I am going to stay with Emily, and then when I return, with the signed employment contract, we can decide what to do.

I can't bear the awkward silence anymore. I stand up, scrape my plate and put it in the dishwasher, then take myself upstairs for a bath. Once I am locked in the bathroom, I call Henrietta's number.

She answers within a few rings.

'Hi, Henrietta, it's me, Lily Leonard. Yes, yes, I will come to France. Book me on a flight as soon as possible.'

16

Nicholas arrived at Blythewood on a chilly October morning clutching a small holdall. The driver his father had arranged to take him to the school was rummaging in the car's boot and retrieved two larger and heavier suitcases.

Nicholas looked at the gargantuan, imposing building looming down at him. Dark-red brick with pillars and steeples jutting out at irregular points made it look like a fantasy castle where witches and wizards hid out. That was how Nicholas would think about it: it was a fantasy building and, therefore, not real. None of this was real. He was sure that after just one term, his mother would be feeling well again, and he could return to his home, and everything would be as it was once more. His soft, cushiony spot on the sofa would still be there waiting for him, and he and his mother would return to quiet companionship, watching their favourite TV shows together.

'Come on, lad.' The driver's voice shook him out of his daydream. The driver had barely spoken the entire two-hour journey, and the sound of him suddenly speaking was a shock.

Nicholas moved as swiftly as his legs would allow him,

hoisting up his holdall so it rested on his shoulder as the driver carried the bags to the front entrance. A bustle of noise came from within: the sound of boys talking loudly and moving about the reception area. Nicholas turned to check the driver was following him in, but he had stopped just at the top of the stairs and put down the bags.

'Right, I'll leave you to it.' And he turned and headed back down the stairs toward the car.

Leave me to what? Nicholas wondered. Was he supposed to carry all these bags in by himself, find where he was supposed to go alone? This was unbelievable. The worry surged through his gut and into his chest. He looked up through the open doors and caught the eye of a small boy who, although petite, looked as though he could be about his age.

'Excuse me,' Nicholas said politely.

The small boy took a step toward him. 'Yes?' he said.

'Where do I go?'

'Are you new?'

'Yes,' Nicholas said solemnly.

'Wicked!' the boy said. 'What house are you in?'

Nicholas thought for a moment and recalled a strange name his mother had used which wasn't Blythewood.

'Sloan?' he tried.

'Great! Same as me. I'll take you there.'

The boy looked at the bags next to Nicholas and gestured to them. 'These yours?'

Nicholas nodded.

The boy hoisted one of them onto his shoulder and began walking swiftly away.

Nicholas grabbed the other heavy case and struggled to get it into a comfortable position with the other small holdall he was already carrying. He began following the boy through twisty corridors until they came out into a quadrangle: lush, green grass framed by a path. They headed through until they were back indoors and wandering through corridors again, and up a flight of steps until the space opened up into a reception area. Nicholas looked up to see the word *SLOAN* on the sign above his head. He felt relief flood through him that he didn't need to walk any further; he was a little embarrassed, to say the least, that the small lad who had just escorted him here, moved at a pace that far outdid his own.

The boy put his hand down on a silver bell and it let out a little *ting* sound. He looked around and grinned at Nicholas.

'Thanks so much for helping; couldn't have got all that up here without you.'

'Not a problem.' The boy grinned.

'I'm Nicholas, by the way.'

'Tim,' the boy said.

Nicholas nodded. Tim. *Nice but dim,* he heard in his head and realised it was something his father said once and he hated himself immediately for thinking something so childish and, frankly, mean. As Nicholas thought of his father, a surge of anger rose into his chest and he began to feel shaky, as though he might pass out. He pushed all the thoughts into the pit of his stomach where they seemed to settle, although he still sensed them whirring away and he wondered if they might always be there.

A woman appeared from a heavy door wearing a bright-pink shirt and a smile.

'Hello.' She looked at Nicholas. 'Who have we here then, Tim?' She addressed the other boy this time.

'This is Nicholas; he's new. I brought his bag for him.' Tim looked pleased with himself.

'Gosh, well I say, that was an achievement, well done, Tim.'

The lady came around from the other side of the desk and Nicholas noticed that one of her buttons was undone on her shirt and he caught a glimpse of white underwear through the tiny gap. He began to look anywhere except at the front of her chest.

'I'm Mrs Paver, the matron. That means I am the person that you come to for anything. If you feel sick, if you want to call your parents, I'm a caring, listening ear for the students here. I'll look after you.'

'That is something that Mrs Paver does very well,' came a gruff, posh voice, and Nicholas saw a heavily moustached man in a thick, dark-green and brown tweed jacket. He had come from the room that Mrs Paver had come from. He looked at Mrs Paver with what Nicholas thought might be admiration, although he had never seen a man look at a woman in that way. Mrs Paver's face looked as though it was turning the same colour as her shirt. And as she began to run her hand absently down the material, she came across the missed button and let out a small gasp. She turned her back on Nicholas.

'Hello, I trust you are Nicholas Leonard?' The man looked down at Nicholas and Nicholas found he was becoming lost in the mountain of moustache. It was like a small rodent had attached itself to this man's upper lip.

'I am,' Nicholas said.

'Jolly good. I'm Mr Peterson, the head of Blythewood. So after Mrs Paver and of course your tutor, I am the one you come to with any woes or dealings you feel cannot be dealt with along the line with your other senior staff members. Is that clear, Master Leonard?'

Nicholas felt he needed to click his heels and stand to attention as Mr Peterson had just referred to him as master.

'Yes,' Nicholas said instead, and a little more meekly than he should have done.

Mr Peterson's eyes were no longer on Nicholas.

'You boys, why are you here?' Mr Peterson's voice had grown louder by about a thousand decibels and, already, Nicholas felt the presence and power of this man in the school. He would have scarpered at that but when he looked around, he saw three boys, all wearing blue ties, staring at Mr Peterson.

'Sorry, sir, we were walking and talking and took a wrong turn.' The tallest of the boys spoke, confidently and without so much as a flinch.

Mr Peterson mumbled something under his breath which sounded as though he didn't believe the boys. 'Well, I am pleased you have acknowledged your mistake. Now, if you would kindly rectify it and return to your own houses and dormitories.' Mr Peterson stood tall as he spoke.

Nicholas observed the three boys. Whilst the other two retreated into the corridor, the boy who had spoken remained where he was and slowly began to remove his tie and whilst he did, he averted his attention to Nicholas and began looking at him with curiosity, a small smile playing across his lips.

Mr Peterson cleared his throat and adjusted his own tie.

'Hector Cunningham, please return to your house immediately,' came Mrs Paver's voice.

Nicholas looked back at her, noticing her button was fixed, and then back at the boy who Mrs Paver had just addressed by his name.

Hector looked at Nicholas and narrowed his eyes a little before turning and following his friends into the darkness of the corridor.

Mr Peterson cleared his throat once more and as Mrs Paver passed him to return to her place behind the desk, she muttered,

'Really, Martin, why on earth do you allow that boy to get the better of you?'

'Right, Master Leonard, I will assist you with your bags and help you to your dormitory where you can unpack and then hopefully join us for lunch. I believe it's gammon, eggs and chips, and jelly and ice cream today. How does that sound?' Mr Peterson picked up one of the suitcases leaving Nicholas with just his holdall.

Nicholas had found the situation with Mr Peterson and the boy he had called Hector a little uncomfortable, but at the mention of jelly and ice cream, he felt instantly better.

Tim scooped up the remaining suitcase and as they walked up the steps that led to the dormitory, Nicholas thought about the boy, Hector, and the way he had stared at him so intently. It was as if he was looking straight at him, with some sort of venom or anger and on top of the funny feeling in the pit of his stomach over his father, he now felt a new niggle and it had Hector's mark all over it.

17

The flight is booked for next weekend. That will be long enough for Stig and me to live in enough awkward silence. It is also enough time for it to become too unbearable to live with one another any more and a short break will be what we both need to assess everything. Our feelings, our love for one another and our hopes for the future. I am sure a few days in France is going to give me the perspective I need.

The doorbell rings on Saturday afternoon, a week after we left Hector's Cotswolds mansion. When I open it, I am surprised to see Ruby there. It isn't that I forgot about her or that she exchanged on the house around the corner; it is that I have been so absorbed in the Hector proposal and thinking about Stig's lies and deceit that she has been simply pushed to the back of my mind. But now I need to address it and accept that she is officially a neighbour, and as she is part of the Hector Bolson-Woods clan and I now feel that I am too, I feel I must truly embrace her.

'Hi, Lily!' She grins at me with a childlike expression and

tone. 'I thought I would call on my neighbour and see how she is doing.'

I am thankful Stig is out playing golf all afternoon and therefore we won't be disturbed. It wouldn't hurt to invite her in. Stig has told me enough lies; I don't need to tell him Ruby has been here.

'Hi.' I step back from the doorway. 'Come in.'

She trots in, her heels making a loud noise on the tile-less hallway.

'Doing some DIY?' she calls as she makes her way confidently into the house and into the kitchen.

'Always,' I call back, the exhaustion apparent in my tone as I close the door.

I find her in the kitchen already seated at the table expectantly.

'Coffee?' I ask, and she grins.

'Lovely.'

I fill the kettle and flick the switch. Then I turn to face her. 'How's the new house?'

'Just lovely. I cannot wait to make my mark on it; it will be a perfect family home.'

I didn't know that Ruby was looking to start a family. I know she is older than me, I can see it in the lines on her face and the streaks of grey in her hair. She has to be at least forty, if not older. When is she planning to start this family, when there is no man on the scene?

'It is a lovely house. You chose well.'

'I did, and a total bargain.'

'What is it you do again?' I ask Ruby. I can't remember ever having a conversation about what she does for a living. How does she support herself and this single lifestyle? How does she afford a house alone?

'I don't do anything,' Ruby says. 'Well, I might find some voluntary work, keep me out of mischief, but other than that, I don't do anything. As a job, which is what I presume you meant?'

'I... did.' I suddenly feel awkward and silly, as though having a job is the only thing that defines a person. I haven't ever imagined that there are people who can simply exist on money which is handed down from generation to generation, which I presume is the case with Ruby. But I am not about to ask any more questions because there is a tone in her voice that suggests she isn't happy to keep discussing her finances.

'Well now you know. I live without the restraints of a job, which some might see as lucky but actually, it can be a bit dull. Of course, it certainly wasn't how it was always supposed to be.' She drifts off and stares out toward the window.

I want to ask her more about what it is she had wanted to do or what she did do and how she ended up with a pot of cash which allows her to live this way, but it all suddenly feels inappropriate; it's not my place to ask just yet. I can't help but recall the way Stig had been talking at her to make her raise her hands up in the air outside of Hector's house. Did it mean he'd said something to offend or upset her? Yet here she was, sitting at our kitchen table, ready to drink coffee and have a nice chat.

When the coffee is made, I bring it to the table, cream and sugar all on a tray, very civilised. I pour a cup for Ruby and lift the jug.

'Yes, please,' she says as I pour the cream.

She lifts the sugar bowl. 'Oh.' She notes the lack of spoon.

'Oh sorry,' I say, 'I forgot the spoons.' I pour cream into my own cup and go to stand.

'No bother.' She stands faster than me and she is over on the other side of the kitchen, opening the cutlery drawer, then she is back at the table with three teaspoons. She places one in front of me, one on the side of her cup and one in the sugar bowl. I am still holding the cream jug in my hand, and Ruby looks at me and clocks my confused expression. For a moment, something passes between us: a knowing look, a silent acknowledgement. Ruby had gone to the drawer on the other side of the kitchen. It is a bigger drawer and when we first moved in, I made that the cutlery drawer as it held everything so easily. It confused people as their first port of call was the drawer right under the kettle. But Ruby hadn't gone there. She'd known exactly where to go without even checking the obvious drawer first. It suddenly becomes clear to me that this isn't the first time Ruby has been in this house. And as this is the first time I have hosted her, it can only mean one thing. She has already been here alone with Stig.

18

It didn't take Nicholas long to unpack and begin to make friends with his fellow students in his dormitory and Sloan. A few days passed and he slunk into his lessons, began to lark about with Tim and a couple of other boys, a hilarious boy called Sags from Pakistan, who had lived here since he was two, and another boy called Harry who made Nicholas feel much better about his weight as Harry carried a stomach that he could mould into shapes at the request of his fellow students at any time, having them all in absolute hysterics.

They were to attend a lesson on the other side of the school today as there was a flood on their side of the building, something which Nicholas seemed to gather happened quite often due to the age of the building and the lack of funds to maintain such a grand, old building. Even though every pupil was paying extortionate fees to attend here.

'I need a number two,' Tim declared as they passed one of the toilets en route to lessons.

'You know where to go; just follow the signs towards the

pool, it's just next to that,' Tim called before bursting through the toilet door and was gone.

Nicholas looked around for the other two of his small clan, but they had already marched off.

Nicholas stood and looked down the corridor, bustling with students from all houses. He felt confident he could find where he needed to go without Tim holding his hand.

Once outside in the quadrangle, Nicholas looked for signs to the pool and headed off in that direction. When he suddenly found himself at a dead end with nothing more than a whirring generator attached to an outside wall and a door that didn't look as though he would be able to open it unless he had a key, he turned to go back, realising he might have just found his way to the rear end of the pool, where the maintenance took place.

But as he turned, he saw he wasn't alone in the dead end and three people stood before him, blocking his exit. He recognised them instantly as Hector from his first day at Sloan and the two boys who had been with him at the time.

'Well, well, well, what do we have here?' Hector spoke as though he were the artful dodger in *Oliver Twist* and Nicholas knew it was put on and not his real voice because he had heard him speak to Mr Peterson, and Hector had a very plummy accent, as his mother would refer to it.

The other two boys laughed, and Nicholas felt his stomach turn to jelly. He didn't like the fact that he would now have to assert himself a little to pass them.

He moved forward a few steps and found himself an inch or so taller than Hector; he surprised himself as he presumed Hector was taller, having only seen him from a distance a few days earlier.

'What are you doing in these parts, Leonard? This is where the rats hang out; are you a rat?' Hector said spitefully.

Nicholas glanced around at his surroundings, wishing he was more agile and one of those people who could scale walls with just their bare hands and jump from high ledges.

'I asked you a question. Are. You. A. Rat?' Hector said again, this time pausing between each word as though Nicholas was some sort of simpleton.

'No, just trying to get to my lesson, actually.' Nicholas spoke and the three boys burst into laughter.

'He doesn't sound like us, does he, lads?' Hector looked round at his crew, and they nodded and grinned like prize twits. 'What kind of accent is that, Leonard?'

'My name is Nicholas,' Nicholas said and began to push forward again. This time, his chest touched Hector's shoulders. A silence descended across the group and Nicholas felt it hard. There was a change in the atmosphere and the two gimps who stood just behind Hector looked uncomfortable. Looking back, Nicholas realised that was his window of opportunity, the moment when he should have just punched Hector Cunningham in the face and gone about his day. The atmosphere had become charged, and if Nicholas had ever been a fighter, then he would have done it. But he wasn't. As much as he was trying to settle in here, he missed his mother, the dinners she cooked him and the nights they spent seated on the sofa next to one another. He wished he were back there again and not standing in this dingy, stinky part of an old building he had never heard of until a few weeks ago, facing a boy who, for some reason unbeknownst to him, had instantly taken a dislike to him the moment he laid eyes on him.

Instead, Nicholas took a step back.

'I'd like to pass.'

'Oh, you'd like to pass.' Hector looked back at the two lads. 'He'd like to pass, lads.' The other two boys grinned, but

Nicholas could sense they didn't have nearly as much confidence in the situation as Hector did.

'What say we give you a password? In the future, should we find ourselves in this situation again, you'll know what to say?'

Nicholas inwardly rolled his eyes. He was beginning to feel anxious; he was going to be late to his lesson and it was only his first week.

'I think Alley Rat might be a good password, what do you think?' He looked at Nicholas.

'Whatever you say,' Nicholas said.

'Right then. What's the password?'

'Alley Rat,' Nicholas mumbled.

'What?' Hector said, laughing.

'Alley Rat.' Nicholas spoke up this time.

'Good. Now off you pop, Alley Rat, to your class. Scuttle along like the vermin you are.' And Hector stood back to let him pass.

Nicholas felt he had gotten off quite lightly, but as he passed, he felt his foot catch on Hector's – or rather, Hector had pushed his foot out purposely to trip him. Nicholas put his hands out to protect himself, but the force with which he landed sent pain soaring through his palms and wrist.

Hector stepped over him, just to add effect to the departure.

'See you later, Alley Rat.'

Nicholas rolled over onto his back and groaned as he tried to get himself to stand. There was a pain searing through his right wrist and blood on both palms. His knees also hurt where they had taken the brunt of the fall. He felt tears prickle in his eyes and he felt anger at himself immediately.

'Don't you bloody dare,' he heard himself say out loud. He did not need to cry. This was not a catastrophe. These boys would soon be bored of him and move on with someone else because that was what happened, wasn't it?

But even as Nicholas thought it, he realised that wasn't to be. Because whatever issue Hector had with him, it seemed to be more than just a new-kid-to-pick-on scenario. He seemed to hate him. Nicholas could see it in his eyes, and he knew what that look meant, because he had seen it before in someone else's eyes. His father's. And his father had sent him here. And no man who had any love for their son would send them away to an institution far away from their friends and family. Nicholas knew that his father could only have hate for him, just the way Hector did, and even though the tears threatened to come again, he pushed them down, brushed down his trousers, and walked out into the quadrangle, hoping and praying he would find his way to his lesson and not be late.

* * *

'What happened?' Tim whispered after Nicholas had got himself settled at his desk. 'I did the quickest number two, thought I'd find you just in front of me, but you were nowhere to be seen.'

'I...' Nicholas looked down at his palms.

'Someone do that to you?' he asked. 'You should report them. Zero-tolerance bullying policy here,' Tim said with a matter-of-fact tone.

'I took a wrong turn. Rushed to get back and tripped.'

'We need to get you familiar with this school ASAP. It will only add to your weaknesses if you can't even find your way to a lesson. The bullies pick up on everything. Start paying attention; we'll study the map and do some mock walkabouts at the weekend.'

'Oh, I won't be here at the weekend,' Nicholas said.

'Really? What's happening?'

'I'll be going home.' It was the first time he had heard himself say the words Because he was sure he would be.

'What? Cos, that's not what it says on your boarding card. I sneaked a look on Mrs Paver's desk. It says you're full boarding. That means you only go home for half-term and the summer holidays.'

Nicholas felt a lump shoot into his throat so fast he thought he might be sick. The next half-term was weeks away; he was expected to stay here for weeks at a time, only traveling back to see his mother when the school term was over. How was his mother even coping, he wondered.

'Did your parents not tell you?'

'Of course they did; I just thought I had this thing on this weekend, but it doesn't matter.'

'Oh, well, I'm full board, so you get to see me all the time too. It's not as bad as you think. It's quite fun.'

Nicholas wasn't sure that the tone in Tim's voice was entirely convincing. But that was by the by. Nicholas had no choice now; he was stuck in a boarding school day after day, week after week until he was finally allowed to go home for a few days. He knew that when he returned home, he should be feeling excited, but already, he could feel a burning in his stomach. It was resentment, and with every passing day and week, that resentment would build until eventually, he would begin to despise not only Hector but his father and his mother too.

19

I saw Ruby out after we continued our coffee, having chatted amiably about nothing in particular, keeping it light and not veering toward the obvious, which was, why had Ruby known where to go to get the teaspoons?

Ruby left, promising to visit again. After she had gone, I sat at the table, remembering Ruby going straight to the cutlery drawer without a second thought and the look we shared. A part of me wonders if she did it purposefully and had not tried to disguise her familiarity with our kitchen and hadn't checked the obvious drawer first to show me that she was a newcomer.

It would have happened when I was at work. At a time when Stig was at work when in fact, he was here and in cahoots with Ruby. But I still cannot work out why Stig has not made so many things obvious to me: his private education, his knowing Hector Bolson-Woods, and now this: his private contact with Ruby. Then there are the text messages from Delilah, someone else he doesn't wish me to know about. There are so many secrets and lies weaving into a giant spider's web and it has all come to light since Hector came into our lives. Or rather into mine, as he was already in my husband's life.

I am not sure how long I have been sitting there, but when I hear the front door, I jump up and grab the coffee tray, quickly placing both cups in the dishwasher so Stig won't suspect I've had a guest and that guest was Ruby. I'm not ready to get into a discussion about anything until I've had some distance from everything.

I am washing up the coffee pot when Stig comes through.

'You're back early,' I note. I hadn't expected him for at least another hour.

'Couldn't focus. My shot was all over the place.'

I don't say anything. I wait to see if Stig instigates talking about the real reasons he is so frustrated over the Hector proposal, but as usual, he doesn't.

For the next few hours, we skirt around one another, only speaking if we need to and when it comes to five o'clock, I ask Stig what he might like to eat for dinner.

He says he will cook, and I am grateful because I have a lot on my mind. While some seek therapy in cooking, my meals turn into disasters when I am picking through issues and problems.

I leave Stig in the kitchen, go upstairs and open my laptop. I stare at Google, knowing that I want to look for something, but I am not sure where to start. I want extra proof that the image I saw of my husband wasn't just a one-off, spoof, or fake. That he had been a student at Blythewood, the same school that Hector went to. I suppose I can only find out if I call the school to see if they will disclose that information. But I am doubtful that will be the case. The only other option is to go there, fake an appointment, and do some digging. But Blythewood is a three-hour drive away and even if I arrive there, how would I extract that kind of information from a staff member?

I stare at the screen a little longer, and then eventually, I type in *Hector Bolson-Woods*. Wikipedia is the first page on the screen and so I click on it. I look at the one photo of him at the top of the page, his signature starched, white shirt and tanned face, the way he looks slightly to his left as though he has been told something funny and the way he is slightly smiling. I have always been curious about him and always thought he was attractive and nice to look at. I appreciate his status and how he pleases people with what he does, but also how he is able to keep out of the limelight and just focus on himself. He attributes this to his success: his ability to ignore distractions such as the media and the things they would write about him.

I click out of Wikipedia and scroll down the page, seeing articles about his food, reviews, etc., and then click to the next page and then the next, and then I stop. The first few words of the article jump out at me.

> I was deserted by my father when I was twelve years old.

What? I click on the article. It is from a site I have never heard of, which makes me wonder if it is true or a spoof. It is just a few short paragraphs, and it looks as though it should have read longer and is not the entire article.

> My father and I had been close, and although he wasn't a very hands-on person, he respected me. We had a good relationship until he brought his new girlfriend home. I knew nothing about her other than she had a son from her previous marriage and was to move into my house very soon.
>
> My mother had moved out six months earlier, and so I

was understandably fraught. I was still a child. From the moment I met the new love of my father's life, she made my life hell, always saying things to put me down. Eventually, she began to put barriers between me and my father. The biggest problem came when she blamed me for a paint spill in the hallway. I was sent to live with my mother, and she and her son moved in soon after.

The article ends there, but underneath, there is a link to the *Daily Express*, citing it as the source of the original article. I click, but the page no longer exists.

Damn it, I wanted to read more about this vile woman. She is the reason why Hector Bolson-Woods and his father, Conroy Bolson-Woods are estranged. It has never occurred to me to delve into the background of their relationship. I assumed it was a standard case of parents and offspring falling out; it happens in all classes all over the world. I know very little of Conroy Bolson-Woods other than he is a multi-millionaire businessman, has done very well for himself and occasionally is mentioned in the news.

A shout from downstairs makes me throw the laptop to one side. Has Stig hurt himself cooking?

I find him in the kitchen leaning on the counter, his back to me, his fists pressed hard against the wood.

'What happened?' I ask.

He doesn't turn. 'Nothing,' he snaps.

'Well, it's something.' I take a step forward, notice his phone on the counter, open on his messages. *Delilah*. The name stares at me from the top, but before I can decipher the barrage of messages sent from both her and him, he snatches the phone up, stuffs it in his pocket, and carries on cooking.

I wait to see if he might turn back or say something. But he does not. Stig wants to keep secrets from me. Is he seeing this woman, Delilah? Does she want to have a baby with him? Is that the reason? I am becoming a burden and I refuse to yield to his demands.

But right now, I feel we are lucky that we don't have children; we don't have responsibilities except for the mortgage and bills. It's just us, and that means we have the luxury of leaving town whenever we feel like it. This is another reason I am able to go to France and accept the job that Hector is offering me.

20

Despite Nicholas's growing resentment, anxiety and frustration toward his family, and his general distaste at having been abandoned by the only two people he had ever relied upon for care and love, six weeks passed without anything too dramatic happening. There had been several other incidents with Hector and his two gimps, whom Nicholas now referred to in his mind as Thing One and Thing Two after the Dr Zeus book he read as a much younger child. They had cornered him that very first weekend and demanded he use the passcode; it seemed Hector wasn't welcome at home with his family at weekends either. And even though Nicholas felt an aching in his very core when he saw Hector Cunningham approaching, he also felt a simmer of sadness for him which mirrored his own unhappiness at having parents who didn't wish to spend time with their offspring and could only bear to see them for short intervals throughout the year. It wasn't that Nicholas felt sorry for Hector; it was only that he somehow felt a smattering of empathy, knowing that Hector was going through similar feelings as he was. Nicholas remembered his mother once saying that it was the sadness in the bullies themselves that came out when they attacked someone verbally or physically and that whoever was the aggressor, it was they who were tormented. It was hard to think about that whenever he was being kicked or punched, jeered at, called names or spat at. But it was a good piece of advice he had received from his mother all the same.

Once half-term finally arrived, the same driver who had dropped him off at Blythewood the first time picked him up. Nicholas felt a glimmer of happiness at the familiarity and felt a tiny amount of relief that he was going home, even allowing himself to look forward to seeing his mother when he returned.

The roads were slow and busy with holidaymakers. Nicholas was as weary as a newborn kitten when he finally arrived home after three long hours in the car.

The driver popped the boot and took out the one large holdall that Nicholas had packed to return home for the February half-term. One week with his mother. As Nicholas hauled himself out of the car, he thought about what they might do together and felt a flutter of excitement at dozing on the sofa as they watched their favourite TV shows.

The front door flew open and there stood a woman who, although she resembled his mother in some ways, could have been an entirely different person in other ways. For starters, her hair was different. It had been cut shorter and was styled in a way that made her look younger than her forty-three years. She wore tight, black jeans, which stretched across her calves and thighs as though they were her skin. She looked different in her face as well. He hadn't ever thought his mother fat, but her face had always been rather round; now it was less so and almost rectangular-looking, her jaw jutting out at an angle he had never noticed before. When she rushed down the stairs to greet him, she flung her arms around him as though she might never let him go and Nicholas, as he responded, also felt that the roundness that had been on other parts of her body was now gone and in its place were other poky-out bits he had neither felt before, nor welcomed now. His mother also smelt different. He had seen spray cans of Impulse in the bathroom cabinet and he knew what that smelled like, but this scent was different; it was denser and heavier, it lingered for longer, and as Nicholas removed himself from his mother's pointy grip, he took some of the scent with him on his own clothes and skin.

'Oh, my darling Nicholas, how are you? I have missed you so much,' his mother squealed. Her eyes shined brightly, he noticed; she was wearing more make-up which accentuated them.

'You've grown, I'm sure you've grown.'

'I'm sure I have grown,' Nicholas said.

'I'm so excited you're here; we are going to do so many exciting things. Starting with dinner tonight.'

Nicholas's mother took the bag from the driver and then, despite the tightness of her trousers, she somehow extracted a cash note from the pocket and handed it over.

The driver nodded and took the note, which looked like twenty pounds to Nicholas.

'Let's get you inside and have a nice cup of tea.'

Once inside the threshold of his house, Nicholas instantly felt the changes. The clutter that had once been the essence of their hallway and greeted them every time they returned home was gone. In its place was a large, oversized vase with a selection of walking sticks and umbrellas. This was the first thing that Nicholas felt was odd because even though they lived quite close to greenery and woods, his mother had never once ventured out with a stick. There was also a strong smell of paint and the walls, which had been a dark blue, were now a bright white and a funny-looking picture in a frame hung above the vase; it looked as though it was a woman but her body was all distorted and wiggly, as though she were a genie trying to get out of a lamp.

Nicholas's bag was abandoned in the hallway, and they went through into the kitchen which again bore an entirely different look to how it had been before. Everything was tidy and there were chairs around the island which had never been there before. It now looked as though it was a place where people might eat when before, they had eaten on a small, wooden table with three chairs that had been in the corner of the kitchen. Nicholas looked again, but it was gone. In its place, though, was a funky-looking sofa, and on the wall on the far side of that was a TV, actually on the wall, not like the big TV they had in the sitting room where they watched their programmes each night. Nicholas's mum had written to him occasionally and there had been a phone call a week, but she had never mentioned that the house would be different when he returned home.

His mother saw Nicholas looking around.

'It looks a little different, doesn't it? I thought it was time to get straightened up and make the place look a little more homely.'

Homely, thought Nicholas; the house he had been swept away from several weeks ago was no longer somewhere he could call home. It was stark and bright and soulless. Where was all the stuff? He wasn't sure exactly what it was he was referring to when he thought of stuff but he knew it was what had represented them as a family: himself, his mother and father when it was the three of them, and then eventually, just the two of them after his father left.

'You will love the sitting room. Come.' His mother took his hand as though she were an excited friend of his and not his mother. When they walked through the sitting-room door, it was as if Nicholas had been transported to another place entirely. There was no sofa, no TV, no sideboard or mirror or any of the things that represented who they were as a family. Instead, there was a large, dining-room table with six chairs around it. It was all white and cream and silver. Three large candelabras were in the middle of the table.

Nicholas was confused.

'It's great, isn't it? A proper dining room. This house looks like a proper family home now, doesn't it, Nicholas?'

Nicholas supposed it did if the family who would be occupying the house were soulless creatures from another planet and had no concept of home comforts.

Nicholas's mother laughed and ruffled his hair.

'Come on, let's get you fed; you must be starving!'

His mother left the room with a real spring in her step, something he had never seen before. Nicholas was left alone feeling dumbfounded in a place he was supposed to call home, but barely recognised at all.

* * *

Dinner, it turned out, was at a restaurant on the other side of town. This was again unusual as Nicholas's mother had always been frugal with her spending, choosing items that had been reduced in the supermarket whenever they shopped there and cooking meals from scratch rather than buying pre-prepared ones. It wasn't that they were particularly poor, but they were not well off, and Nicholas's grandparents on both sides were of what he had heard his parents refer to as 'working class', so he had never been spoiled either.

The food in the restaurant was good and Nicholas scoffed his way through three courses. His mother nibbled a salad and then drank some green tea. He wondered what happened to the blocks of chocolate they used to share on an evening and if they might share one tonight watching a movie. He thought about that uncomfortable-looking sofa in the kitchen and the odd-looking TV on the wall; it would be like visiting the cinema. Not cosy at all. His mother asked him questions throughout dinner; she generally seemed very upbeat and happy. At one point, she brought out a big phone; it was a mobile phone, she told him, and he was intrigued, having never seen one in real life before. Then it rang out a very loud, invasive noise and a few people in the restaurant turned and looked. Nicholas's mother turned a shade of red and rushed out of the restaurant to answer the call just as Nicholas was finishing his pudding. When she returned, she looked even happier than she had been before.

'Nicholas,' she said. 'How would you like to go out to dinner tomorrow night?'

Nicholas thought that would be okay and so he nodded. The food had been good. The sticky toffee was very good.

'Great. Because I would like to bring a friend for you to meet. That was him on the phone just now.'

'Him?' Nicholas parroted back.

'Yes. He is a man. A male friend. He is very nice, and I think you will really like him.'

Nicholas let out a sigh. His stomach was full, and he was tired from travelling. 'Sure,' he said. His mother clapped her hands together and Nicholas felt as though he were having dinner with a sister and not a mother that he had known for the thirteen years of his life so far.

21

A week passes, and Stig and I speak very little. When he comes home from work on the Thursday before I am due to travel, he makes himself a sandwich in the kitchen as I do a long yoga class and never want to eat afterwards.

'I'm going to stay with Emily for a few nights,' I say, hating the lie as it leaves my lips, but reminding myself that Stig has lied constantly for years.

Stig turns and looks at me, then goes back to his sandwich. 'Right,' he says, accepting that the decision was mine yet still unhappy about it. 'And may I ask why?' he continues, adding ingredients to his sandwich: gherkins, pastrami, mayonnaise.

'Because I think a bit of breathing space between us would be good. I think the whole Hector thing got out of hand and I think you seem stressed about it all, disproportionately so given that it isn't you who has been offered a job. You seem inordinately consumed with your phone, which is unlike you, and we barely say two words to one another in a day. And Emily is my friend, and I fancy a trip to Hampshire to visit her.'

I wait to see if Stig will object, try to address some of the issues I raised, but he is quiet and focuses on his sandwich.

'So I'll see you on Sunday,' I say. I have been quietly packing a bag for a few days and booked today off work as a holiday. I will stay with Emily tonight and then catch an early flight to France from Southampton tomorrow. I will be with Hector at his chateau by mid-afternoon Friday.

By travelling to Emily's tonight, I do not feel the lie is as weighty. It is as though I will be spending the entire time there, and Emily will vouch for me once I fill her in on the entire story, which she will inhale like oxygen.

I go upstairs, collect my suitcase and handbag, and go downstairs. Stig has devoured the sandwich and left the kitchen table covered in crumbs and is nowhere to be seen or heard. I experience a moment when I think this is all a terrible mistake, that I should tell him what I know about him and Hector at school together and that I am onto him over this Delilah woman.

But this is the right thing to do. Stig will try and stop me; this is my decision.

I notice Stig has left me a note.

Gone for a run.

I am dubious. Unless he packed the sandwich away or threw it, he had eaten it, and he was not going to be running on a full stomach.

I know Stig is angry with Hector. I know he is uncomfortable with Ruby living so close to us now. He has shown an instant dislike to her, and I wonder if that is where he has gone.

I put my suitcase in my car and slowly drive the two minutes around the corner to the cottages. I park my car in a small lay-by opposite, tucked behind a tree, so I cannot be seen if anyone comes or goes to Ruby's house. I turn off the engine, and the car falls silent.

I feel lucky where we live because it is quiet enough yet not so quiet that I feel isolated. But out here, just a short drive from where we live, it feels so remote. The three cottages were previously a part of the farm and lived in by staff when it had been a bigger, busier, working farm. Now it is just a few sheep and most of the land has been sold off. There is a security light outside the house next door to Ruby, and it keeps flashing on and off in that way when a wild animal is on the prowl, but it doesn't look as if anyone is in, and the third one is lying empty, either to be sold or rented. So Ruby is very much alone out here, and I suddenly feel sorry for her that she is living here alone with some expectation of creating a family life. Yet I saw the way Gordon dismissed her that evening and it seems she has not had a good run of decent men in her life. I decide that when I return from France, I will make some effort with her, at least make her feel as though she has someone keeping an eye on her. It is a big step to break away from the clan she has been a part of for so long and suddenly try and make it alone, no longer in the hustle and bustle of London; this sleepy part of Oxfordshire is a far cry from the life she has become accustomed to where she can step out of her front door and have everything she needs at her fingertips. But Ruby was adamant that she was ready to step away and I had to wonder if it is one thing or a combination of many that has sent her on this path. She had been at Hector's Cotswolds house, so she is still a part of their lives. I wonder if they would ever visit her here, the people she spent so much of her time with. And somehow, I can't imagine Henrietta or Hector or Tristan rocking up here to see her, to check in on her, which is why I will make it my responsibility to make sure that she is okay from time to time. Despite how much Stig has lied to me and knowing that Ruby has already spent time with him in my house, I still feel that Ruby is a precious creature who needs to be taken care of. Maybe this is what she is seeking in Stig. It's certainly what she had sought in Hector and Co.

I let out a breath and then another five, and then ten, minutes passes. I am anxious to get on the road, to get to Emily so we can have a glass of wine before bed. I have purposely chosen to get there after her children are asleep, so I don't have to endure the madness. It isn't that they aren't cute, but I can never finish a sentence when they are up and hanging around Emily's feet, demanding this, that, and the other and testing her patience so I can tell she is only half listening to me.

It is almost dark now. A noise outside the car makes me gasp and I shuffle down in my seat, now unable to see what is outside the window without shining a light. I am just about to turn on the engine and get going to Hampshire when I hear a door slam. I look up, and there is Stig on Ruby's doorstep. He has just come out, and the door has been closed behind him. He checks his phone, the light illuminates his face and then he begins jogging in the direction of our house. I look at the house and see a light come on upstairs then the silhouette of Ruby through the window. What have the two of them been doing? The more I consider her here all alone, the more I wonder if she is just getting away from it all in the way city people do when they relocate to the country or if she is getting away from Hector and everyone. Suppose she does not want to have anything more to do with them. Perhaps the partying and drinking have all become too much, and this is her time. I support her dream, her desire to be free and to start a life here for herself.

But why the hell is Stig here and what does *he* want with Ruby?

22

The man arrived in a car with a number plate that looked different to any other number plates he had seen before. It had just two numbers and two letters. Nicholas noticed that the man also had a driver, but by now, that didn't seem so weird as Nicholas had had a driver take him to and from Blythewood.

The man towered over Nicholas and his mother stared up at him as though he were Christ the redeemer.

'Good evening, young Nicholas. May I introduce myself; my name is Conroy Bolson-Woods. You may call me by my first name,' Conroy said and held his hand out. Nicholas took it; now used to the formative ways at Blythewood, this was second nature to him.

'Your mother said you were a fine-looking boy and she was not wrong. I am very pleased to make your acquaintance. I am sure your mother has mentioned that we have become good friends these last few months and I am very fond of her. Therefore it is imperative that you and I get along, wouldn't you say?'

Nicholas felt a stirring in the pit of his stomach. He nodded and his mother moved closer to his side and put a reassuring arm around him. 'I am sure once you both get to know one another, you will get on like a house on fire.' His mother laughed softly.

'Oh, Martha, you are so very sweet,' Conroy said just as softly, and then the pair of them looked at one another as though Nicholas was nowhere near, and they were both somewhere alone.

It was also strange to hear his mother's name fall from the mouth of someone other than his father.

The dinner was at a restaurant even fancier than the one they had eaten at the night before and Nicholas was sure that people were looking over at them and whispering. Could they see that this man was not his father? Did he really look that uncomfortable and out of place? he thought. But he soon began to forget about the stares because the food was so delicious and when the desserts arrived, they came on a trolley and Nicholas was allowed to pick whatever he wanted. He chose a slice of Black Forest gateaux and Conroy said it was an excellent choice.

When the car dropped them back to the house, his mother spent a long time in the hallway as he went to the kitchen to put the TV on and pretended he couldn't hear the girly laughter drifting down the hallway to the echoey kitchen.

His mother joined him about fifteen minutes later and sat down next to him. Although it wasn't the same as when they used to settle in the living room together, this was okay, Nicholas thought. There was something very different about his mother and he put it down to happiness. Something that she hadn't felt in a long time.

* * *

The next morning, Nicholas woke in his large, airy bedroom, another room which had had a makeover: white walls and new bedspreads, not quite as serious as the rest of the house; at least his mother had left all his knick-knacks in there.

Nicholas had not woken naturally; something had woken him. He stepped out of bed and went over to the window, peered down to the front garden, where he saw a man with a large stick hammering it into the grass next to the fence. Had his mother employed a gardener now as well? But when the hammering ceased, the man pushed a large, rectangular piece of wood onto the stick. There were several bits of print on the wood, including the name of a business and a telephone number. On the top of the sign were the words:

FOR SALE

23

I arrive at Emily's house near to nine. She opens the door and silently screams, and we hug each other. She bundles me through into their kitchen/lounge and pours wine.

I look around at the chaos on the floor and every surface: empty baby bottles, toys, wrappers, half-eaten packets of raisins. But Emily is so comfortable amongst it, I can't fathom it. How would I ever be able to give in to the mess?

'Tell me everything,' she says, taking a long gulp of wine.

I had already informed Emily about some of what had happened so far with Hector, but only up to the second invitation to his Cotswolds manor.

I include everything from discovering Delilah's messages on his phone to Hector's proposal. She almost drops her glass of wine.

'Holy shit, Lil, what the actual?'

I shake my head, still finding it all a little too much to believe now I am telling it to someone else.

'My God, Lil, your life is suddenly so exciting. I miss my old life, the excitement.' Emily is referring to her job as a solicitor for one of Oxford's most prestigious firms.

'You'll go back, right?'

'Yes, but not for at least another year; the baby needs me, and you know...' She gestures to the house; it is huge, twice the size of mine and Stig's, and all paid for by her husband, a barrister. Emily does not need to work except for her pride and sanity, and I have no doubt she will be back again at some point. The new baby has been a game changer; she has evolved into a proper mum, something she struggled to do the first time around with Milo. Her struggles are another reason to have reservations about having children; it had been challenging to witness four years ago just how hard Emily found it.

'My life is: feed the babies, sleep when I can. I am exhausted and your tales, as bizarre and slightly unorthodox as they are, are a welcome relief. Show me the business proposal.'

I hand her the paper from my bag and she reads it once.

'I mean, it's all there. Thorough.'

'I want to do this; I feel like I want control. I found out about Stig's lies before I was offered this deal and before I made my decision. I think the money will help me a lot. Especially if I need to make a decision about whether I am to stay with Stig.'

'I see what you mean but are you sure it isn't a knee-jerk reaction?'

'I don't think so. Only hindsight can reveal that in the next few months. Maybe I will regret not telling him.'

'You still on the pill?'

I nod.

'You two are really in a pickle. I'll help as much as I can when you get back and you've made your decision.'

'Thanks,' I say, 'although I feel it will be a decision based on all I know so far as getting Stig to tell me anything is like drawing blood from a stone. I'm not even sure he will open up and want to talk.'

'He is a closed book, that one.' Emily sips her wine. 'I am your friend; I know you and I this isn't all you think it will be. I sense stormy waters.'

'Are you a psychic now?'

'No,' she says seriously this time. 'I am a woman looking at this with a fresh eye. I am not emotionally involved.'

'I don't intend to get emotionally involved either,' I say defiantly.

'Oh, Lil, don't tell me you haven't thought about Hector at all in this and how he feels about you?'

'Of course.'

'And you don't think any of the decisions you are heading toward are not influenced by the honeyed words of a man you just met?'

I am quiet for a moment whilst I think.

'I think I don't know my husband and perhaps I never have.'

* * *

I creep away from Emily's house at dawn, leaving my car in the car park at the airport then heading to departures.

When the plane takes off just after 7 a.m., a slight terror creeps through my body. I manage to shake it off with a vodka and tonic once we are in the air, and I am unable to decipher exactly what caused it. However, by the time the plane touches down in Bordeaux, I am just feeling nervous, and that is expected.

I know, now I am here, I can't have any negative thoughts. I need to feel in control, I need to feel I am going to move on with my life after this; this needs to be a step forward. And everything that happens after this, I need to be in control of.

I am picked up by a driver in arrivals and we speak a mixture of a little broken English and French. He is able to tell me that the chateau is approximately an hour's drive away.

Just over an hour later, we drive along a very long driveway in the middle of the countryside. Immediately, the reception on my mobile begins to dip. I send a pin drop to Emily, just as a precaution, in case I am needed and no one can get hold of me on my mobile as I am pretty sure the reception could be touch and go here. I am surrounded by a lot of trees. I feel that spike of terror return again and then I think of where I am and how much wine will be on offer. Hector is a nice man, a lovely, kind man. He is a lonely man; his father disowned him. That must have been very hard for him at such a young age too. That is the age when kids need their parents. I find it difficult to believe that any man can throw their child out and never speak to them again. Hector spoke of his mother a lot in the media and when he was interviewed, and what she had done for him over the years to make him into the man he is now. He struggles with relationships, which is why he isn't married. I hope that the charity he is proposing will also be good therapy for him, because despite the endless crap I am dealing with back home, I am ready to put it all behind me for now, to live in the moment, with Hector Bolson-Woods, a man I already trust and who I am becoming very fond of.

24

Nicholas returned to Blythewood after the half-term feeling as though his life had truly been turned upside down. The man, Conroy, wished to marry his mother, and they were to live together. His mother told him that he would be as welcome at the new home as he was in his old home, but she understood that it would take some time to adjust to the new place.

'You will have your own room, so you know, whenever you are ready,' his mother had said, brushing his head, and Nicholas had never been so keen to get back to the boarding school.

There was a general buzz and excitement as all the children returned to their dorms after a week away. And all too soon, Nicholas found himself face to face with Hector. He looked different. He had a tanned face, so Nicholas presumed he had been to a hot country for the half-term.

Hector stared at him for a moment. 'Alley Rat, you're back; you didn't fall off a mountain or something as I had hoped and prayed you might.'

There was a difference to the tone in Hector's voice; maybe it was because he did not have Thing One or Thing Two with him, but he almost sounded as though he really could not be bothered. It unnerved Nicholas and it almost felt as though they were engaging in a gentle banter rather than the bully and the bullied.

'Well, I am sorry to disappoint you,' Nicholas retorted.

Hector stared hard at him for a moment and then punched him in the gut, so fast that no one would have noticed. Nicholas bent over and wailed internally at the wrenching inside his abdomen. 'Funny, because you always so manage to disappoint me, Alley Rat, by just being you.' And then he spat next to Nicholas's feet where he was crouched over. Nicholas stared at the glistening saliva, feeling as though he might throw up.

He felt too ill to go down to dinner that night, so Mrs Paver brought up a tray of soup and bread and a little fruit.

She touched his forehead in a motherly way before leaving him.

When Tim and the other five boys he shared a dorm with all came careering into the dorm after dinner and their Sunday-evening TV time, Nicholas pretended to be asleep, so they all reduced their whoops and cries to whispers.

'I think it's that Hector; he gives him such a hard time,' Tim whispered.

'Well, his dad abandoned him, didn't he?' said one of the others.

'Do you know why?' Tim said.

'Must have been something terrible; you don't just abandon your kid for no reason.'

They continued to whisper, and Nicholas thought about his own father, who he rarely considered these days, and wondered what exactly he had done to deserve to be abandoned by him. And now his own family home was to be sold, more things were changing. Nicholas felt he barely knew himself any more.

* * *

A whole academic year passed in the blink of an eye and before Nicholas knew it, he was moving into the next year and would be beginning his GCSEs.

He had spent the summer at his new home, even though it felt strange calling it that; they had all taken a holiday to Barbados as well as Florida. He felt incredibly lucky and was now almost glad that his mother had met Conroy. Everything had turned out just fine. He still had run-ins with Hector, but the anger seemed to have subsided, and Nicholas had grown over the year. He had stretched and wasn't so chubby; he was doing so much sport every day that he was leaner and almost gaining muscle now. He still enjoyed his food and received regular care packages from his mother – which she now signed from her and Conroy – which contained treats from all around the world, as Conroy travelled regularly for his work. He had now also come to realise that Conroy was often recognised as the multi-millionaire businessman he was. Nicholas had had no idea, but he had been on TV and in magazines and anyone who read them or watched the programmes would know him. Nicholas decided immediately to keep this information to himself; he didn't want anyone to know that his mother was going to marry a well-known business tycoon. Although he enjoyed the luxuries he now experienced, he wasn't about to begin to declare that to world. A part of him still missed and longed for the simplicity of his old life, when he was the only person in his mother's world, and he felt totally adored. As much as Conroy was a nice enough man and kind and generous, he often wished he could have his mother back for himself.

In the first week of January there was a rugby match planned to ease them into the beginning of term and a new year, a friendly, and Nicholas, feeling fitter and healthier than he ever had been and fresh back from a two-week trip to Thailand with his mother and Conroy, was geared up and ready for it.

It didn't even faze him when he was informed that the match would be Sloan against Waldon; it had been so long since Hector had even approached him to cause trouble.

The match got off to a good start with a successful drop goal from Sloan.

Hector had barely even looked Nicholas's way and Nicholas was lost in the moment of the game, not thinking about anyone or anything except getting the ball over the line.

During half-time, he stood around with his housemates, swigging water, rinsing out his gum shield, and then they wandered back onto the pitch.

'My God, you're tanned,' a lad called Mike commented. He was Waldon, but he and Nicholas had struck up a bit of a rapport. His father was also a multi-millionaire from what he had gathered, and he often went on long and expensive trips abroad during the holidays. 'Where was it this time, you lucky sod?' Mike said, as though he himself was not used to the finer things in life and exotic trips all year round.

'Thailand,' Nicholas said.

'Wow, nice. Where?'

'All of it, pretty much – we stayed in a hotel and then chartered a boat to island hop.'

'My God, you're a lucky git,' Mike went on.

Nicholas and Mike stopped on the pitch and as they did, Hector walked past. Had he been walking right behind them? If he had, Nicholas had not noticed.

'We've done it a few times, but not the island hopping; my folks are far too into their comforts. They love a hotel and dry land.'

'Yeah, right,' Nicholas said, still finding these conversations odd, that he was now one of these lads, that he could discuss expenses and trips to Thailand as though he were talking about what he had watched on the TV the night before. It was laughable really, to think what his life had been before. It was now apparent to Nicholas that it was Conroy who paid for his school tuition fees. He was embarrassed to say that he did not realise that the school and his education had to be paid for when he first arrived at Blythewood. And he also now understood that his mother was way into a relationship with Conroy before his mother and father split, hence why a place had already been secured here for him at the point when his father left. He always found it odd though how his mother had appeared so sad that day when his father announced to him that he would be leaving for boarding school. He wondered how his father felt about that. But that was all he could do, wonder, because his father had not been in touch with him since.

The second half of the game commenced and within minutes, Nicholas found himself back in control of the ball, and at the same time, he was aware of someone very close to his heel. He managed to turn his head slightly enough to see how close they were and when he did, he was surprised to see it was Hector. Nicholas was much faster than Hector, something he never realised in the early days of attending Blythewood. If he had had known, he would have simply just run away from him. So it was a surprise to find Hector within a hair's breadth because he must have been trying very hard to get this close to him and so quickly. It must have taken all his effort to have done it. Yet somehow, Hector still had enough energy within him to perform a pretty hard and fast, dirtier-than-dirty tackle which took Nicholas down with such force, he forgot who and where he was for a few minutes.

He was carried off the pitch on a stretcher to the medical room where, after a thorough examination by the school doctor, he spent the rest of the afternoon recovering. He lay there falling in and out of consciousness, waking slightly only to sink back into a hazy half-sleep. It was when he was slumbering in a half-awake state that he heard the voice of one of the nurses speaking with someone else, who he eventually began to place as Mrs Paver. They were both in the office which was just off the day room where Nicholas lay resting.

'We'll have to keep an eye on him; that was nasty fall,' the nurse said.

'I know, terrible thing to have happened.'

'I just don't understand that boy. He has a lovely life, a mother who cares for him, and let me tell you, some of them don't,' the nurse went on in a stage whispered voice. 'Hector Cunningham is nothing but a bully.'

'Oh I know, Pam, but there is a little more to it than that,' Mrs Paver said.

'Oh, is there now? Tell me what I'm missing.'

'Hector's father disowned him a few years ago; that's why he only lives with his mother now.'

'Yes, I know all this, and I've met Mrs Cunningham several times now. She is a splendid woman.'

'She is,' Mrs Paver continued. 'But Hector took his father leaving very badly. I don't know why he no longer has contact with him.'

'Well, a lot of them don't, do they? That's why they are here, and we have to pick up the pieces for them, the poor souls.'

'Yes, but who his father is with now makes this situation so very difficult.'

'Okay?' the nurse said, inquisitively.

Mrs Paver now dropped her voice a little quieter. 'Martha Leonard.'

There was a gasp which Nicholas presumed was from the nurse. 'Conroy Bolson-Woods and Nicholas's mother?'

Nicholas's heart sped up, a rate so fast that he felt he might need to press the bell for assistance but he knew he wasn't supposed to be privy to this conversation, never mind that the two women should not have been gossiping about him when he was situated so close to them, and they had only presumed he was fully asleep.

'Yes, and last year, he took up with Martha Leonard, Nicholas's mother. Christ knows how they crossed paths when their worlds were so far apart, but there we go, love is found in the most unlikely places.'

'And does Hector know his father is living with Nicholas's mother?' The nurse scraped her chair and was now sitting down, Nicholas presumed, engaged in the story as though it was a soap opera. Nicholas felt his throat swell and wondered if he was coming down with something or if maybe the fall had triggered something more serious.

'Hector does and poor Nicholas does not know that Hector knows. They wanted to keep it from Nicholas, to protect him.' Mrs Paver let out a short sharp laugh.

The nurse let out a loud tut and a sigh. 'The poor mite.'

'But it's not our place to tell him, is it?'

Well I bloody well know now, Nicholas wanted to shout from his bed but remained completely still, terrified to move an inch should he cause the bed springs to react and draw attention.

'I believe Hector's mother pays the fees for him to attend here, she is very successful in her own right, but it was her mission to make sure he received the best schooling,' Mrs Paver went on.

'And Conroy decided to send Nicholas here, what, as another kind of punishment for his son? To rub it in his face?'

'I don't know exactly. It is the best school in the country, Pam; you know that people would kill to get their children in here.'

There was a silence before Pam, the nurse, spoke. 'Well, let's hope they haven't,' she said and let out a slight snigger, followed by another one which came from Mrs Paver before they said their goodbyes and Mrs Paver left.

Nicholas's heart was racing, and he wanted to jump from the bed and run but he heard the nurse enter the room and he had to pretend to be fast asleep, again not moving a muscle until he was sure she had left the room. When he heard her pull the door and leave it ajar, then heard the sound of the kettle being boiled in the office next door, only then did he move, letting his body shudder as the tears fell hard and fast.

25

Hector's house finally comes into sight, and it takes my breath away. It is like a fairy-tale castle. White windows with white shutters against a light stone building. My phone alerts me to a message. It shows I have a voicemail. It might be Stig. I am not ready to hear his voice. Maybe he has found out where I am and is trying to get me to come home. I am not ready for that yet. I want to stay and see this out. I need to be in control of my own life from now, regardless of what happens with Stig and me.

The car pulls into a long-arched driveway around the back of the chateau. I can see orchards on either side, and just to my right, I can see into a kitchen garden where things grow up walls and trellising or encased under nets. *You could live off this land*, I think.

A small, stooped woman as brown and wrinkly as a prune comes out of a small gate and approaches the car. The driver steps out and opens the door for me. After an hour or so in an air-conditioned car, the outside heat hits me like a wall. The woman mumbles something in broken English and jabs a hand out toward my bag. I shake my head.

'Oh, no, honestly, I can carry it,' I say as the driver places my small suitcase on the ground. I snatch the handle, flip it up to waist height and try to pull it across the gravel path.

The woman shakes her head and snatches it off me, puts down the handle, lifts the case to her waist height and stomps off to the house.

I wave at the driver and he tips his cap at me. I wonder if I should have given him a gratuity. I don't have any euros, and my purse is in the bottom of my handbag and that elderly French lady who is quick on her feet is away with my bag. I race after her and find her in a cool, terracotta hallway.

'Ahh,' I say, pointing at my bag. 'Shall I take it?'

'*Non*,' she replies sharply. And begins walking again. I follow her along corridors and winding staircases until we stop at a door, and she opens it. It is a large suite, with a four-poster bed and a balcony. I rush to the window to see that it overlooks the gardens, straight borders on either side, with pruned bushes and a glimpse of the sea. It is too perfect. How will I ever want to go home again?

The lady leaves me without any instructions for what I what I am to do, or where I am to go. I feel a surge in my gut. Does she know why I am here? Has Hector forgotten me?

I would put her in her late seventies. Even though she does not speak English very well, that does not mean she is not privy to the comings and goings of the chateau. I imagine she is the eyes and ears of the place.

I unpack, placing a few dresses and shoes in the wardrobe. Then I put some of my toiletries in the bathroom and my make-up on the dressing table.

I could live here, I think again. I have no idea how the next two days will pan out. Will we discuss business all weekend? Will we do some excursions? Will I have an opportunity to sunbathe before my flight home on Sunday?

It is still early in the day, and the grounds are calling me; I am sure it will not be impertinent to start to feel my way around the place. It is huge and might take me several hours. I pop my phone into a small handbag and wear it across my chest and step out into the corridor. For a moment, I can't remember which way to go, then I recollect coming in from the left which means I need to turn right. Soon enough, I come to the same stairs I remember coming up with the French housekeeper. I meander the hallways and follow my nose until I am back in the little hallway.

So far, the little French lady is the only person I have seen. I anticipate seeing Henrietta and her arriving with her briefcase and a clipboard to go through the particulars of the next few days. But it seems as though it is just going to be us, Hector and me. I get a sense there are few, if any, other staff in the chateau this weekend. But I presume this is how Hector wants it, and it makes sense. I think about how much we will get through, just the two of us, as well as getting to know one another better.

I go outside and am in the driveway. I want to be at the front of the house, so I begin walking around the side of the building. I look up at the brick, which, now close, looks tired. I can't imagine the cost of maintaining a building this size. Beyond the vineyards on either side, the grounds become woods, before they open up onto the gardens at the front again. It feels a little claustrophobic and I am thankful for that sea glimpse from the window; otherwise, it would be easy to feel isolated.

As I make it around the building, I glimpse wood panels tucked within the foliage, and I take a few steps closer. I can see it is a hut of some sort. The door is ajar, so I make my way closer, wondering if it is a gardener's hut. I pull the door, and it creaks.

Inside is sparse. A few shards of light shine through the one window and there is nothing except an old mattress on a dusty floor. *Strange*, I think. Perhaps the gardener naps there in the day.

I wander until I make it to the front of the house, and I see the gardens in all their spectacular glory. I stand, take them in for a while, and wish I had a cool drink; I am suddenly parched. I look at the grand front entrance and wonder if I might be able to navigate my way to the kitchen from here. Something catches my eye. I glance up. I am sure I saw a figure dash from view in the third-floor window. Could it have been the French lady housekeeper. I have not seen any other staff around yet. I am sure there will be a few in the house and I will also bump into Hector soon no doubt.

I walk up to the entrance and into a stunning hall. Black and white chequered flooring, a giant cherub statue in the centre, a chaise lounge beside a winding staircase with a black, iron-railing banister. A red, velvet chair to my right looks inviting to sit on but I need refreshments after my journey. I am starting to feel a little put out that there is no one around to greet me and hand me a refreshing fruit mocktail. This is not like Hector's last two houses I have visited, where there was a drink in my hand before I'd had time to even say hello to anyone.

Each room is brightly decorated, giving a light, airy feeling, and as I go from room to room, and there are a lot, I see how each one is heavily furnished. Some of the items must be worth a lot of money.

I stop in one room, one of many sitting areas I have come across, and wonder what each one is used for. Then I begin to head back the way I came, and when I reach the hallway, I take the door on the other side, which leads into a sizeable, provincial-style kitchen with oak beams in the ceiling, a restored island with highchairs with metal backs and although they have soft seating, they don't look that inviting. But I notice in the centre of the island there is a large bowl of fresh fruit: grapes, peaches and oranges. I open one of the long cupboards that looks like it might be a fridge, and I am thankful to see it is, and well stocked with meat, cheese, more fruit, and a large jug of what looks like orange juice. I locate a glass, fill it to the top, and drink thirstily. I feel rude helping myself, but it feels indulgent, and the juice is sweet and fresh. I wonder if they have been grown locally as I know it is possible in some microclimates.

The weather is so inviting, I want to get back outside and explore a bit more.

I take myself off along the driveway until I find a gate that leads into the orchard. After a walk picking a few raspberries, gooseberries, and blueberries, I find myself in the kitchen garden. There, I am greeted by every vegetable and salad I can imagine. I see rainbow chard, endless herbs, rainbow carrots, and every coloured tomato and lettuce leaf.

The heat begins to get to me. I feel sure if I went back inside, I would find Hector. But when I return to the grand hallway, the house is still eerily quiet.

'Hello,' I call, but all I hear is my voice echoing back at me. I nearly laugh at the sound of it and at the absurdity of the situation. Then my laughter fades as I turn around and realise that I might be quite alone here. I haven't even seen the elderly housekeeper who greeted me at the back door, and I am now beginning to think I imagined her.

When I get back to my room, I am ready for a nap, yet my body is tense, and my mind a whirlwind. I knew it would not allow me rest. My eyes clock a sheet of white paper on the dressing table which wasn't there before, I sit at the stool and see it is a letter.

Dearest Lily,

I am so glad you are here. Please take the rest of the day to relax and settle in, and I would be honoured if you would have dinner with me this evening.

I will have the main dining room set. It looks out onto the front lawn, and it is a beautiful space.

See you at 8

Much love, H

I'm not sure how I feel about Hector being in my room unless he asked the housekeeper to do it. Then I think back to when I was out in front of the house and I looked up and saw movement. I realise that it had been my room.

Despite that, a wave of relief washes over me. Hector is here, somewhere, ready to receive me this evening. I can rest easy for the next few hours.

I look at my phone; it is coming up for 2 p.m. I have plenty of time. I notice the message again, indicating an answerphone message. I am feeling less anxious and a little more in control of the situation; I have got my bearings now, and I can handle a message from Stig.

And I know I need to answer it in case it is an emergency.

I dial in and I'm surprised to hear Emily's voice, given that I had only left her a few hours earlier. I wonder what I have left behind at the house that she was calling to tell me about.

'Lil.' Her voice has an urgency to it. 'I was just looking at a few things last night in bed. I was curious after we spoke, and I wanted to make sure you were okay and had made the right choice. Anyway, I started surfing like you do and then I was looking at things about Conroy, Hector's father, after you told me about their relationship, and Stig attending Blythewood. I found something, Lil: a very old image way back in the archives.

It's an image of Conroy back in the nineties. A journalist had probably snapped it of him coming out of a restaurant; he is with a woman, tall and blonde, a bit of a bombshell, and next to her is a young lad, about fifteen or so. It's Stig, Lil; I'm ninety-nine per cent sure. There's more to this than meets the eye. Stig also had a relationship with Conroy, Hector's dad. Hector is estranged from his father; there's a correlation I haven't quite worked out yet, but it feels relevant, a hidden connection. I wanted you to know. Call me if you need anything, and please just let me know you got there safely, and everything is okay and kosher. God, I wish you'd come to me sooner; I would have flown out with you so you had someone nearby. Anyway, love you. Call me soon.'

26

Once Nicholas knew that Hector's father was his stepfather, he felt very different about everything. He didn't feel sorry for Hector as such, just that he felt he shouldn't be in this position at all. It was Hector who was Conroy's own flesh and blood, yet Hector had been banished by his own father from the family home, which Nicholas now resided in for some of the year. There has not been anything in the house to suggest that there had been another son. The last time Nicholas went to Highlake, for that was the name of the estate, he even discovered a photo of himself on the wall: the annual school photo. The photo looked lonely with a mass of space around it and Nicholas presumed that subsequent annual photos would follow. He had felt honoured that Conroy had allowed him to be hung in the library room, with all the photos of the family that went back centuries.

Nicholas knew that, at some point, a conversation would need to be had between him and Hector. But he was just fourteen years old; how did one broach that subject and what would he possibly say?

I live with your dad now, sorry about that.

There was nothing that Nicholas could say or do to make it better. It would simply be a case of acknowledging that he knew and that maybe that would reduce some of the stress. Perhaps, Nicholas could use it to his advantage. Perhaps Hector was scared of Conroy; perhaps he could tell Conroy that he was getting bullied.

But that wasn't an option. Conroy had never mentioned anything about Hector, he was obviously well and truly out of the family and perhaps bringing him up would anger him, and Nicholas was settled, finally relaxing at his new home and at school.

But he questioned all the time why he hadn't been told, why he was expected to go to school with Conroy's legitimate son. But then again it came back to Conroy and if he had wiped Hector from his life, that would mean he would not want to bring it up. It was the price to pay for the riches and luxuries his life now entailed.

However much Nicholas tried, he knew that he would be unable to keep holding on to this information forever. At some point, he needed to tell Hector that he knew and let bygones be bygones. Maybe, deep down, Nicholas thought, Hector wished to be brothers and maybe there was a chance that Nicholas could be the one to reunite father and son. It sounded like a bit of a long shot in theory, but people forgave one another all the time, and whatever it was that Hector did, how could it have been that bad? He was a child, for goodness' sake. How could a child wrong an adult to the point that they no longer wished to see them again? But again, Nicholas realised he was thinking nonsense as it had been such a long time since his own father had walked out and never been seen again.

And besides, there never seemed to be an opportunity to be with Hector alone. He was always with Thing One and Thing Two, or any other of his many friends. They were in separate houses, separate dorms; it would take Nicholas to find his way over to Waldon and ask to speak with Hector alone, and he did not feel confident enough to do that.

But as chance would have it, Nicholas found himself in the office with Mr Peterson over a piece he wished him to recite in the upcoming school play. It was something close to his heart and so he had brought Nicholas to his office to go over the prose to make sure he did its justice. Nicholas was not so keen on performance, but he wanted to be seen as trying lots of things, and not just becoming a typical sports geek.

As he left the office, feeling that much more confident about giving the words the gumption they deserved, he collided with someone and when he looked up, it was Hector. He looked momentarily stunned and when he saw it was Nicholas who had crashed into him, his face changed from nondescript to pure contempt.

'Christ sake, Alley Rat, watch it.'

Nicholas took a step back. 'I know,' he blurted out.

'What?' Hector snapped impatiently.

Nicholas realised that whilst *I know* sounded the right thing to say in his head, it was entirely out of context. He took a deep breath and registered the aggravation on Hector's face.

'Your father. I know your father is Conroy Bolson-Woods.'

'Well done, Alley Rat, good of you to catch up.' Hector barged past Nicholas toward Mr Peterson's door.

'I didn't ask for any of this,' Nicholas called and Hector looked back, anger and frustration etched across his face.

Nicholas walked back toward Sloan, not feeling as though he

had used the moment to the best advantage and that maybe he should have said something more meaningful. Had Hector even understood where he was coming from? He hoped whatever had just occurred between him and Hector had sealed the rift between them, at least in the short term, even if it was just a plaster across the wound for now.

* * *

It did seem to do the trick because Hector kept his distance from then on. The years went by and Nicholas, about to begin studying for his A-levels, found that he barely had any contact with Hector. Hector could only be taking a wide berth after that awkward interaction. There were times when their paths would cross but Hector seemed to go out of his way to avoid Nicholas.

By the time Nicholas's schooling ended, he was about to come out of Blythewood with two A's and an A star and a beautiful girlfriend. It was unbelievable, considering he had never dreamed of having such an experience and opportunity and that when he first attended Blythewood, he had cried himself to sleep every night for a month. Coming away with outstanding grades meant he now had options that he might not have had before. He could only feel grateful for the sudden change in his life circumstances and that he could now call himself a Bolson-Woods. From here on in, his life was going to be far better than he could have ever imagined.

But before all of that, he was grateful for the time to kick back, relax and enjoy a well-earned end-of-term, end-of-school, beginning-of-life party. He had heard about the Blythewood prom send-offs, but they seemed like a myth because he could only ever hear them and not see them. All the rest of the students would leave to return home for the summer and the final year students were the only ones left on the grounds.

The party would take place that evening; it took place in a huge gazebo on the front lawn. There was a bar, and the leavers were allowed to bring a guest. These were usually female. And so Nicholas was to bring his girlfriend, Delilah. He had heard about the aftermath, the remnants of the parties over the years: the discarded bottles, dicky bows, wigs, pools of vomit, and even once, an actual student, still laying under the table in the gazebo, alive, just asleep.

But now it was his turn. Nicholas could hardly believe that the time had come for him to transition from child student to adult and via the most epic way he knew.

The party was due to begin at six thirty with a formal dinner, followed by speeches from the headmaster, the housemasters and mistresses, as well as a couple of the well-respected tutors. They seemed to believe that by starting early, the students would all be wrapped up, suitably drunk and exhausted by midnight. But Nicholas had never heard of a final year party ending before 5 a.m.

Nicholas had been dating a girl on and off for the last year. Delilah attended the all-girls school three miles down the road, and they had met at a mini triathlon. Delilah was fit and into her sports, and she was also a keen ballet dancer.

He, Tim, Sags, and Henry had been down to a local gentlemen's store to have their dinner jackets fitted and even Henry had managed to bag a date, having never been seen with a member of the opposite sex since they began puberty. Tim came out as gay two years ago and was bringing his boyfriend from Portugal, who was staying with him for the summer. A foreign exchange that evolved into more than an educational trip.

Only Sags was date-free, which he was fine with as many students attended alone.

The formalities were over and soon it was time to get down and party. The bar was open, just beer and cider and wine. No spirits, but there was plenty of that hidden in the back pockets of the students and in the handbags of their girlfriends, plus much more in the form of pick-me-ups, Nicholas was certain.

The final dinner was held in the grand hall of Blythewood, and after the speeches, the students and guests made their way down the path, which was adorned with lanterns in the trees on either side, and out across the lawn to the large gazebo, which had been set up, lights flashing and music pumping from it already.

Delilah had arrived looking as beautiful as she could ever be, and Nicholas was thrilled and intimidated by her beauty. Yet overall, he was proud to have her as his date this evening.

He had caught a glimpse of Hector across the grand hall, and he saw him again as he made his way, hand in hand with Delilah, to the party. Hector had glanced his way as he passed him on the steps leading down to the front lawn. Nicholas, who hadn't had much interaction with Hector for the last few years, did not like the interaction, as momentary as it was; Nicholas felt it carried a weight with it that he had not seen in a while. And the glare he saw as Hector glanced at Delilah. It was so brief, but it was the way it happened directly after he had looked at Nicholas. Nicholas had not brought Delilah to the school before, as it was not allowed, even though some boys did sneak out to meet girls on the grounds; Nicholas wanted to keep Delilah to himself and would not have even brought her to the leavers' ball tonight, but Delilah had insisted on coming and Nicholas was happy that she had. He would be lying if he didn't think there was still animosity between him and Hector; for some reason, Hector had managed to suppress it for the last few years. But Nicholas felt that same twinge in his gut that he had not felt for a long time as Hector passed and made eye contact. But Nicholas suppressed the sensation because tonight was a night to celebrate, have fun, kick back and forget about anything except living in the moment. After tonight, he would never have to see Hector again.

27

I can't rest after I hear Emily's message; she has planted a seed that has got me thinking as much as it has her. We are similar in that way, except her talent for asking the right questions took her to university to study law, whereas mine are still Nancy Drew sleuthing skills. I know my husband has been lying to me our entire relationship. I know there is much more to know about him. Now, it turns out, not only did he attend the most prestigious school in England, but he knows Hector's father, a multi-millionaire. Stig had some relationship with Hector's father when he was a child. The snippet of a story I have uncovered and the image that Emily found, which I am now looking at, are both buried deep in the cyber world as though someone had wanted them to disappear. And to most, they wouldn't mean very much, but to me, the wife of a man who has told me so many lies already and has a link to one of the richest families in England, yet doesn't want me to know, it's big news.

But what I do know is that Emily has not recognised that the blonde lady in the picture is Stig's mother. Because she would not know that. Stig carries a photo of her in his wallet. He has never spoken of either of his parents. He has never delved into why, except that he doesn't talk with either of them. I find it sad that he keeps a photo yet he doesn't speak of her. She is a striking woman with blonde, bobbed hair; she reminds me of a 1960s model. Now I know that the woman who had moved in with Conroy and forced Hector out had been Stig's mother. So does that mean that Stig's mother is not particularly nice, and this is why she and Stig no longer speak? Not only has Stig received an education that is a far cry from the standard school he had once mentioned he had attended, but he has lived an entirely different existence. He attended one of the most prestigious schools in the country and was partly raised by one of the country's richest and most influential men. It is all so messed up: two boys who have both become estranged from their fathers and now Stig is estranged from his mother. Did Stig fall out with his mother because she treated Hector so callously and essentially, in the eyes of a child, stole his father from him?

I can't help but think about the money. The money that Stig might be entitled to, had been given and seen over the years. Or perhaps Conroy has done something terrible and that is why Stig left and never returned. For him, it was a blip in his life he has never wanted to discuss or return to again, that is for sure. But it still didn't get him off for lying to me. No matter his reasons, I am his wife and I have a right to know who he is and where he came from. Especially as this is having a significant impact on my life.

This could explain why the two of them have animosity between them. All I know is that Hector and his father were estranged because of a fallout between Conrad's new wife, who had been Stig's mother. But it seems to me that Hector has been nothing but gracious and hospitable, and it is Stig who has continued to hold the grudge when he had been the one to benefit the most.

I feel uneasy that there is more to this relationship than I had first understood. Perhaps I am a pawn in a game that the two of them are playing?

In a few days, I will be back at home, and now I have a lot more to go on; I can bring it all up with Stig and demand answers. At this point, I have no idea who my husband is. Right now, I have more understanding and empathy for Hector, as he seems to be the one who suffered the most.

I message Emily back to thank her for the image and assure her everything is fine. The chateau is the most beautiful place I have ever been to. I am having dinner with Hector tonight, and he is very gracious. I don't tell her I have yet to see him, and the only communication has been through a note he left in my bedroom. I think, being who she is, Emily would almost certainly find it strange and have something else to say. I want to feel some autonomy, and if I continue to fill her in with every little thing, I feel she would take that away from me.

I have rested as much as I can under the circumstances, so I head to the bathroom and smell every product in the en suite. I choose a bath oil called Omorovicza that looks familiar but is something I would have overlooked due to the price. I pour it generously into the bath and stay there, trying not to think any more about what I am doing here without my husband's knowledge. I want wanted to enjoy myself a little, as well as be as professional as I can be. I have always had a bit of a thing for Hector Bolson-Woods, but it has more to do with his status in the food industry and, of course, his talent as a chef. I try to work out if my feelings could and would stretch beyond that.

Despite the size of the place, despite his lack of presence so far. And if I am really honest, it feels good to be here, to indulge in such luxuries. I am certain Hector is a good man, and I feel safe here. He is going to look after me, and it will all be okay.

28

The party was in full flow. Delilah urged Nicholas to dance and so he did, even though it was entirely out of his comfort zone, and he would have done anything other than prance around in front of his mates and girlfriend. But the alcohol had completely loosened him up and so he weaved his way through the growing crowd and let the beat soar through his body and force it to move in time.

Sags and Henry were both drunk, and Nicholas began to feel sorry for his date, who had sidled over to the corner and looked less than impressed.

'Look at poor Henry's date,' Nicholas half-shouted into Delilah's ear. 'What a shoddy show.'

'I know, he's had far too much to drink,' Delilah called back.

'He can't handle it, which is the problem; he probably only had four or five pints.'

'Well, that would be enough to knock me sideways.' Delilah laughed, and Nicholas pulled her in closer to him.

'You know, you should dance with her, cheer her up. I feel sorry for her just slumped in the corner like that. And Henry is hardly going to mind; he's far too gone. I'm sure he doesn't know his own name.'

Nicholas laughed. 'You're right there and may I say how very kind of you; not all girlfriends would send their man off to dance with another woman.'

Delilah laughed and kissed Nicholas hard on the lips. 'Not all men would go and do it. But I know you will.'

Nicholas kissed her again, but long and deep this time. 'You're a bit of all right, you are,' he said in a cockney accent.

'You're not too bad yourself.' Delilah cackled back, emulating the East End London tone to perfection. And Nicholas walked away backwards at first to keep his sight on his girlfriend for a bit longer, thinking to himself for the first time that he might want to marry her one day. She mimed holding a drink and swigging one back and Nicholas nodded, his heart brimming over with a love he felt for her that had always been there, but he had never known what to do with. He thought that they could both sit down and talk for a while when he had done his gentlemanly duty.

He approached Henry's date, who was still slumped and looked like she was about to nod off.

'Aralia.' Nicholas held out his hand. 'Would you do me the honour of dancing with me?' Nicholas asked as the first few beats dropped to Dizzee Rascal's 'Dance Wiv Me'.

Aralia's eyes brightened at once, and she leapt to her feet as though the whole evening had been leading up to this one moment. The two of them dance/walked to the dance floor. Aralia did a squat and then jumped back up in Nicholas's face and shimmied around him, a great big grin on her face.

'Wow, you're a great dancer,' Nicholas shouted over the music.

'I know,' Aralia said with a hint of laughter.

The two of them danced for what felt like ages when Nicholas realised the song had changed a good few times. Delilah had gone off to get drinks some time ago and he could not see her anywhere in the tent.

'I'm going to find Delilah,' he shouted in Aralia's ear, and she nodded furiously, turning to a bunch of guys dancing next to her and settling into a rhythm with them. Checking that they were treating her respectfully on the dance floor before he turned, Nicholas scanned the tent again before heading out to the undercover bar next door. There was a small queue, but no sign of Delilah. Nicholas surveyed the area outside. It was dark now; several people were milling about on the grass, laid out or dancing. Something inside Nicholas urged him to take a shortcut through the trees, which would bring him out next to the bridge and the brook next to a bothy used for storing old gym equipment. Nicholas thought that Delilah would be stupid if she had come down here alone. She didn't know the school well and was in a minority of females this evening. However, he heard a female scream before he had even come through the trees. He sprinted toward the sound, rounded the corner and saw the bothy in his sights.

'Delilah,' he called as he ran. He stopped abruptly just a few feet away from the bothy's entrance as a figure appeared from the shadows. He was looking dishevelled, his dicky bow hanging at an angle and slightly untied. He stumbled toward Nicholas, and he did not see him in the dark until he was right in front of him. Only then did Hector look upward toward Nicholas and stop right in front of him.

'Ahh, Alley Rat,' Hector said, the mocking tone as thick in his voice as ever.

Nicholas looked over Hector's shoulder as Delilah appeared from the bothy's doorway. Her face was a crumpled mess, and her make-up had run in streaks down her cheeks. Nicholas looked to her shoulder, where her dress was ripped and hanging off in a bundle, which Delilah held in her hand, trying to protect her modesty.

'What the hell?' Nicholas yelled and moved toward Hector. Hector stood in his way and Nicholas, who had height over Hector, gave him a firm push as he made his way to Delilah.

'Are you okay? What happened?'

Delilah was crying, and although she looked up at Nicholas, she seemed unable to speak.

'God damn it, Hector!' Nicholas turned around and bellowed. Then he roared.

Hector looked at Nicholas. For the first time, he seemed genuinely scared. Was this why Hector had kept his distance from Nicholas for the last few years? Nicholas had shot up, had become athletic, and his shoulders were broader than Hector's. He knew he had strength now and that he could take Hector down at any time, should he want to. And now, maybe after years of torment and abuse and the pure frustration this act, whatever sordid activity had just taken place before he came through the trees to the sound of his girlfriend's wails, perhaps this was the time, to take it all back and reclaim the power.

Hector had begun to back away. He now looked like a startled deer, not knowing what was about to happen terrifying him the most. It even terrified Nicholas, but that terror was morphing into more anger so fierce that Nicholas wasn't sure what to do with it. But he charged anyway, like a raging bull about to take down his prey. And as he charged, Hector turned and ran.

29

I find the dining room Hector referred to earlier in his note. I stumbled upon it on my solo tour of the chateau. The doors are open and lead onto a large patio area overlooking the formal gardens. The huge dining table is set in just one corner for two. It looks beautiful and intimate. I note just three sets of cutlery, so perhaps we won't have many courses this time. But I am happy about that. This is a dream come true in many ways, being able to dine alone with Hector, if I can put out of my mind the reasons I am here and the web of lies surrounding this whole event and just appreciate this experience.

I stand at the patio doors and look across the vast garden. The sun is beginning to set in the distance. I hear a sound and turn. Hector stands in the doorway, his signature white shirt this time paired with a fetching pair of blue chinos, his face tanned from the French sun. How long has he been out here? I wonder.

'Lily.' My name comes out of his mouth as though it were just air.

'Hector,' I say.

'You look radiant. I'm so pleased you came.' He walks toward me and gently kisses me on both cheeks. He smells clean with a delicious undertone of tobacco and vanilla, a scent I have noted on him on each occasion we have met.

'I thought we could eat a little less extravagantly this evening. That way, we can focus on talking. I think it's important that we talk, don't you?'

'I do; it would be rude if we didn't.' I laugh. I am nervous; on the three other occasions I have dined with Hector, I put alcohol in my system before I arrived.

'That it would. The food can so easily become the focus of the evening, but we are just two people today. It seems a little showy to create something I might make to gain a Michelin star. You and I know it's not why you are here.'

I feel a tiny flutter of nerves in my stomach at his reference. *So we are actually doing this*, I think. *I will be working for Hector soon.*

'And may I ask if you have informed Stig of your whereabouts?'

Hector holds a chair out for me to sit and moves it in toward the table as I do.

'We were in disagreement about it in the end.'

Hector appears nonchalant hearing this news, but I wonder if he is secretly happy Stig is not here and I am here alone.

Hector lifts a bottle of champagne from a silver bucket next to his chair and pours us both a glass. He looks me in the eye as he holds his glass close to mine.

'To us and this,' he says quietly.

I repeat his words back to him before we clink glasses, and I take a bigger gulp than I had intended. The bubbles fizz in my nostrils and make my eyes water. But Hector doesn't notice; he places the bottle back in the bucket and then sits.

'I thought about serving everything this evening, but have

you seen how far the kitchen is from here? I would barely see you,' he says jovially. 'So I roped in a local girl to plate and serve. I presume you met Anna earlier? She is the main housekeeper here. She is getting on a bit now but refuses to retire.'

'Yes, I met her. She carried my case like a Russian shot-putter,' I say, and Hector laughs.

'That's exactly what Anna is like; she is freakishly strong for such a small lady. She barely speaks a word of English, but fortunately, I speak fluent French, so I can converse with her very easily. She refuses to learn English. No matter how many of my English guests are here, she never tries to pick it up.'

'Doesn't need to, I suppose, at her age; she has gotten by just fine up until now.'

'Indeed. Stubborn old mule,' he says jovially and sips his champagne.

'She must have served you well? How long has she been with you? How long have you had this beautiful chateau?'

'So many questions,' Hector notes.

I laugh. 'Sorry, I have so much I want to ask about this place. I have never seen anything like it before, except on TV.'

'I bought it in the early noughties when these places were going for ridiculous money. I mean it was cheap. I got an excellent bargain. The cost of running it is more expensive than what I paid for it. I invested in the orchards and gardens and most of the furniture is local. I supply a local winemaker, so I reap some of the costs back. I'm thinking of making my own cheese.'

'Bolson-Woods brie,' I say, and Hector laughs.

'Precisely. That is exactly what I will call it.' He tops up my glass with more champagne. 'We can move mountains with your skills.'

I wait to see if he might bring up the business proposal, but he doesn't, and I don't want to push it; he did invite me here after all. I'm sure we will talk more later about it.

A young woman walks into the room, pushing a trolley with silver dishes on board. She is possibly in her early twenties, with dark hair and a meek look as she stoops over the trolley.

She speaks English to us with a French accent. 'Good evening.' She does a little curtsy and removes the lids on the trays, revealing two beautiful parfaits with melba toast, chutney and fruit.

'Wow.' I can't help myself. I haven't eaten all day. I am famished.

'Local chicken-liver parfait, home-grown fig and apple chutney, and I think the melba toast is local sourdough. Am I right, Sienna?' Hector says.

The girl suddenly looks up at the sound of her name, and her face is perplexed. The way her eyes widen makes me wonder if she is scared of Hector. She puts the place down in front of me and then one in front of Hector.

'Other side,' he says quietly, through his teeth; it sounds a little menacing, and I let out a giggle because I think he is joking. Then Sienna dashes to the other side of Hector, puts the plate down, and hurries back to the trolley. As she passes me, our eyes meet, and that slight look of terror is there again. She is scared of him.

As she wheels the trolley away, Hector looks down at his plate, and without looking up, he says, 'Some people just can't be taught. I've tried my best with her.'

'She seems fairly young?' I say, and Hector looks up at me and seems to assess me for a moment.

'She is. You're right.' Then he begins spreading the parfait onto the melba toast. 'I offer the work, and I am trying to train her so she can work in some of the more prestigious restaurants in France. But sometimes, I feel people don't want to be taught.' I hear an irritation in his tone, and I don't want to press him further. It appears it is a touchy subject; perhaps he finds teaching people difficult. However, I have never heard of any bad reports in the press of staff mistreated by him. An unease creeps over me; it's probably because Hector and I are alone together. As much as I was excited about the trip, I am trying not to tap into the side of me that is feeling a tad nervous and anxious now it's just us. My hand twitches to reach out for Stig's, and I remind myself he is a liar and that's why I'm conducting this meeting without him.

I pick up my knife, spread some of the parfait, and bite.

'Mmmm, delicious,' I say to Hector, hoping to distract him from his irritation over this girl.

The praise works and we can move comfortably on to discuss my work. I thank him again for the donation and I speak more about the plans I have with the money and how far it will go. I want to press him on many things, such as his relationship with his father and how Stig's relationship with Conroy affected him growing up, but I don't feel close enough to him yet to discuss such intimate matters. I wonder if I might be able to ask him at some point in the future.

Hector tops up my champagne again and Sienna comes out a few minutes after we have finished our starters to collect our plates. She doesn't make eye contact this time, swiftly removes the plates and leaves the room. I can sense an atmosphere each time she has been in the room, making me feel a little uncomfortable, but I try not to let it show or mar the evening. For whatever reason, Hector is irritated by her. Perhaps it is the perfectionist in him. But I can't get the look in her eyes out of my head.

Sienna brings the next course on the trolley: a delicate-looking fish dish with salmon mousse, samphire, and tiny vegetables. Hector tells me the sauce is lobster bisque, and the fish is a local bass.

'It's so light and flavoursome,' I tell him, and we eat and talk more about the chateau and the area and the orchards. Still, he doesn't mention the business proposal again, even after I raise the Family First and the donation, which would have been a perfect time to begin discussing it.

I excuse myself after the main course to use the facilities. Hector says he will seek a decent dessert wine from the cellar and heads off that way. I wander through the hallway, thinking I am confident about where I am going, but the champagne has made my head light and airy, and before I know it, I am back in the main hall.

'Oh.' I look around. I am sure I saw a small cloakroom on my earlier tour.

I hear a clang from the kitchen and wonder if Sienna is there. Feeling confident after the champagne, I push the door open, thinking I might ask Sienna if she can direct me to the toilet. When I open the door, Sienna stands there, and with her is a woman. She is a little older but looks exactly like Sienna. She has the same dark hair and slim frame, and when she hears me at the door, she has the same terror in her eyes.

She was holding on to Sienna maternally, but when she sees me, she lets go of Sienna and dashes from the room like a startled rabbit. I am left looking at Sienna.

'I... sorry to interrupt, I am just looking for the facilities?'

Sienna stares at me, that same fixed expression.

'The lady's room?' I try again. Sienna just stares. I don't have my phone with me for Google Translate, but by some miracle, probably caused by the loss of my grey matter with the alcohol, words come to me.

'*Les lavbos!*' I call out as though I have just got a full house in Bingo.

Sienna jumps at my sudden increase in volume but then seems to understand.

She walks tentatively to the door. I stand back, and she points toward a door at the far end of the hallway, barely lit up by a small lamp on a table a few meters from it.

'Ahh, *merci*,' I say and turn to walk to the facilities. I glance back for a moment, and Sienna is still in the doorway, looking at me. I reach the door and look back once more. She has closed the door and is no longer there.

'Everything okay?'

I physically jump at Hector's voice in the dark hallway.

'Jeez,' I hiss and look where he stands near the toilet door. He must have come from a small door behind him; I can just about make it out in the darkness.

Hector wears a neutral expression, and for a moment, I worry I have done something wrong; perhaps he heard me asking Sienna for directions and disagrees with me disturbing the staff when they are working.

'Yes,' I say. 'Just getting lost in your big old chateau.' Then I point to the door. 'Found it.'

He looks at the door, which I hope is the toilet, and nods.

'Good.' He holds up a bottle in front of me. 'Our dessert wine.'

'Ooh,' I say, inspecting it in the barely lit space as though I might see it well enough or even know what I am looking at.

'I'll see you back at the table?' Hector says with a hint of a question, as though he thinks I might not come.

'Yes, just give me a moment to powder my nose.' I hear a strangled note in my voice, and Hector hears it too; I can tell by the way he looks at me. I have been startled, that is all; I don't know why my heart is still racing.

I open the door, and Hector remains where he is, smiling at me until I close it. I stand in a heavily decorated space, with plants dotted about. A French-style dresser is above the basin with a huge mirror above that. I lock the door and stand silently, not daring to breathe. I haven't heard Hector move as I stand as still as I can. I am sure I can hear his breath on the other side of the door, out of sync with mine, but my heart is beating so fast, it is hard to know. I don't move for a full minute until I hear Hector's shoes clicking on the concrete floor as he walks away. Then I let out a huge breath and stand in front of the mirror. I look at myself. My heart is a charging horse in my chest, and I am confused. I feel a sudden wave of emotion, a sadness, and the panic that has risen through me from nowhere. It is the strength of the champagne maybe and the combination of that with the travel and early start. I like to drink, but not usually in such vast quantities. Surely that has to be the reason. Because I am safe here, I remind myself.

But something about how Sienna has looked each time I have seen her, and how the other woman, who looks so similar and can only have been Sienna's mother, rushed off as though she was not allowed to be there. And the way Hector appeared in the hallway just now. I must put it down to the language barrier between Sienna and me. The vast yet empty feeling of the chateau is putting me on edge. I can't get my bearings yet, and I dislike the sensation it brings.

I leave the toilet and find my way back to the dining room.

Tarte Tatin and clotted cream is already on the table and Hector is pouring the dessert wine.

When I enter the room, he looks up at me, and when I sit down, he puts a hand on my arm.

'Are you okay, Lily?'

I let out a breath. 'Yeah, I think so. Just tired, I guess.'

He hands me a glass of dessert wine. 'You don't need to be nervous around me. Tonight is a way for us to get to know one another better, and tomorrow evening, we'll talk business.'

I feel a wave of relief. I thought he had forgotten about it or changed his mind.

We finish our desserts and drink the wine and then we stand out on the balcony looking into the dark gardens. I wish we were closer to the sea so I could hear the swoosh of the waves. Then Hector turns to me and kisses me lightly on my cheek.

'Goodnight, Lily. I look forward to seeing you again tomorrow.' Then he turns and leaves me standing on the patio, looking into the dark.

30

It didn't take Nicholas long to catch up with Hector, his long strides outrunning Hector's small, fast ones. By the time he had reached him, Nicholas had his hands around his collar and was yanking him backwards. Hector stumbled and fell to his knees. Nicholas grabbed him by one arm and pulled him back up. Hector took a swipe at Nicholas, but it was feeble; he was drunker than he looked, and he fell forward. Nicholas managed to grab his arm, but this time, Hector found some strength, and Nicholas, who thought he was on top, was clipped on the chin by Hector's fist. It shocked him for a second but gave Hector enough time to run. By the time Nicholas had realised what had happened, Hector was heading for the bridge. Rage still burned through Nicholas as he caught up with him and stood in front of Hector.

'You need to calm down, Alley Rat,' he slurred, but Nicholas could only see and feel the years of torment, and even though the taunting had subsided over the years, this was too much. It was as though it was one last act before they parted ways. Hector wished to get his revenge on Nicholas for the final time. Well, he wouldn't let him. He grabbed him by the jacket on both sides and shoved him hard against the bridge. Hector slid down and crawled away a few feet, but Nicholas bent down and dragged him to his feet. Hector looked Nicholas in the eye and laughed, and Nicholas punched him, his fist landing on his cheek. Hector fell against the wall, and as he did, Nicholas heard the crack of bricks falling away and hitting the brook several metres below. Hector looked at Nicholas, his face awash with fear. He reached out his hand to grab something, a hand or a piece of Nicholas's clothing, but there was nothing to grab hold of, and Nicholas's reflexes, which had been on fire until seconds ago, suddenly halted. Nicholas watched as the wall gave way entirely on one side, and Hector with his back against it, leaning into it, could do nothing to stop it. He was helpless, and Nicholas stood, aghast, as he watched him fall.

The sound of Hector hitting the brook was excruciating. Nicholas felt sick.

'Nicholas, what have you done?' came Delilah's raspy voice behind him.

Nicholas shot around and looked at Delilah.

'I don't know,' he murmured. 'The wall, he was leaning against it, it fell.'

'You pushed him!' Delilah said.

'I didn't. I swear, it was an accident; I was mad at what he did to you.'

'We need to call an ambulance. Immediately.' Delilah turned and ran to the main house. Nicholas could hear groaning from below and felt a glimmer of relief that Hector was alive. That he wasn't just about to begin his adult life as an inmate in the local prison.

He went further along the path until he was able to skid down the bank which took him to the brook. He could just about see Hector's legs in the half-moon light. He was still groaning, which was a good thing Nicholas supposed, but he was also imagining all sorts of horrific scenarios such as a broken back, perhaps a smashed face.

He reached Hector, who was looking in a bad way. His leg was jolted out at an angle; he could make out a dark mass on the stones around him, and to his horror, he realised it was blood.

'Oh Christ,' he murmured.

'Alley Rat,' Hector spat; the pain was evident in his voice.

'Steady up, old chap, we'll have you sorted soon.' Nicholas removed his dinner jacket and lay it over Hector like he had seen people do in movies. The edges were instantly wet from the water.

Hector remained quiet for a while, and Nicholas eventually found the courage to lean across and listen for breathing.

As he did, Hector reached out and grabbed his arm.

'You... will... pay. I... will... make... sure... you... pay... for... this,' Hector hissed and spat the words out slowly, using every ounce of energy he had before he apparently passed out.

Nicholas was relieved to finally hear the sound of a siren and, minutes later, the sound of running feet as the paramedics arrived.

* * *

Nicholas returned to Highlake for the summer and was unable to rest and relax as he waited for news of Hector's recovery. He had a smashed pelvis, a broken leg, a fractured rib and a severe impact to his skull; they weren't sure if there was any brain damage yet.

Nicholas tried to relax into his holiday and the beginning of his life as an adult, but despite the delicious foods and promise of an upcoming extended holiday to India, he could not focus on anything else except Hector's recovery. He had also tried calling Delilah several times, to no avail. She was avoiding him, it was clear, as each time he got different responses from the housekeeper. She was indisposed, out with friends, and on another call. Eventually, after two weeks, he stopped calling.

When Tim's message came a few days later that Hector had been released from the hospital and that, with a lot of physiotherapy, he was going to recover, Nicholas was finally able to feel relief. But no sooner did he feel the relief he had longed for for so long, it faded as quickly as it had arrived, and he was once again filled with an uncontrollable rage.

He got straight into his Land Rover, which Conroy had bought him as a congratulations present, and headed straight to Delilah. It was Sunday afternoon, and he knew that she always ate Sunday lunch with her family at home; he was praying that she would be home now.

When he arrived at Delilah's house, which was on par with Highlake, albeit slightly more modern, he parked his car in the driveway and headed up the steps to the front door. Their Filipino housekeeper, Sofia, answered the door, and a look of shock came over her face as Nicholas said hello but forced his way into the hallway.

'Please tell Miss Delilah I am here to see her,' he said.

Sofia did a little nod and scuttled away. A minute or two later, Delilah arrived in the hallway. Nicholas felt his breath catch in his throat when he saw her. She was a glorious sight to behold after so many weeks apart.

She walked right up to him but did not attempt any contact.

'Nicholas, why did you come here?' she said, trying to sound cool, but Nicholas could hear a hint of exasperation in her voice.

'Because you refused to return my calls and I needed to see you, to speak to you.'

Delilah looked away.

'Hector is fine. Well, not fine, he will be okay, so I heard. He'll be getting physio and whatnot, but he should be on the mend.'

'I know. I heard,' she said coolly.

'Oh. Right.' Nicholas moved in closer. 'Listen, Delilah, what happened that night? You were with him, you came out of the bothy, your dress was ripped, you looked a state.'

Delilah looked down at her bare feet.

Nicholas reached out to touch her arm, but Delilah snatched it away.

'I know he did something to you, or at least tried. You were crying, your make-up it was all over your face—'

'He didn't do anything to me,' Delilah interrupted.

Nicholas frowned. 'What, wait a minute, I didn't imagine it, that was why I was so mad, Delilah; I was protecting you.'

'You didn't need to protect me; he did nothing wrong.' Delilah cleared her throat and looked down at her feet again. 'It was me. I instigated it.'

'What?' Nicholas choked.

Delilah finally looked up and met Nicholas's confused expression.

'It was me. I have fancied him for ages. An opportunity presented itself, and we went for it.'

'But we... we were together.'

'I'm seventeen years old, for Christ's sake, Nicholas. We're not married. We're kids. I was never tied down to you, nor were you to me. We were both free to do exactly as we pleased, and I don't doubt you were doing the same. I know what you boarding schoolboys are like.'

Nicholas let out a sound of disgust. 'Well, you clearly don't know because we are not all the same, and I am certainly not one of them, as you know. And you, Delilah...' Nicholas choked on her name. 'You were special to me, and I had not been with anyone else. You were my first,' he whispered for both their dignities.

'Well, you were not my first, and I doubt you thought I would be yours forever.'

Delilah looked around as if she were ready to finish the conversation and return to her lunch.

It was obvious to him now that she saw through him to the working-class boy who had got into Blythewood because his mother married a millionaire and that Hector was the one with the real aristocratic blood, and that was what girls like her needed. It was innate, passed down the bloodline. Marry your kind only.

'Well, I guess I will go then. But let me just say one more thing before I do.'

Delilah had turned to walk away, but she stopped and looked back at Nicholas.

'You were the one and that night, before you went to him, I had thought of you and us, and I had imagined us together and that one day, I might like us to marry.'

Delilah closed her eyes briefly. 'Goodbye, Nicholas.' She walked away, leaving Nicholas standing in the hallway, a torrent of emotions rushing through his body.

* * *

Several weeks later, after Nicholas, his mother, and Conroy had all returned from a tour of India, a letter arrived and was waiting in the hallway for him. Along with several other correspondence, this one was handwritten and looked the most enticing, so he opened it first.

Dear Alley Rat,

I know you will be shocked to hear from me and that you thought all this was behind us, but I need you to know that it is not.

I have suffered substantial injuries to many parts of my body, and it will take months if not years for me to properly recover. There is no guarantee that I will be able to live a life which is free from pain. I could be suffering from the damage done for the rest of my life. As for the plans I had for travel and the sports opportunities I had available to me, they will all be on hold, who knows how long for. The point is, stepbrother, dear, you have, in short, ruined my life. I have no idea what the future holds for me and right now, the pain is quite unbearable.

I don't think you knew what you were doing that night. You were undoubtedly drunk, you were certainly enraged, and you were totally out of order. You crossed a very big line. You could have killed me.

As you well know, the police were involved in the early stages, and I was asked repeatedly if I would like to take it further. But guess what, Alley Rat? I saved your tail. I told them I don't remember who did it and that it was all a silly, drunken accident. Two overexcited boys, ready to make the transition into adulthood, and a silly accident occurred. Tragic as it was, it was only an accident. And I made it all go away for you.

So what do you have to say to me? You must be feeling thankful, I imagine, ready to bow down to me, all that relief rushing through your body, knowing that your life will continue as it was always supposed to. Well, with the help of my father, it will, because let's not forget where you came from and what you have already taken from me.

You see, all I see you as is someone who takes and seems to get away with it, while I must be the one to sit back and watch you move along with your life – the life that I should have been living.

I thought about it for a while, you little creep, I really did. I thought I could just carry on with my life undisturbed by the fact that you stole my life and then tried to kill me, and then I thought, what a total idiot I must be if I let that happen. I have spared you a criminal record and given you the chance to live a life so far removed from anything you ever imagined.

But let me tell you that I cannot allow this to happen. I did not tell the police anything and will continue to honour that. But what I will tell you is this. There will come a time in your adulthood when you think all this is behind you, and I will be there, ready to wreck it all for you. It will happen, so watch out, Alley Rat. I am right behind you and coming to get you.

31

I slept well, considering how much I drank and how I felt just before dessert, and I can shake off any feelings I had the night before once I look out of my window and see the spectacular view and the sun shining.

I shower, dress in shorts and a vest, and go downstairs. I am not sure where I am to go, as Hector didn't mention joining me for breakfast, so I might not see him until dinner this evening. I don't have anyone to ask and I hadn't thought to ask Hector last night. Perhaps he isn't a morning person.

I make my way to the dining room. I don't feel hungry after last night's meal, but I am ready for some coffee. I am pleased to see that the place where I had been sitting last night is set, but the place next to me is not. So I am to dine alone.

Pastries, a glass of fresh orange juice and a coffee cup are on the table.

I sit and sip the juice, looking out across the gardens, wondering what I might do today as I may have hours ahead of me until I see Hector again this evening.

Sienna enters the room, and I brighten at her arrival, glad of the company. I hope to communicate with her better today.

'*Bonjour*,' I say, and Sienna manages a look that resembles a smile, but it is only her eyes softening a little at the edges and she looks less stressed. *Is it because Hector is not here?* I wonder, then dismiss the thought because that paints Hector as a villain who terrifies his staff, and that isn't how I see him. But for the first time, I consider his words to me at the Cotswolds manor. He told me he could not have normal relationships due to the media attention and so on, but I can't recollect any stories in the papers about Hector and other women. Sienna picks up a silver pot from a trolley, which I hope is coffee, and when she pours it, the aroma fills the room, and I inhale the chocolatey, nutty scent.

'*Comment vas-tu?*' I ask Sienna, hoping my French for *how you are* translates well enough.

Sienna looks at me, and for a moment I feel as though she wants to tell me so much, and if the language barrier wasn't there, we might be able to have a conversation. Hector had said she was from a poor family, and I want to know if the terrified woman in the kitchen last night was Sienna's mother, and what kind of troubles they have experienced in their life. I want to ask if she is happy here learning a skill and if she is looking forward to going and working in the French restaurants Hector mentioned and how that would help and assist her family. But I have no words to use and so I am left with only a few sparse French words I can remember from my GCSE days at school.

Sienna leaves the room, and I am left alone with the pastries, fruit, coffee, and my thoughts and time.

A noise outside on the lawn startles me. I jump up from my seat and look out through the patio doors. It was a scream I had heard and when I look, I realise it had come from the woman I had seen in the kitchen last night. She is wearing the same clothes I had seen her in and is running across the lawn, in a slow, stumbling way, as though she has no energy to do so at all. Then Hector appears, in a pair of shorts and a T-shirt, running at a quicker speed so he can catch up with her. When he does, he grabs her arm and the woman half falls. I feel a surge of shock rush through me. What is going on? For a moment, I think Hector is angry, and there is to be a confrontation, but then Hector gathers the woman in his arms and turns her back toward the house. She is upset and crying loudly. But Hector holds her up and begins walking her back toward the chateau. From where I stand, they would not know that I saw anything, but I also can't tell if they are coming back inside or going around the house to the back. There are so many areas to get lost inside, but when I saw the woods on either side of the chateau yesterday, I knew that the grounds went on beyond what I could see.

I think of the way Sienna was last night, and now this woman. It seems they are both clearly miserable. I want to find Sienna and ask what is going on, but I feel it isn't my business. Hector seemed disappointed that I had been in the kitchen last night, so he might think I was interfering. I take my seat once more and try to concentrate on my breakfast, but where I hadn't been very hungry before, I have now completely lost my appetite. All I can see is the image of the woman falling against Hector. My mouth is dry, so I take a few sips of orange juice, but the acidity makes me want to wretch.

A few minutes later, Sienna comes back into the room. She is holding the coffee pot, but her hands are shaking.

I stand up and go to her. I take the pot from her hands. 'I'll take this. Leave it here,' and I place the pot on the table. She is still shaking, so I squeeze her hands in mine.

'It's okay,' I say. Perhaps Hector is right; some people are not able to be trained.

Sienna looks at me and in a hushed tone says, '*Le mal.*'

I nod, not understanding, but I need her to know I appreciate everything she is trying to do.

Then she turns and walks out of the door.

I sit back at the table and finish my coffee. At least Hector is in the building, and I hope I have the pleasure of his company later today. The day stretches out in front of me, and I consider the things I can do. I could explore the grounds some more and try to find my way to the beach, which doesn't look too far away, but my phone shows no reception this morning, which is strange because yesterday it gave me a little. So that is the GPS out of the window. I have brought a book, but I am not sure I can concentrate. So maybe a walk in the woods before lunch would be the best thing. I enjoy woods; I find them as relaxing as a beach, and I noticed a little path next to the shed yesterday. I am good at wayfinding, and I am sure I can follow my nose to find a pleasant route and take in some of the French nature.

I leave the chateau after breakfast. Having found a spare water bottle in the kitchen, I fill it up and put it in my handbag and phone, which will now only help take photos.

I find my way to the chateau's back entrance and take a left toward the woods. I see the hut I saw yesterday and walk over to it, again intrigued, wondering if I might meet a gardener or any other staff member.

I go to push the door again but find it locked this time. I hear a sharp noise like something scraping across a hard surface and look around to see what it is. There is nothing and nobody there. I spot the path I saw yesterday and set along it. It is wide enough to look like it is walked along often. I wonder if Hector ever walks out this way.

It is a pleasant walk, and I take in the fauna and listen to the sounds of birds in the trees, feeling the familiarity of walking through a forest at home. I wouldn't have known I was in France if it weren't for the insatiable heat.

I can sense that the path will take me to the far side of the front garden as I am veering too far from the side of the chateau. If I look carefully enough, I can just about make out the walls of the old building through the trees. I have been walking for about five minutes when I hear a commotion, coming through from the side of the chateau. I can hear a deep, male voice, but I can't place it. I hear the sound of a woman's voice. She is speaking in French; it has to be Sienna or her mother or the housekeeper. Then I hear a noise which shoots a jolt through my body. It is the sound of a hand slapping skin. I peer through the trees to see what I have heard. I see the figure of a man I am sure is Hector and the recognisable dark hair of one of the women: either Sienna or her mother. But the figures are moving, and the chirping of birds drowns out their voices in my ears. I stare long and hard until the woman moves away, but the male figure stays. His face turns, and he stares into the woods as though he can see me. Then, I see that it is indeed Hector. I stumble backwards and the back of my leg collides with a tree stump. The pain sears through me, and I want to cry out, but Hector has possibly seen me, sensed I am standing in the shadows, watching. Hasn't he? I keep quiet, allowing the pain to rage through my body and I hold in the scream I so badly wanted to expel.

Have I heard what I thought I had? Did someone hit someone? I saw Hector rushing to the aid of the woman – who I presumed was Sienna's mother – and showing her support and care. But so far, she seemed quite unhinged, the way she ran away from the kitchen last night and across the lawn this morning.

I slowly right myself and walk forward a few steps. Not seeing anyone, I continue the walk until I am out of the woods and on the front lawn. I feel the back of my leg is wet, and when I hold my hand up, it is covered in blood. I look down and see a nasty graze seeping red.

Damn it, that is going to look hideous in a dress tonight. Despite the graze and the odd behaviour of the staff, I feel a smattering of excitement. Finally, I will do something worthwhile that pays me a decent wage. I know Hannah and Michelle will be disappointed to lose me, but at least I left them with a hefty donation from Hector.

It seems pretty extravagant to do business here, but I will never forget this large, lifeless chateau, which seems far too big for one man to stumble about in all day. It is a little odd, I suppose, and when I leave, telling the tale of where I signed the contract to work for Hector Bolson-Woods will be a fascinating story to hear.

Will I add in the other peculiarities? I ask myself.

I guess they began with Hector leaving me a note in my room and knowing that it was probably him I had seen when I was in the front garden yesterday as I looked up at the window. Then there is the oddness of the two women and the way Sienna stares at me with her big eyes as though she is in a permanent state of terror. Even though Hector assures me she is in training, there is something else that I am sensing, and I feel she wants to tell me more. I freaked out yesterday as Hector had startled me outside the WC, and even though the scene at breakfast this morning seemed caring and compassionate, I'm still not entirely sure what I just heard and saw through the trees. I think I will feel better if I connect to the outside world and get some recep-

The Dinner Party

tion on my phone, and maybe tap into my voicemails and check my messages. I am beginning to feel detached, and I need to hear the voice of someone familiar.

I take myself up to my bedroom. I need to clean my leg up and maybe try to relax before lunch. I use a flannel to wipe the blood and dirt and then look in the toiletry bag for the little tub of Sudocrem I brought with me. I dab big blobs onto my leg, and then I look out of the large window. I notice little clasps at the top and bottom and realise that two separate windows will open up; when I release them and push them back, it is like a little balcony. A tiny brick wall juts out, giving the impression of safety, but I could easily topple over the edge. I pull over a plush chair from the corner and place it at the edge of the window. I sit down, looking out across the gardens and beyond. I take my phone out of my bag and look at it. There are a few bars. My heart leaps. *My goodness.* I edge closer to the little wall and another bar pops up. This is the place, this is where I need to be to get reception, high up and as close to the window as possible. I hadn't thought about that before. A few messages pop to life, and I see ones from Stig.

> Hope you're okay. Not much happening here.

Then earlier this morning:

> Text me to let me know you are okay. I haven't heard from you, and it looks like my last message didn't get through.

I decide to message him back quickly.

> I'm fine, my phone was switched off. Back online now

We don't use kisses even though my finger is ready to automatically type one.

He reads it immediately and begins to type back.

Good good

I see there is the voicemail, so I dial in and listen.

'Hi, Lil, it's me again,' comes Emily's voice. 'Listen, Lil, I've done a little more digging and I know you'll be irritated with me, but only initially I hope. This whole situation has not been sitting well with me. I called in a favour from a couple of friends at some local solicitors in Oxford. With Hector's restaurant being in Oxford, I just thought there was a bit of a connection with all of them to the area, and Blythewood not being that far away. Anyway, I found something, Lil. A long-hidden, dropped case. A woman called Delilah Ashley-Cooper, a former student of Brixworth girls' school not far from Blythewood; the girls were often known to have spent time with the lads at Blythewood, with many of them ending up having relationships with them. A claim was brought forward against Hector, by Delilah. It was only made a few years ago but based on an event several years before.' Emily pauses, presumably to look at a date. 'It was February 2015 she put in the claim, and the alleged event happened in 2001. It didn't get past the preliminary; the claim was struck out due to no reasonable grounds. The claim was rape, Lil.'

I suck in a breath and hold the phone closer to my ear, my heart thudding in my chest.

'I'm worried about you, this contract, this arrangement. I wish you had come to me earlier before you went there, and given me more time.' There is a wail in the background on the message. 'I have to go, baby is crying, but listen, when you get this message, please call me; we need to talk about this. It's fine for you to just come home. Please, I love you.'

I hold the phone in my hand and stay motionless. What does this mean? And is it the same Delilah that was texting Stig? I know it has to be, but what is the connection? If the claim was rejected, it was because there were no firm grounds for the allegation, and therefore, Delilah could be one of those women who come forward with allegations when someone starts to become famous. I think back to 2015 when Hector was rising up as an established chef; his face was everywhere. This is why Hector conducted his relationships this way, he told me himself. He probably has a ton of women making allegations and trying to make a quick buck out of him. He likes me because I am a good person, I work for a small charity and that is why he donated the money to Family First.

Bang bang.

I jump from my chair and clutch my phone to my chest.

Someone is at the door. Could it be one of the French women checking on me?

Bang bang.

I walk to the door and slowly open it.

Hector stands there in his shorts and T-shirt, his hair swept to one side. He is wearing an easy smile.

'Lily. Good morning,' he says. 'What are you doing locked away in your room on such a beautiful day? The French countryside awaits you.'

'I... um.' I clutch my phone in my hand and feel my palm go sweaty. What if Hector heard the answerphone message through the door? My mouth is suddenly dry. 'Well, you see, I was out earlier, taking a stroll, and I grazed my leg.' I turn my leg slightly to show him, although it is all covered in thick, white cream.

'Lily,' he says, as though I am a child caught doing something naughty. 'You really should have come to me. I have a range of first-aid boxes; I could have dressed that properly for you.'

I shake my head. 'No, honestly, it's fine, just a little graze. I always come prepared.'

'Do you fall and hurt yourself often?' Hector asks, and I am confused by his response. He looks at me as though I am a dainty woman; his tone says the same.

I laugh. 'No, this was a one-off.'

'So you were being careless?' he says, and I feel a stirring in the pit of my stomach. 'What had you been doing to catch your leg like that?'

My stomach tightens and my hand gripping the phone becomes wet. I switch hands and wipe my palm on my shorts. I shake my head.

'Just new surroundings, I guess. I wasn't looking where I was going.'

'The woods can be treacherous. Please let me know if I can help in any way. Get yourself out in the sun. Get some vitamin D on your skin.' He lifts his hand and brushes his finger across my cheek. 'I'll see you at dinner. Say 7 p.m. this evening?'

I gulp hard and nod. 'Seven is perfect.'

He smiles again and then turns and walks away.

I close the door, the sweat now building in my left hand as Hector's words play back at me.

I hadn't mentioned where I had been earlier.

I think back to when I was in the woods earlier and the slap I had heard. And the way he had peered towards the foliage. He had known I was in the woods. He had seen me.

32

After school had finished, Nicholas decided to get away. He went back to Thailand and revisited some of the places he had travelled to with other friends and Conroy. But he was alone and that was how he wanted it to be. His heart was broken. It had to be because there was an aching there whenever he thought of Delilah. There had been a while when he had thought he loved her, when he thought they might go on and become something together, but that was never going to happen because she had betrayed him. She had taken up with Hector, had sex with him in the bothy, and he had stupidly tried to protect her, and in the process, almost killed Hector. Nicholas was a criminal. He could have gone straight to the police and Nicholas could have a criminal record; his whole life would have been taken away from him. A life he had never expected to have, that was gifted to him. He was incredibly lucky because this was Hector's life he was living. He should be where Nicholas was now, living with his father, taking regular trips to exotic countries, chartering boats, living on a huge estate. Nicholas had somehow slipped into the role of Hector and had replaced the son Conroy had. Yet no one would ever tell him why; no one would give him the reason as to why Hector had been banished from his home, what he had done to deserve that. But he knew that he didn't deserve this life, that he was never supposed to be the one who had grown up in place of Hector. He didn't condone the things he had done to him or the way he had been treated, but he did understand Hector's frustrations that he had suddenly stepped into his life the moment he had been banished. Hector had grown up riddled with anger and frustrations which he had taken out on Nicholas, and on top of that, he had almost killed Hector.

Whatever Hector wanted from Nicholas, he would simply have to wait and see. Hector was not the sort of guy to give up easily. Maybe he would wait years to try and get his revenge.

Thailand was as beautiful as it was the first time Nicholas had travelled here, but this time, the trip was tainted with the repercussions of his actions, of everything he had done, either under his control or out of his control. But he stayed there all the same for many months, some might say 'finding himself', but he knew who he was, and wanted to forget himself. Forget Nicholas, who was associated with the Bolson-Woods family, and discover the person he was supposed to grow up to be. Not someone who had been showered in luxuries and given everything they could ask for. He grew his hair long. He met a guy who said he reminded him of the character Stig of the Dump from the children's TV show, so that stuck. By the time he left Thailand, 'Nicholas' had been well and truly buried, and he was now known as Stig to all he met from there on in. And as he no longer had any contact with Conroy or his mother, it was all new people, it was easy for them to begin to know him as Stig. He was not a kid any more, he was a man, and he had to face up to what was real and what wasn't. Stig didn't want to hide behind the protection of a man who acted like his father but who was never supposed to have been. He had to take responsibility and accept the consequences. At some point in his life, and he did not know when, Hector would come for him. He would find him, take something precious from him and there would be nothing Stig could do to stop him.

33

I feel sick. The words from Emily's voice message are still ringing in my ears and the unsettling tone of Hector's visit at the door just now and the way he referred to the woods, are lingering. Why am I allowing the doubts to creep in when I am so sure of Hector? Introducing the name Delilah to this constantly evolving conundrum is now taking up my concentration. Why is Stig in contact with a Delilah? Can it be possible that this Delilah, who had accused Hector of rape, is the same woman who was contacting Stig? I know it has to be, it cannot be a coincidence. They are all connected in some way. What I need to know is, why now? Why is this Delilah getting in touch with Stig and why would someone wait fourteen years to report a crime?

Suddenly, I see a vision of the slap, and it is as if I physically experienced it. I am sure I saw and heard it earlier, and I remember the way Hector stared into the woods and the way Sienna seemed terrified when she was around him. I presumed it had to do with her training, but what if I am wrong? What if Hector has a temper? What if Sienna and the other woman are terrified of him?

I remember the last thing Sienna said to me in French, which I didn't understand.

I presumed it was a thank you or a goodbye as it was such a short phrase.

I return to the chair by the window, pick up my phone, and type in *le mal*.

The word that appears in front of me is *evil*.

I drop my phone in my lap. This is too much. I am suddenly riddled with worry that I may have made a mistake; I shouldn't be here. There is too much ambiguity, too many unanswered questions, too much I need to know to piece it all together, but I can't ask Hector. Not now, not after he has invited me here.

I use the opportunity of being next to the window to check my bank balance. Can I afford to pay for a plane ticket to get myself home early? I tap in my passwords and wait for the screen to load which shows me my balance.

It will be very tight and impact my contributions to this month's bills and food, but if I need to do it, I can do it. I begin to feel silly for ever thinking it was a good idea to come and do this alone, without anyone – apart from Emily – knowing I am here. To lie to Stig, despite what he has done or was doing with this Delilah; perhaps I have made things worse. If I tell Hector that there is a family emergency, I am sure I can slip away without having to have too much of a discussion. Suddenly, I realise that the best place I need to be is at home, asking Stig some questions outright, to his face, and speaking with Emily to see what else she has uncovered as I am sure there will be more by now, the way that woman worked.

I creep out of the room, anticipating Hector might be lurking in the corridor, and I go downstairs. I hear a clanking coming from the kitchen. I imagine that Sienna is in the kitchen preparing lunch.

I push open the door to the kitchen and Sienna jumps at the sound of me. I walk in.

'Don't be scared.' I hold my hands up at her but she has that same terrified look in her eyes. 'I'm just coming to tell you that I won't be staying for lunch; I need to get back to England.'

Sienna stares at me.

'*Avion*,' I say and stick my arms out and make an impression of a plane.

Sienna continues to stare blankly at me.

I hear a shuffle at the back of the kitchen, and a figure moves forward: the woman from yesterday. She looks terrible: her eyes are puffy, her shoulders hunched. I now realise that this is not how I expect the staff of a multi-millionaire to act. I would expect them to be well-kept and happy, like his London and Cotswolds staff. I was temporarily blinded by Hector and the alcohol and the food last night when I should have been listening to my instincts, realising that these women were not incapable; they were terrified.

'She does not speak,' the woman says in a French accent. 'She says only a few words.'

'Okay, well, I was just saying, I need to get home to England, so don't worry about cooking for me. Can you let me know about calling a taxi or a driver to get me to the airport?'

I will try and change my flight on the way and stay at a local hotel if needed.

'I do not know how I can help you with that,' the woman says.

'Are you two mother and daughter?' I ask outright, needing to know why these two women look so similar.

The woman nods.

Sienna jumps again and looks toward the window.

'*Père*,' she whispers, and the woman scurries away through

the back door of the kitchen where she presumably appeared from.

'*Père?*' I ask Sienna, but Sienna is back at the sink, scrubbing potatoes as though her life depends on it.

Suddenly, the door behind me opens, and there is Hector.

'Ah, Lily,' he says brightly, and if nothing else had happened since I had arrived, I might feel comfort from his greeting. But I cannot feel any comfort in this situation any more.

'Are you helping my staff prepare lunch?' he says with a laugh which sounds forced.

'I did not intend to. I was coming to let you know that I need to get back to England.'

Hector looks perplexed. 'Immediately?'

'I'd like to, yes.'

'But you've only just arrived. We have our dinner this evening.' He sounds genuinely forlorn, and guilt rises through me as though I have done something terrible to harm him and hurt his feelings.

I don't say anything. I am not sure what I am supposed to say.

Hector looks around the kitchen.

'Well then, I suppose you must do what you must do.' His voice is small now.

'I... erm, it's just, I have some things I need to deal with at home and staying here in this beautiful chateau is... I just need to get home. I'm sorry, Hector.'

'Don't be.' He rubs his hand across the kitchen surface. 'This is unclean,' he calls across the room.

Sienna drops the potatoes she is holding, rubs her hands on her apron and rushes across the room with a cloth in hand, rubbing at the spot where Hector has his hand.

I watch and hate every second because I think Hector is

making Sienna do pointless tasks because of how I had just made him feel.

Sienna walks away and Hector looks at me.

'Well I guess you had better go and pack, if you have even unpacked, that is.'

Then he turns and walks out of the kitchen.

'Can I get the number of that driver?' I call after Hector.

'I'm afraid he doesn't work Saturdays, but if you want to wait an extra day, he can hopefully take you back tomorrow as planned,' he says.

I swallow hard. Sweat pools in my lower back. 'I wish I could, I'm sorry I...'

Hector holds up his hand and I stop speaking.

'No need to say more, Lily. All is well. A taxi will take you back to the airport if you can get through the language barrier.' He laughs as he walks away.

'Oh,' I say to myself. I had hoped he would be a bit more helpful than that, but then he hadn't been here to greet me when I arrived, and now it doesn't surprise me that he won't see me leave.

I turn and look at Sienna, thinking of something to say and wondering what I can say in English that she might understand. But when I look at her, she is shaking so violently that I think she is having a fit. I rush to her and place an arm around her.

'Are you okay?' I ask. 'Please sit down.' I point to a chair, but she shakes her head and carries on scrubbing the potatoes. I think back a moment to the word she said when she knew that Hector was coming. And now I know that the two women are terrified of him.

I leave the kitchen and go to my room, where I can get reception at the window again. I type in the word I had heard Sienna utter.

Père.
My phone does its duty and translates.
Father.

* * *

I came here on a stupid whim, not thinking through anything beforehand. I had been trying to get back at Stig, and I had been swept away by Hector. I had enjoyed being seen; I had wanted Stig to see me as an equal earner. But mostly, I was angry at Stig, and I thought I might get some answers, and if not, I could distract myself with Hector's attention.

I want to apologise to Emily for being so rash and making her worry; she doesn't need my idiotic behaviour affecting her on top of all the stress she has going on in her life. I feel silly and selfish.

I begin throwing things into my suitcase. As I do, my phone alerts me to the news. I subscribe to the reports local to my area. There is usually very little: roadblocks, the odd break-in, or vandalism. Often, there are happy reports of local students' or traders' achievements. Even though I am rushing, something makes me stop what I am doing to look at the report.

Woman Found Dead at House in East Littlemore

'What?' I say to myself as I tap the phone furiously to get into the story. The damn internet. I race to the window and hold the phone aloft for a moment to grab some reception. Then I click again on the link. There are no images, just words and it is short.

A body was discovered this morning at East Littlemore. The

woman, believed to be in her early forties, was found at the property by the postman.

The police are treating the incident as suspicious at this time and further enquiries will be made.

Further enquiries. Dead? Ruby? My heart speeds up. The area East Littlemore runs from the three farm cottages along the path where the main farm is and then into a stretch of countryside. There are no other houses that it could be. There is no other woman it could be, and if I am right, then the person I know who has seen Ruby recently is Stig. Why had he been there that night? Poor Ruby. I feel my legs go weak, and my stomach feels tight. She's dead.

A few moments ago, I had been keen to get home to make right the wrong I had done but now I was stuck between a rock and a hard place. I don't want to stay here and I no longer want to go home.

34

Stig had tried his best to forget all about Hector and Delilah and for many years, he did. He began to see Hector's face pop up everywhere. When had he decided to become a chef? Cooking wasn't something he had ever known Hector to show an interest in at school. So he must have enrolled in a cordon bleu course and done some travelling. He must have made it his mission to become a famous chef, no doubt so Stig had to see his stupid face everywhere he went, Stig thought.

So when Stig returned to England and tried to settle in London, he couldn't because of the restaurants that Hector kept putting his name to. London was a big place but he was sure he would bump into him at some point. So he moved to Oxford. Where he eventually met Lily when he did the web design for the charity she worked for. He told her nothing of the life he had left behind because it had never been his life to have in the first place. And he didn't wish to lie to her. So he kept quiet and said nothing when she asked the questions. He did not mention the money he had had access to for much of his teenage years. He could talk about the places he had travelled to, as he had crammed in a fair bit between leaving school and his late twenties. He cut all ties with his mother and Conroy. He could never look at his mother again after the way she had lied to him. They both knew that Hector was at school with him, yet they kept that information from him, and he had suffered at the hands of the frustrated little bully. He had never shared that information with his mother or Conroy. His mother had tried to reach out to him a handful of times and the money continued to arrive in his bank account every month until he closed the account. He transferred the money into another account where it had stayed gaining interest all these years.

If he had known that he was to be getting a surprise anniversary present in the form of a meal at the new restaurant of his arch-enemy then he would have found a way to get out of it. But Lil had seemed so pleased with herself. And so he'd had to play along. He ignored the jibes that Hector made when Lily wasn't listening and continued to play the role of shocked but thankful husband. Then he could be honest afterwards because Lily knew he wasn't down with all the celeb stuff. He liked his quiet, unassuming life. He had thought he was safe; he had thought he had escaped the consequences of his actions. But he hadn't. Hector had found him, and he had to accept that whatever he was due was coming to him.

35

I have to go home. That was the decision I made, and I need to stick to it. There is so much more to deal with now.

I will ask Sienna's mother if she will mind calling a taxi for me if there is any reception. I don't know which firms come out here, and after some futile googling, I give up.

When I arrive downstairs, there is no one in the kitchen. I leave my suitcase in the hallway and begin calling for Sienna. I have no idea where Hector is. He could be off-sulking somewhere.

After twenty minutes of walking up and down corridors, I find my way back to the hallway. I go outside and walk around the side of the house. I begin calling Sienna again. Panic rises in my throat at the prospect of being stranded here alone. What if Hector leaves? What if Sienna and her mother have gone too? I have shoddy reception, I speak no French and I am pretty sure the walk to the main road is long. And I don't remember seeing many, if any, houses for miles before we turned down the driveway yesterday.

Then I hear it: a noise to my right, coming from the hut. It had been locked earlier, so I try and open it.

The handle won't move.

'Hello?' I say.

'Hello,' comes the French accent which I know is not Sienna but must be her mother.

'Why are you in here and the door locked?'

'Because he locks us in here!' comes her hissed, angry voice. 'Can you let us out?'

'I don't know.' I think I am going to be sick. Hector locks his daughter and the mother of his daughter in this hut. Is that why there is a small mattress there? Does he expect them to sleep there? I notice two bolts at the top and the bottom of the door. Could that be all that is holding the door shut?

I release each bolt and then turn the handle. It opens.

On the other side of the door stands the woman. Behind her, Sienna sits rocking and sobbing on the mattress.

'What the hell is going on?' I ask her, exasperated.

'He has gone mad.' She shakes her hand to the ceiling to emphasise her point.

'What is your name?' I ask.

'I am Anna, this is Sienna.'

'Is Hector her father?' I ask.

Anna nods shamefully at first and then looks at me. 'I had no choice,' she says, this time with anger.

I put my hand to my mouth. *Rape.*

Emily's words come back to me: *The claim was rape, Lil.*

I want to believe her. But all the while I have been here, it has been quite obvious these two women are under his control. Anna looks beyond me, and her mouth opens to scream. I turn around, but I feel the full force of weight behind me and I am thrust into the hut, causing me to fall to my knees.

I hear the door slam behind me and the sound of two bolts being drawn across.

36

Stig had to go through with the first dinner date to please Lil. She was so happy they had managed to make the acquaintance. Stig could feel she was slipping away from him. He knew that she did not want to have a baby with him yet and it was understandable. He had kept too much of himself to himself. That is not what you do in a marriage and Stig knew that. But she thought he was stupid and that he didn't know why those silver, rectangular packets of pills kept appearing in her drawer and that the pregnancies never happened. He knew he had to do anything he could to keep her. And if that meant going along with Hector's stupid invitations to more dinners, then so be it. Let him have his fun, Stig thought, as he was sure that he would tire of it soon the way he had tired of it before. But he didn't. it went on and on and when the second invite came and he found himself at the Cotswolds manor watching his wife being presented with a business proposal, he knew he had to step in and say something. It was too much. He couldn't have Hector in his life permanently – if Lily were working with him, it would mean he would be back in his life. But Hector was rich, well-known, and well-liked, and Lil was sucked in. It was too late; there was nothing he could have done.

But the biggest shock for him didn't come in the form of that proposal; it came when he walked into Hector's house that first time in his London pad.

He hadn't expected to see her there. She looked the same but much skinnier. Malnourished, even. He knew she hadn't been looking after herself, but she, unlike him, had stayed in touch with Hector. He had wanted to say her name, which was on the edge of his lips, but before he even had to stop himself, she introduced herself as Ruby. She, too, had tried to shake off the past with a new name the way he had. But what were her reasons? Ruby was a nice enough name, but the other name, the one he had known her by all those years ago, was far superior and far more beautiful, just like her. He'd longed to open his mouth and call her... Delilah.

37

I look around for something to break down the door with.

'Girls,' I say to the two of them. 'We can't just sit here hoping he'll come back and let us out. We need to get out of here, so start thinking.'

Anna and Sienna look at me hopelessly, so I stand up, feeling the impact of the fall on both of my knees.

There is nothing except the mattress in the corner of the room. I think about pulling it apart for the springs but what good will that do? Eventually, I look at the tiny window and then at Sienna. 'She's a tiny slip of a girl; at a literal push, we could get her through that window,' I say, pointing to it.

Anna looks at me like I am mad.

'What if she gets stuck? What if he is out there?'

I hold Anna by both of her arms. 'She won't and he won't,' I tell her with absolute conviction. But I have no idea if what I am saying is true. It could fail miserably, but it could also work. And we didn't have any other options.

'First of all, we need to smash the window,' I say. I look at Sienna. She is wearing her apron still; it looks thick.

'Ask her to give me her apron.'

Anna says hurriedly in French and gestures to her daughter's waist. Sienna stands up and takes it off. Anna gives it to me, and I wrap it several times around my hand. It is something I have seen on TV. Again, I have no idea if it will be successful, but I have no other options.

'I need to get on your shoulders,' I say to Anna.

'What?'

'Bend down.'

She does as I ask and when she is on her knees I climb onto her shoulders.

'Sienna, help your mother to her feet,' I call and Anna translates into French, her voice already weak.

Sienna stands to one side of Anna and after a count of three, Anna tries to get to her feet. But we do not budge an inch.

'Anna, remember when you gave birth to Sienna? Remember how strong you felt then? Think of that, and when I count to three, push from your legs as hard as you can.'

I count to three again, and this time, Anna lets out an almighty roar, and I am face to face with the window. I can hear her moans and protests, and she is wobbling beneath me, so I aim and punch the window, once, twice, three times. It smashes. I use my protected fist to push as much of the glass out of the way as possible, leaving just about a big enough gap to slide Sienna through.

I slip from Anna's shoulders, and she falls against the wall and then to her knees and topples to the ground.

'Come on,' I say, gasping, 'we haven't got time to waste.'

I kneel this time and gesture for Sienna to get on my shoulders. 'When she is outside, tell her to walk around to the front door and unbolt both bolts top and bottom and open the door.'

Anna looks at me; I can see the terror in her eyes. I am asking a lot of her baby girl.

After Anna has translated, adding a lot more of her own words which I presume are words of encouragement, Sienna tentatively steps forward and climbs onto my shoulders. Anna holds on to both me and Sienna to balance us and I push myself to my feet. Sienna isn't very heavy, but it is an effort all the same.

'Now go through the window. You might hurt yourself, but I think you need to go headfirst so you can see. It's only a slight drop.'

I line Sienna up and then lift her off my shoulders as much as my biceps will allow to encourage her through the window. She is moaning and crying but eventually, I am only holding on to her legs.

'Can you reach the floor?'

Anna shouts something in French, and I let go of her legs. There is a thump and then a moan.

'Sienna, Sienna,' Anna calls. But there is silence.

I look at Anna. What have I done to her child? What if she is right and Hector is out there?

Then a noise at the door. Two locks scrape back, and the door creaks open.

38

Stig had to pretend again. Not only that he didn't know Hector and that he was an amiable man, one he was content with spending time over dinner with, but that he didn't know her. Delilah. It helped that she had changed her name to Ruby.

After that night, she found his phone number on his website, called it over and over during the day until Stig agreed to see her. They met for coffee in Oxford. She was all over the place, a bag of emotions, one minute raving about her life and how busy she was going to this party and that invite and the next, breaking down into tears and apologising over and over for what she had done.

Stig told her not to worry; it was the past, she seemed happy in her life and Stig had Lily now. Nicholas didn't want her to be sad about what had happened all those years ago. But Delilah, now Ruby, had been a witness; she had seen what had happened between him and Hector that night after the final prom. It had never been spoken of again; Nicholas had avoided Hector as best he could, but now there was another fly in the ointment. What was he going to do about Ruby?

39

'My goodness, are you okay?' I pull Sienna into my arms, and she stays there like a plank of wood, not reciprocating the hug. I let go of her and Anna and I walk out of the hut, but before we do, I grab a piece of glass and slip it into my shorts pocket.

Sienna is holding her wrist; she must have landed on it when she dropped to the floor.

'You'll be okay; we'll get you to a doctor.' I look at Anna. 'What do we do now? Where do we go?'

'My grandmother's car,' Anna says. 'She lives a mile down the hill; we walk that way.'

We begin walking along the drive we had come down when I arrived yesterday and I wonder how so much has changed in twenty-four hours. Yesterday, I was so happy to be here, thinking of the prospects and future.

'There is a path along here that cuts down the hill to the right that leads to my grandmother's house.'

'So do you both live here?' I ask and Anna looks solemn.

'I stay here when he wants me. But I was worried for Sienna

this weekend; she has never been alone with him before but he wanted her here, to wait on you.'

'I see.'

'She is only fifteen.'

'Fifteen?' I had thought she was about twenty.

'So I hid around the grounds to keep an eye on her, but he found me.'

I thought about the two incidents between Hector and Anna. When I had thought he was coming to her aid, she was running from him. The second time when I had seen from the woods, a slap.

We make it quite far down the driveway, and I ask Anna how much further; Sienna is walking just behind us.

Suddenly, at a loud noise, we all turn. There is a small sports car racing toward us. Hector. We barely have enough time to jump to the side of the driveway when Hector stops the car and jumps out, his hair unkempt, his face red and contorted.

'Run.' I point to the path that I now see veering off to the right. Anna and Sienna begin to run at a pace. I stay where I am.

But Hector is out of the car and he has Sienna.

I take a few steps back, My hand hovers over my pocket where the glass is.

'Lily,' he says, trying to sound endearing. He sweeps his messy hair back with his hand.

'What do you want, Hector?'

'I want you,' he says, trying to hold his cool but his voice is wavering.

'Hector, you have everything: you have all of this, your other houses, your friends, your business. What is it that you need? Please let go of Sienna,' I ask.

'I need peace. I need peace in here.' He pounds at his chest.

He opens the passenger door; he is about to throw Sienna inside. The girl is trembling.

'No.' I step forward. 'Take me.'

Sienna has been through enough. I am stronger. I have the glass as a weapon if I need it.

Hector pushes Sienna forward and she runs to Anna. It is hard to believe that she is his daughter the way he treats her.

Hector stands there with the door open and holds his arm out, gesturing for me to get inside. I turn and face Anna and mouth 'Police' to her before I step into the car. Hector slams the door behind me, and then he is in the driver's seat. Without looking at me, he speeds off down the driveway.

'Where are we going?' I ask quietly, and silently praying that everything will be okay. How have things ended up this way? I arrived yesterday and had a lovely meal with Hector. How could I have been so naïve and put my trust in someone that, in all honesty, I do not know at all?

'To a little spot I know.' He pushes his hair back again; I get a whiff of body odour.

The car continues along the drive until we reach the open gates and he speeds out onto the road. I hold on to the sides of my seat. I don't dare say a word in case I say the wrong thing but eventually, as we career around corners at a speed I am uncomfortable with, I say, 'Is it a favourite spot?' I hope I can somehow talk him around if I remain calm. But my heart is galloping at a ridiculous rate; I am sure I might pass out.

'I wouldn't say favourite, but I go there from time to time.'

My gut wrenches and my mouth is so dry, I can barely speak. I cling to the side of the door.

Eventually, Hector pulls the car into an alcove. I look to my right; I can see the cliff below and the sea. Is he going to drive the car off the edge? I want to scream and cry out, but appearing calm is the only control I have right now. I need to try and talk Hector around if he's thinking of doing that to us both.

Hector is quiet, and I am sure he must be able to hear my heart thudding.

I go to speak. 'Hec—'

'Just shut up!' he bellows. This is the other side of Hector, the one I have never seen. I shrink back into my seat and tuck my hand into my right pocket; the glass is poking into my thigh.

'You don't understand; she replaced my mother. She had it coming.'

This has come from nowhere. 'Hector, I'm confused; who are you talking about?'

He looks at me as though I am mad. 'The bitch that is your husband's mother.'

I nod. I knew this about the family. But what had he meant? She had it coming.

'You'll need to elaborate, Hector. I don't understand,' I say gently.

'She waltzed into my house as though she bloody owned it. A scummy little woman from a scummy council estate, weeks after my mother left. He didn't care how I felt.' Hector is grabbing at his hair.

'You mean your father, Conroy?'

'Yes,' he spits. 'She had it coming. They've all had it coming since.'

I tried to think about how to probe him.

'Did you do something to Stig's mother? Is that why you were made to leave?'

'Of course I bloody did! She didn't get those marks around her neck from my father, did she? No, he was such a good, kind man,' Hector says spitefully.

'You tried to kill her?'

'Tried to.' He laughs demonically. 'I was just a kid, but she was small, and I was strong. She put up a good fight, I'll give you that.'

So Hector had attacked Stig's mother and that was why he had been removed from the house.

'Have you harmed anyone else since then?' I ask Hector, thinking of Anna when she told me how Sienna had been conceived. And then Emily's words again.

The claim was rape, Lil.

Had Delilah's claim been right all along?

'They all had it coming,' he says, and he fumbles with the door. I grab onto the door handle, move my legs to the side, and squeeze the glass in my hand so I am ready to jump from the car and run. Hector kneels on the gravel path and looks at me through the door.

'I saw you and I thought you would save me.' He laughs again. 'How stupid I was, thinking that you might be different, that I could see you differently. But I can't, Lily. I still want to do the same to you. And I can't be that person anymore. I can't keep looking in the mirror and seeing a monster. I am sick.' He clenches his fists on his knees.

'You can get help, Hector,' I call through the door. The sinking feeling increases.

He shakes his head and stands up. I jump out of the car. *Don't you dare put me through this, Hector*, I think. But he is already running so fast, as though he is about to win a race. He keeps on running even though it is obvious the gravel ground is about to end and give way to nothing, a space. But he knows what he is doing, and he doesn't stop; even when his body leaves the edge of the cliff, his legs still move as though he is running. Still going right up until the end.

40

Ruby kept calling Stig. He had her name saved in his phone as Delilah. That was who she was to him and always would be.

Then there were the texts. He had tried to answer one once when he was driving to the Cotswolds and Lily knew he had done so as well. He was always so careful never to drive and mess about with his phone.

> I need to see you.

His reply came:

> I can't do this now

She tried to confront him at the Cotswolds house when they left. He told her he couldn't see her again.

But then she bought the damn house right next to them; they were practically neighbours now. How was he supposed to move on when she was right under his nose?

Then she called him the other night and begged him to

come over. And he did. He told Lily he was going for a run and went to the farmhouse cottage. It was nice inside, nothing like the riches they had both been used to as children, her more than him. It seemed she had also wanted to walk away from all of that.

'Why?' he had asked her. She wasn't going to leave him alone, so he might as well know.

It was all a mistake, her mistake. She had messed up big time.

She took him back to that night at the leaving prom.

'He just came at me from behind; I wasn't sure what was happening,' she said. 'And then, before I knew what was happening, I was on the floor, my dress ripped, he was in me, he was hurting me, calling me every name, horrible names. Then he finished and got up and walked away and then there you were. And I was horrified and ashamed and shocked, and you presumed you knew and you were right. I wish you had killed him that night. He has made my life miserable ever since. I have tried so hard to get away from him, but he just kept luring me back. I disowned my family. I have no one. He was all I had. Even though he continues to treat me wrong. I made a claim once, but it was dropped. I was, in the eyes of everyone, Hector's bit of stuff, his friend with benefits. How could I tell them that when I was still a teenager, he raped me, and I had been returning to him ever since because I am weak because he is all I have. Until you came back. You came back for me, right, Nicholas?'

Stig's heart fell. He had been right at the prom. Delilah had been attacked by Hector. Of course, what he did was still wrong, but he had been right in his heart to protect Delilah.

'Why did you push me away? Why did you tell me that I was wrong, that you gave yourself to him?'

'Because I was ashamed; I thought it was my fault. I had flirted with him; I thought he liked me. I didn't know what love was or that you felt the way you did. I didn't know you were the better man. I was a kid.'

Stig wanted to take her in his arms but he knew that it could escalate. Ruby wanted him.

'I know you have your life, but Hector wants Lily, he can have her, and you and I can pick up from where we were. I bought this house so you don't even have to move.'

Everything she was saying was like listening to a foreign language. How could Delilah... Ruby, want him after all this time? How could she think that he would give up his marriage? Why would she presume that Hector could have Lily and that everyone would live happily ever after? She wasn't well. She probably hadn't been for a long time. But Nicholas had tried back then, to tell her, to help her. But she had pushed him away. She might have been a kid, but he knew what was right and wrong. What had she been taught that had made her into this?

So he had left.

Stig wasn't to know that he would be the last one to see her alive.

EPILOGUE

Stig brings two glasses of beer from the bar back to our table. The condensation is dripping down them from the heat. I have the paper in front of me, the story about Hector Bolson-Woods's funeral is open and we have been reading it together. This holiday in Greece is a way to put all the past behind us, reconnect and try to make sense of what had happened to both of us.

There had been a good turnout, and everyone had good things to say about the man who had done so much for the community and for charities. Wasn't it a terrible shame that someone so good was gone? Even in his death, Hector is still able to hide the things he did, the truth about the life he led and the unhappy upbringing that caused so many other people's unhappiness, including my husband's. But we understand it now.

Stig kept some of the money from Conroy all this time, never wanting to spend it as it was money from a man who was never really a father to him, a man who had lied and put him in a difficult position for years, a man who he thought had simply disowned Hector and withheld the details from him.

'He can't hurt anyone any more,' Stig says after he has finished reading it. I have already read it three times. Still, even in his death, after everything I know about him, I am still craving details about him. There is so little left to hold on to now and I know I will need to close this chapter soon.

I don't talk much about poor Ruby and her taking her own life. Because Stig feels so guilty about all of it. He left her there that night and didn't know about the concoction of drugs and alcohol she planned to take after he left. She had looked to Stig to save her, but he couldn't.

The only thing we have now is our future. No more looking back.

I have stopped taking the pill. I am going to make it up to Stig, to us and myself. We will start a family and maybe one day, we can forget all about this episode.

Until then, we both raise our glasses and clink. I am sure we are both toasting the same thing. My thoughts are with Ruby, the vulnerable woman I met, and Stig's for Delilah, the girl he once knew and loved.

Neither of us are thinking of Hector…

* * *

MORE FROM NINA MANNING

Another book from Nina Manning, *Her Last Summer*, is available to order now here:

https://mybook.to/HerLastSummerBackAd

ACKNOWLEDGEMENTS

Like all my books, they begin with a tiny seed of an idea that eventually evolves into the full story after a lot of sweat and headaches.

This time, the little seed came from my friend, Jordan Marsh, who told me about a time he went to the restaurant of a famous chef and asked if the chef was working. It turned out he was, and he and his wife were invited to the kitchen and cooked for by him. As much as I enjoy listening to my friend's life stories, I am always thinking... what if? And that was the case here. What if the chef knew one of the couple, but they both kept quiet, and why had they kept quiet? Had something happened in the past? And so the writing process begins. So firstly, thank you, Jordan, for giving me a nugget to chew on, I hope you enjoy telling this new and evolved version of your story to others.

Thanks, as always, to Emily Ruston, who is always the first to hear about the ideas in my head before I begin writing them and who always gives the best structural edits.

Many thanks to all at Boldwood Books. I am grateful for all you have done in the last six years. It's been an adventure.

Thanks to my wonderful three children, who always understand when I need time and space to write and edit. I love you Savannah, Bodhi and Huxley.

Finally, thank you, lovely reader, for picking up this book. I hope you enjoyed it; your support is everything.

ABOUT THE AUTHOR

Nina Manning studied psychology and was a restaurant-owner and private chef (including to members of the royal family). She is the founder and co-host of *Sniffing The Pages*, a book review podcast. Her debut psychological thriller, *The Daughter in Law*, was a bestseller in the UK, US, Australia and Canada. She lives in Scotland.

Sign up to Nina Manning's mailing list here for news, competitions and updates on future books.

Visit Nina's website: https://www.ninamanningauthor.com/

Follow Nina on social media:

- x.com/ninamanninguk
- instagram.com/ninamanningauthor
- facebook.com/Nina-Manning-100083674816362
- bookbub.com/authors/nina-manning
- tiktok.com/@ninamanningauthor

ALSO BY NINA MANNING

Psychological Thrillers

The Daughter In Law

The Guilty Wife

The House Mate

The Bridesmaid

Queen Bee

The Waitress

The Beach House

Her Last Summer

The Dinner Party

Women's Fiction

The 3am Shattered Mums' Club

The 6pm Frazzled Mums' Club

THE *Murder* LIST

THE MURDER LIST IS A NEWSLETTER DEDICATED TO SPINE-CHILLING FICTION AND GRIPPING PAGE-TURNERS!

SIGN UP TO MAKE SURE YOU'RE ON OUR HIT LIST FOR EXCLUSIVE DEALS, AUTHOR CONTENT, AND COMPETITIONS.

SIGN UP TO OUR NEWSLETTER

BIT.LY/THEMURDERLISTNEWS

Boldwood

Boldwood Books is an award-winning fiction publishing company seeking out the best stories from around the world.

Find out more at www.boldwoodbooks.com

Join our reader community for brilliant books, competitions and offers!

Follow us
@BoldwoodBooks
@TheBoldBookClub

Sign up to our weekly deals newsletter

https://bit.ly/BoldwoodBNewsletter

Printed in Great Britain
by Amazon